P.I.

Apprentice

Second Edition

P.I. Apprentice

Second Edition

Mike Faricy

Library of Congress Control Number: 2023918911
paperback ISBN: 978-1-962080-57-6
e-Book ISBN: 978-1-962080-58-3

MJF Publishing books may be purchased for education, Business, or promotional use. For information on bulk purchases, please contact the author directly at mikefaricyauthor@gmail.com

Published by

MJF Publishing
https://www.mikefaricybooks.com

Acknowledgments

I would like to thank the following people for their help and support:

Special thanks to my editors, Kitty, Donna and Rhonda for their hard work, cheerful patience and positive feedback.

I would like to thank Ann and Julie for their creative talent and not slitting their wrists or jumping off the high bridge when dealing with my Neanderthal computer capabilities.

Special thanks to Ann for her patience.

Last, I would like to thank family and friends for their encouragement and unqualified support. Special thanks to Maggie, Jed, Schatz, Pat, Av, Emily and Pat for not rolling their eyes, at least when I was there, and most of all, to my wife Teresa whose belief, support and inspiration has from day one, never waned.

Prologue

For the past fifteen minutes I'd been in my office watching through my binoculars as the two women in the third-floor apartment across the street sipped coffee and applied makeup. They were standing next to one another with makeup mirrors on the island counter and mugs of coffee next to the mirrors. The topless blonde had a white towel wrapped around her head. The redhead's hair was pulled back, and she was wearing a black bra.

They got me thinking it might be a good idea to phone my close personal friend Crystal and set up a play date. She answered on the second ring. "Well, Dev Haskell, I was beginning to wonder. What have you been up to?"

"Oh, nothing much. I wanted to see if you might be interested in getting together tonight." I had the binoculars up. The blonde said something, and the redhead nodded excitedly.

"I'd love it, say dinner around 7:00, and it might be a good idea to bring an overnight bag. I've got a new toy you can help me try out."

"More than willing to help, Crystal. I'll see you to-night."

"Rest up," she said and disconnected.

A car had just parked across the street behind my car, and a young woman climbed out. She draped a large tote bag over her shoulder. The bag looked like it was made from a southwestern Indian rug, and I figured she was probably heading into the hairdressers across the hall from my office. As long as it wasn't my office mate, Louie Laufen, I could keep watching the ladies across the street.

The staircase creaked ever so slightly as the young woman made her way up to the second floor. Now, both ladies in the apartment were laughing as the redhead brushed some sort of powder onto the blonde woman's cleavage and blew her a kiss. Just as I adjusted the binoculars for a closer view, the office door opened.

"Oh, excuse me. I'm looking for Mr. Haskell. Is this his office?" the young woman asked and then looked at the door for my name. There was nothing on the door identifying either Louie or me, except for the unit number 200.

"What? Err, umm, good morning," I said and spun around in my office chair. The binoculars hung around my neck by a black leather strap as I pushed the chair closer to the desk. "What can I do for you?" I asked as I studied the woman, her age couldn't have been more than mid-twenties. She may have looked familiar, but I couldn't place her. Morton, my Golden Retriever, was off his pillow and in the process of attempting to place his nose up her skirt.

"Are you Mr. Haskell?" she asked as she twice brushed Morton away.

"Yes, I am. No one else would want to be me," I laughed. She responded with a confused look. "What can I do for you?"

"My dad told me that if anything ever happened to him, I should talk to you."

"Who's your dad?"

"John Carter."

"John? I know or knew a Jack Carter. He passed away a while back."

"Yeah, that was my dad. Both my parents were killed in a car accident."

"Oh, wait, are you Melissa? No, you can't be. You should be in high school and—"

"Yeah, that's me. I graduated from high school eight years ago. Now, I work in the city attorney's office.

"Melissa, oh, please, please come in and sit down. Your parents were such wonderful people. Umm…belated condolences. I've been out to the cemetery to pay my respects. I know, because of Covid, there wasn't a funeral. It must have been very difficult, losing both parents in a car accident. It was labeled a hit and run, wasn't it?"

She nodded and said, "Yes, that's what I wanted to see you about."

"Okay, here, umm…take a seat and let me get you a cup of coffee. Do you take it black?"

She nodded. "Black would be fine."

I pulled out one of the client chairs in front of my desk, and she sat down. She took a manila envelope out of her tote bag. I grabbed Louie's coffee mug off his picnic table desk. I poured what was left down the sink, rinsed it out and refilled it with the remnants in the pot. The coffee had been on since yesterday morning, and I had meant to turn it off and make a fresh pot when I came in, but then the women across the street had served as a bit of a distraction. I quickly set my binoculars on the file cabinet and grabbed the mug.

"Here you go, Melissa," I said and set Louie's mug down in front of her. "Sorry, but we're fresh out of pastries," I joked.

"That's okay. Thanks." She ignored my attempt at humor and took a sip from the mug. She seemed to shiver for a second or two and then placed the mug as far away as possible.

I settled into my desk chair. "So, how can I help you?"

She looked at me for a long moment, took a deep swallow, then handed me a manila envelope. She was visibly shaking. "I'm pretty sure my parents were murdered."

One

It took a long moment for that last statement to sink in. Finally, I came back to reality. "Murdered? Melissa, that's a pretty strong statement. Obviously it's upsetting. In fact, I can't imagine the pain you must be going through, but—"

"I didn't make an offhanded comment. Look, my folks are gone. They're dead. Okay. As much as it pains me to say it, I accept the fact. I don't like it, but I accept it. They're not going to answer my phone calls. They're not going to open the door when the doorbell rings. That said, I've been checking some things out, and it's all in that file. You don't have to read it now, but I'm hoping you'll take a look at it sometime and tell me what you think. I know you did some work for my dad, and if you feel up to it, I'd really like you to check things out. I need someone like you to confirm the information I've assembled."

"You said you're in the city attorney's office?"

She nodded, "Let me stop you right there. No, I didn't run that file past anyone in the office if that's what you're thinking. People there are too connected. As a matter of fact, other than me, you're the only person who will have seen the file."

"What do you mean? Too connected? I'm not following."

"I can't afford to have someone go off the deep end based on the information I've put together. Please, just take a look and tell me what you think. If you go through it and you decide you don't want to be involved, that's not a problem. I won't like it, but I get it. Oh, and I'll probably never talk to you again. Just kidding," she said and smiled.

"All right. Don't say anything else. Let me take a look and I promise you this. I'll go through it and do the best I can. Fair enough?"

She nodded, and her eyes suddenly looked watery. I passed her the Kleenex box I keep on my desk for just such an emergency. Five minutes later, I watched out the window as she climbed into her car and headed down to her office in the St. Paul courthouse.

I took a long look at the manila envelope, eventually took a deep breath, and took out the multi-page file. It was more than just a few pages, probably about twenty. I pulled out my phone and placed it in airplane mode. I'd met Jack Carter years ago when I'd dropped out of college after my first semester. He was a real estate developer, and he offered me a job instead of enlisting in the army, but of course, being nineteen, I knew better. When I got out and came back home, he steered me toward a couple of job opportunities that I immediately screwed up. He was always supportive of me, shook his head when I got my Private Investigators license, and sent me the occasional case. I usually checked out an insurance claim or the work history of someone he wanted to hire. Over the years, his office grew from four people to, maybe fifty or sixty, and he made millions.

Me? Well, I share an office with Louie Laufen, who handles DUI cases, and our local crime lord Tubby Gustafson drives me crazy on any given day.

It was close to four in the afternoon when Louie finally made it into the office. He'd had three court appearances, the last one at 3:00. "Oh, man, what a day," he said as he tossed his briefcase onto his picnic table and settled into his desk chair. As he turned on his computer, he asked, "Everything okay on your end?"

"Mmm," I said and turned to the next page in Melissa's file.

It was close to 5:00 when Louie shut down his computer and asked, "You thinking about going over to The Spot for one? Dev? Hey, earth to Dev."

"Oh, sorry, checking out some stuff here. What did you say?"

"Asked if you were interested in going over to The Spot for a little relaxation?"

"Yeah, let me just finish up here. I'll take Morton on a quick walk, and we'll join you in fifteen or twenty minutes."

"See you over there." He rose from his chair, grabbed his briefcase, and gave a quick wave as he hurried out the door. I watched out the window as he crossed the street and headed into The Spot.

I glanced at the clock on the wall. Louie had left over an hour ago. I was on my third read of Melissa's file. I placed it back in the manila envelope and grabbed Morton's leash. As soon as I grabbed the leash, he was off his pillow and standing at the door. I clicked the leash onto his collar, and we went outside. We crossed the street, I tossed the envelope on the front seat of my car, and we walked for three blocks. Morton investigated every other fence gate and registered his visit on both fire hydrants.

Once we entered The Spot, Morton nearly pulled my arm out of its shoulder socket as he strained on the leash. We headed toward Louie on his stool at the corner of the bar. As we rounded the corner, Louie reached down with a handful of pork rinds and said, "Well, Morton, you had me worried, afraid Dev had fallen asleep or was scanning the apartment building across the street again."

"Sorry about that, Louie. I got involved in a file, and the next thing I knew, an hour had gone by."

Louie checked his watch. "Actually, it's been an hour and a half, but who's counting? Oh wait, I'm counting because it's your turn to buy."

"How 'bout a beer, Dev?" Mike, the bartender, asked.

"I'll take a Summit and better give Louie a refill before he starts to throw a hissy fit."

"He's been complaining ever since he came in." Mike laughed and headed down the bar.

"You seemed really into whatever you were reading. Everything okay?" Louie asked.

"What? Oh, yeah. Just a file someone dropped off that I'm going through."

"Oh, so then you're not being sued. Or are you?"

"Me, no, the file has nothing to do with me, well, other than the woman wants me to check some things out."

"You going to do that?"

"Yeah. I owe it to the family. Her father gave me a lot of good advice, not that I ever followed any of it, but he was a friend, a mentor of mine as a young guy. So yeah, I'm going to check some things out. How'd the day go for you? You had three appearances in court today, didn't you?"

Louie gave a nod and went on to tell me about his day over the course of two beers and another handful of pork rinds for Morton. It was after eight when we headed home. I tossed Morton a biscuit in the kitchen, warmed up some pasta that had been in the refrigerator for a few days, and we settled in front of the TV. We headed up to bed around 11:00. I was wide awake at 2:00, and after lying there for fifteen minutes, I went downstairs, grabbed Melissa's file, and started reading it for the fourth or fifth time.

TWO

y alarm woke me at 6:30. I turned it off, and Morton woke me an hour later. I went downstairs to the kitchen, let him out the backdoor, then grabbed a shower and put on a reasonably clean t-shirt and jeans.

We were down in the office just after 9:30. Louie was on his computer, and amazingly, a fresh pot of coffee was going. I poured a mug and topped off Louie's.

He gave me a friendly nod. "Thanks, Dev. Long night? You look tired."

"Oh couldn't sleep and ended up reviewing that same file for a couple of hours."

"Oh, you're kidding. Here I was thinking you had some incredible erotic night lined up with a beauty queen."

"No, not by a long shot. I was—oh shit, wait a minute," I said and looked at my phone. It was still set on airplane mode. "Oh, no. I was supposed to meet up with someone last night, and I got so involved reading that damn file I completely forgot. I adjusted my phone, so I wouldn't be interrupted. Oh, God." I checked my recent phone calls, four of them twenty minutes apart, all from Crystal. I wasn't sure I wanted to hear the messages she left. There were six text messages: 'Are you okay? Are you coming over? Did you forget? Please let me know you're okay. Call me when you see this. I don't care what time it is.' And then the last one, 'Dev, please let me know you're okay. Please.'

Her audible messages, there were four, with the last one coming through about midnight, were more of the same. She sounded worried and concerned rather than mad. I had to play this carefully. I thought for a minute and then made the call.

The phone barely rang, and she answered, "Oh, God, Dev, are you okay?"

"Yes, Crystal, I'm okay. It was just a harrowing night."

"Oh, my God, I knew it. I just knew it. What happened?"

"Oh…ah…two toddlers were missing. Three and four years old. The babysitter fell asleep, and when the parents came home from work, the little ones were gone. Somehow they got out of the house. I was so focused on finding them I completely forgot. The police were involved. Must have been fifty or sixty people looking for the little children. It was getting dark. Even the police were starting to think that maybe they had been kidnapped. It was close to midnight when I found them. They had climbed a ladder up to a treehouse in the backyard two doors away. When I found them, they were sound asleep. I carried them back to the parents' house, then had to show the treehouse to the police and a bunch of newspaper reporters. I didn't get home until sometime after 2:00 and just collapsed in bed. I would have called sooner, but I didn't want to wake you after the long night you had. I'm really sorry, Crystal. I was afraid—"

"Oh, Dev. Not another word. You saved them? Those two little ones? Oh my God, it's a miracle they didn't fall out of that treehouse. How old did you say they were?"

"Three and five, I think. I really can't remember, and I'm still so tired." I glanced over at Louie. He was sipping his coffee and shaking his head.

"Oh, Dev. God, I'm so proud of you. I can't wait to read about this in the paper. Which papers were the reporters from?"

"Oh, I'm not sure. They told me, but I was too focused on the little kids. I told them not to take pictures of me carrying the kids. I was afraid the camera flash might wake them."

"The camera flash?" she said.

"I just wanted to get them back to their parents, who, obviously, were very worried."

"And the babysitter. Was it a woman?"

"Oh, no, it was a neighbor girl. I think she was ten or eleven. You know, kids just being kids."

"Any chance you're free tonight? We might be able to catch it on the news before we get down to business."

I nodded at Louie. "Why yes. I'd love to come over. What can I bring?"

"Just bring yourself, and you had better rest up. We're going to be very busy. 6:00 sound okay?"

"Yes, I'll see you tonight."

"Oh, Dev, you're my hero. You're going to see all of me tonight, up close and very personal. We're going to celebrate like you won't believe, honey" Crystal said and disconnected.

I breathed a sigh of relief.

Louie shook his head. "You gotta be kidding me. She actually bought that fabrication?"

"Not bad for coming up with something right off the cuff. Yeah, I should have put it on speaker for you. I'm her hero, and she wants to thank me in an up close and very personal way, and those are her exact words. Oh, and she told me to rest up."

"Unbelievable. And just what are you going to tell her when there's nothing on the news, the internet, or in the newspaper?"

"Yeah, I'm going to have to think about that. Hopefully, something big will happen today, and I can just say it was bigger news and took over the media."

"Just be careful, Dev. These things have a way of getting out of control, and suddenly, you're living the lie. She's going to ask you names, where this happened, and all kinds of stuff. And you're going to have to get your story straight and keep it that way."

"Thanks for the advice, Louie. Not to worry, I'll think of something."

Three

I headed out to one of the main locations in Melissa's file just before noon. A massive multi-unit apartment complex called The White House. I'd heard of it but had never actually been in it. It was just to the east of St. Paul in the suburb of Woodbury. The complex was three years old and made up of five, five-story buildings arranged in a pentagon. Each building housed one hundred units, which rounded out to twenty units per floor, or five hundred units in the entire five building complex. I had passed the place countless times on the freeway but never really paid much attention to it other than they were new and took up a large amount of space along the freeway corridor. I took the exit and drove along the frontage road toward the five-story buildings in the distance.

There was a visitor's parking lot in front of each building. I turned into one of the parking lots and headed toward the door in the center of the building. The door had a box-gable roof over it, extending out about six feet from the building. The sign on the front of the roof read

'Leasing Office' in blue letters. I stepped into the building. The leasing office was just off to the right. Straight ahead was a security door with a phone next to it to contact residents. I headed into the leasing office.

There was a brown leather couch against the wall just to the right of the door. A framed poster of the the White House Apartments hung on the wall above the couch. Straight ahead was a marble-topped counter. The woman behind the counter was on the phone. She signaled me with her hand and nodded, suggesting it would just be a moment.

"But if you'll check your lease, our policy is that you have agreed to pay rent for a twelve-month period, which means you are liable for that rent payment of two thousand one hundred dollars until next November, which is five months from now. Yes, I understand that, and I will be happy to place your unit on the available list once you have vacated and we have restored the unit for the next occupant. No, ma'am, that will be up to our maintenance department to determine. Yes, very well, thank you." As she hung up, she muttered something under her breath that I presumed wasn't all that polite.

She turned to face me, flashed a quick smile, and said, "Good morning. How may I help you?"

"I'm interested in renting a unit."

She looked surprised for a brief moment before she said, "I'd be happy to help you." She reached over to the credenza behind her, grabbed a clipboard off a stack, and handed it to me. "If you would just fill this form out, we can get you started."

I took the clipboard and sat down on the brown leather couch. The form on the clipboard asked for basic information. My name, address, that sort of thing. Among other things, it listed that the building was pet friendly and that smoking was prohibited. There was a second page that displayed two floorplans, a single-bedroom and a two-bedroom unit. It also mentioned a social room on the fourth floor available for rent and a workout room, also on the fourth floor. Underground parking was available for an additional one hundred and twenty dollars a month.

As I was filling out the form, the phone rang, and the woman went through a similar conversation to the one I'd heard minutes ago, explaining what was required in order to move out of the apartment.

She flashed another fake smile when I handed her the clipboard, gave it a ten-second glance, and said, "Are you interested in a one or two-bedroom unit?"

"Oh, definitely a two-bedroom unit. I work from home, so the second bedroom will serve as my office."

"I see," she said and nodded. "And what exactly do you do, Mr. Haskell?"

"I have a marketing firm. I sell items all over the world on the internet. You do have internet access, don't you?"

"But of course. Would you have a moment to tour a two-bedroom unit?"

"Yes, I was hoping to see one."

"Wonderful. My name is Jennifer, by the way. Please follow me," she said as she stepped out from behind her desk. We walked out of the office. She locked the office door and then unlocked the door leading out of the small lobby and into the actual residential area. The carpet in the hallway was worn, and for being a no-smoking building, it smelled an awful lot like cigarettes. The two-bedroom unit was the second door on the right. I figured the first door was probably the one-bedroom unit.

She unlocked the door, and we stepped into the unit. It seemed to be a fairly standard layout. There was a small entry area and a bathroom off to the left. Off to the right was a small dining area with a table and four chairs. Just beyond that was the kitchen with a four-burner stove, dishwasher, refrigerator, and veneer wood cabinets. On the left was a living room area with a couch, a matching wingback chair, and a coffee table. A window looked out onto a large concrete courtyard with permanent tables and benches bolted to the concrete. Four more five-story buildings surrounded all sides of the courtyard. There were probably twenty people outside, but the area was large enough that it didn't appear crowded. A few kids were using the swings, and two boys, ten or eleven years old, were shooting baskets.

"Let me show you the bedrooms," Jennifer said and stepped over to a closed door. She opened the door and stepped inside. The room had a double bed and a chest of drawers. It would have been too small for a king-sized bed and maybe even a queen size. There was a closet with two sliding doors, one of which was opened, displaying not all that much room.

"Very nice," I lied.

"Let me show you the other bedroom," she said and stepped out of the room. The other bedroom was roughly the same, only smaller. A set of bunk beds were against the far wall. There was a double chest of drawers, three drawers high and presumably for two children. The closet had two sliding doors, one of which was open, revealing a similar closet to the other one, only smaller.

From there, we toured the bathroom, which was barely large enough for both of us. A small sink and cabinet with a mirror were attached to the wall. The tub had a shower head and no shower curtain. Two towel bars were opposite each other. One next to the tub and the other above the toilet.

"Any questions?" Jennifer asked.

"No, it's very nice. Very comfortable. Oh, one question, what is the availability?"

"So not a problem. Units are available on every floor."

"Do you have a lot of people leaving?"

"No more than usual. We're in the midst of the moving season. Things come pretty much to a halt from November to April. No one wants to move in the Minnesota winter."

"Yeah, of course."

I followed her out to the lobby, where she turned and faced me. "Now, we can get you started on a lease. It's fifty dollars to complete our credit report. As I mentioned, we have units available on every floor, so once your credit is approved, which takes just three or four days, you can start moving in."

"Let's do it," I said, and we went back into her office.

She gave me another clipboard, this time with a credit form. I filled out the form in about five minutes. I listed my annual income at a quarter of a million dollars. The only accurate information I put on the form was my name, a credit card number, and my phone number. I had to pay fifty bucks so they could check my credit. I handed the clipboard back to her and said, "Thanks so much. I appreciate you taking the time, Jennifer."

"I'll let you know just as soon as we receive credit approval," she said, and I headed for the lobby and out into the sunshine.

Four

As luck would have it, there was a car with a trailer two parking places away from my vehicle. Just now, two guys were lifting a couch onto the trailer. Six dining room chairs were lined up on the sidewalk next to the trailer. The guys looked to be around thirty. I walked over to my car and waited until they were finished with the couch. "You guys moving out?" I asked.

They looked at me like I was nuts after watching them move the couch onto the trailer. "Yeah, I am, this is our third load, and we've got four or five more after this," a guy with the goatee said.

"How long have you lived here?"

"Just a year, one of the worst years of my life."

"I just had a tour of the two-bedroom unit. I was thinking of moving in. I guess they've got openings on every floor."

The goatee nodded. "That would make sense. The internet is out a couple of times a week. We've had power outages every month that last for hours. No garbage disposals, the sinks back up, and sometimes the toilets. The place is a dive. Whoever built it cut costs everywhere they could. The garage door for the underground parking wouldn't work over Christmas, so no one could leave. That didn't make people very happy."

"I guess not. The place is only a few years old, and you've got power outages?"

"Oh yeah, every month, even in nice weather, all of a sudden, everything goes off, including the elevators. They've got all sorts of lowlifes living here. Did she have you fill out one of those credit forms?" he asked.

"Yeah, I just finished filling it out."

"Well, don't worry. They'll wait a bit and call you, tell you things are filling up, and you'd better act fast. It's all bullshit. When you pay the fifty bucks for the credit report, they keep the money and never actually send the report to be verified. They'll call you later today and tell you that you've been approved. God, my car has been broken into three separate times in the so-called secure underground parking. The last time whoever did it broke the driver's window. You'd think they'd have security cameras down there, but they don't. The alarm went off for hours in my car, and no one did anything. There are some decent folks that live here, but there are some real jerks, too. Save yourself the hassle and go somewhere else."

"Are you moving to one of the other buildings?"

He shook his head. "They're all the same. Lousy internet, the plumbing is half-ass, and the phone lines are out from time to time too. I had three different friends in the other buildings, I'm the last one here, and I can't wait to get out. You'd be better served if you could qualify for low-income housing."

I chuckled at that.

"I'm not kidding, man. Oh, did I mention they apparently don't pay the trash hauler on a regular basis? Twice in the last six months, it wasn't picked up for a couple of weeks. God, we could smell it up on the fourth floor. My wife threatened to leave me if we didn't move. She's been living at her parent's house for the last month. Won't come back here."

"We need to keep moving, Donny," the other guy said.

"Yeah, why don't you watch this stuff, so no one takes it? I'll get that other cart down here." He turned toward me. "Sorry to be such a downer, dude, but take my word. You don't want to be here." With that, he grabbed the cart and began to push it back toward the building.

I climbed into my car and headed back to the office, stopping at McDonald's on the way to grab a couple of cheeseburgers that I ate while driving. Back at the office, Louie's car was nowhere around. I tossed the McDonald's bag in the trash bin in front of the building and headed up the stairs. I wrote a note reminding me of my dinner date with Crystal, telling me to leave by 4:00 and take Morton for a long walk before getting cleaned up

for my wild night. I checked out the White House Apartments online and read the reviews, largely complaints
echoing what the guy with the goatee had told me. Louie
was still out of the office when it was time to leave.

Five

I took Morton for a long walk. Once we were home, I tossed him a biscuit, headed upstairs, and hit the shower. I gave myself a close shave and stepped into some nice trousers and a button-down shirt fresh out of the dry cleaner's bag. On the way over to Crystal's, I picked up two bottles of champagne. I didn't really care for the stuff, but I knew she loved it. I could sip a glass, and she'd empty the bottle and get in the mood, although based on our phone conversation, I figured she was already in the mood and might just meet me at the door wearing only a smile.

As I drove, I reworked my story about the two kids in the treehouse and decided to add a line about them being scared and that they cried themselves to sleep. I came up with the two names, Adam and Eve, just so I wouldn't forget. I figured I could tell Crystal that their father was a minister, and that's where the names came from. Since Crystal had a nice little white dog, a Bichon Frise named Princess, I decided to leave out the part about a pit bull barking and growling at the base of the tree. Instead, I added that the minister father wanted to give me a cash reward, but I wouldn't take the money and instead told him to put me on his prayer list.

Crystal and I have had an on-again, off-again relationship for the last few years. I was my usual self, and amazingly, she liked that, well, until she didn't, and then wouldn't communicate for sometimes six months or more. That was fine with me.

She lived in a trendy neighborhood full of homes built around the time of the first world war. Her home, a two-story buff-colored stucco affair, was on the corner. The large living room window, just to the left of the front door, had beveled glass panels on either side of it. The window in her study had four panes of glass and was on the opposite side of the front door. A rectangular flower-patterned stained glass panel was above that window. Both windows had flower boxes with red geraniums, and both rooms featured a lovely fireplace. We had enjoyed ourselves numerous times in the colder months in front of the fire.

I turned onto her street at the opposite end of the block and immediately thought someone must be having a party. There weren't any parking spaces available even though all of the homes had a double garage in the back on the alley, so they couldn't be homeowners' cars. I drove down the block past her house and parked halfway down the next block. I walked back carrying the paper bag with the two bottles of chilled champagne. When I stopped at the corner, I could see a half-dozen kids in her backyard, and my first thought was that some friends had stopped by unexpectedly. I crossed the street and walked up the brick-paved path to her front door. The front oak door was open, and I could see people, lots of people, through the screen door.

As I stepped inside, a friend of Crystal's, a woman whose name I'd forgotten, turned and looked at me as she sipped from a mug, then shouted, "Crystal, he's here. Your hero has arrived!"

Oh no, please God, don't let this happen, I thought and smiled just as Crystal appeared with a half-filled champagne flute in her hand.

"Oh, right on time. I just had to tell a few people," she said as folks began to empty the rooms behind her. A few people looked familiar, but I don't think I'd ever met most of them before.

"Hi, I brought you some champagne," I said and held out the paper bag.

"Oh, thank you, of course, everyone arrived with a bottle. We've got plenty of everything. Come on, get over here and give me a kiss, my hero."

I smiled and stepped over to kiss her on the cheek. She grabbed me, wrapped her arms around me, and shoved her tongue into my mouth. I suddenly felt chilled champagne running down my back as she pulled me closer. I eventually moved a half-inch away as everyone clapped and hooted. "Could we talk privately for just a moment, please?" I said into her ear.

She nodded, grabbed my hand, and led me back toward the kitchen as people patted my champagne-soaked shirt and said, "Well done."

"God Bless."

"Good Job."

"Poor little kids."

I nodded and kept repeating, "Thank you."

Crystal led me into the pantry. She closed the door behind us, drained her glass, and wrapped her arms around me, again.

Once we came up for air, I took a half-step back. "I thought it was just going to be the two of us for a, you know, a private, up close and personal evening."

"Oh, don't worry, Mister. You're going to get everything you want and more. These are just a few of my friends who stopped over for a few minutes and wanted to congratulate you. It's a big deal, Dev. Everyone wants to hear all about it," she said and then sort of stumbled a half-step backward and refocused. That last move suggested she'd been celebrating for more than a few minutes.

"Oh, it's really nice you invited a few people over," I said, thinking there must be close to a hundred folks in the house. "But I was just hoping, you know, it would just be the two of us."

"Dev, they want to hear all about it. I can't imagine how frightened those two little children must have been, and you found them at midnight, no less. You saved them from real and imagined danger. They could have fallen out of that treehouse and broken a leg, or, oh my God, they could have broken their little necks, the poor babies. You saved them, Dev. You're a hero. Come on, let's celebrate. Everyone wants to hear the story."

"I don't want to tell it, Crystal. In fact, I promised the parents I wouldn't say anything. They're afraid they could be charged with parental neglect or something like that."

"How could that be? You said they were at work. They weren't even home."

"Exactly, Crystal. But it's not too big of a leap to think of some self-righteous politician or even just some-one on the street who thinks they should have been home, or the mother shouldn't have been working, and all of a sudden, they've got a lawsuit on their hands. That's why I just want to keep it quiet."

"But Joe is here, and he wanted to talk to you."

"Who's Joe?"

"Joe Humphrey. My neighbor. They live right across the alley. He writes for the paper."

"He's a reporter?"

She nodded. "He's got his own column. Reports on all kinds of things."

"Oh, I really shouldn't talk to him, Crystal. That could work out to not be good at all for the family, and they've already been through enough."

She gave a long sigh, took a deep breath, and said, "Okay. I suppose you're right. Besides, I need another glass of champagne," she said and handed me her empty champagne flute.

"I'll be happy to get that for you. Come on, let's join your friends since they won't be staying too long."

She smiled, gave me another long kiss, then leaned back and said, "Fill my glass."

She opened the door to the pantry. I grabbed my bag with the champagne bottles, and we stepped out.

"That was fast," some woman said and giggled.

"Not to worry, saving the best till last," Crystal replied. Once I popped the cork on a bottle and refilled her champagne flute, she headed down the hall toward the crowd in the living room. There were at least a dozen wine bottles on the table. Most of them were barely full. A number of bottles and beer cans were in the recycling bin that was next to the kitchen table.

I placed both of the champagne bottles in the refrigerator, grabbed a beer, and headed out toward the living room.

People gradually began to leave just before 9:00. It took another half-hour, but the crowd had thinned to just two other women chatting to Crystal in the living room. I was in the kitchen placing empty bottles in the recycling bin and loading the dishwasher when a guy strolled into the kitchen.

Six

The guy smiled and held out his hand. "So, I guess you're the man of the hour. I'm Joe Humphrey." I placed three glasses in the top rack of the dishwasher, and we shook hands. "Dev Haskell, nice to meet you. You're with the newspaper, aren't you?"

He nodded and said, "Yeah, one of the last. Fortunately, I've got my own column and enough followers that they really haven't pulled the plug on me. Not that they won't, they just haven't yet. So tell me about finding those two little kids."

A warning light flashed in my thick skull. "Not really much to tell. Crystal made a big deal about it. Two little kids climbed up into a treehouse, and it got dark. They were either afraid, or they fell asleep. Anyway, we had a bunch of folks looking for them. I happened to check the treehouse, and there they were, sound asleep."

"Where was this?"

"Oh, in town, but, like I told Crystal, I'm really not going to say anything else because the parents are afraid someone might sue them for child neglect or endangerment or something, and at the end of the day, this was just one of those things that happen when you're raising kids, and thankfully, everyone is okay."

He nodded. "I get it. We've got four of our own. Never a dull moment, and if we happen to get a quiet time, well, that's when we really start to worry because peace and quiet means they're up to something."

We both laughed at that. "So, how are things at the paper? I know you've had some staff cutbacks."

"Some staff? Try most of the staff. We're down to twenty-nine people. We're now printed by our former rivals over in Minneapolis. I joke and say if one of the few reporters we have left had a story to cover over on the East side, they'd have to input it on their GPS so they could find their way over there. Hell, any way you look at it, most of our articles on any given day are picked up from the associated press. Unfortunately, in today's world, if people are looking for up-to-date news, they go onto YouTube or worse."

"There's a lot of inaccurate stuff out there," I commented.

He nodded. "Yeah, and a lot of crazies who buy into it. But on the other hand, a lot of it is accurate or at least is accurately covering a particular perspective. Well, anyway, glad you found those two kids, and everything turned out okay. I've got some pals on the force. I'll check with them tomorrow and see if there's any general information they can pass on."

"They may not even know about it. You know, an emergency call that ends up being nothing. The cops must have uncountable ones like that every day."

He nodded and said, "I'm sure they do, and probably glad they end up being nothing. Well, nice to meet you. You said your name was Den?"

"No, Dev, short for Devlin. Dev Haskell."

"Got it. Nice to meet you. Let me see if I can get the missus to say goodnight so we can head home." He flashed a smile and headed out of the kitchen.

I hauled a few dozen glasses in from the backyard. I took the recycling out to the blue bin next to the garage, cleaned up the kitchen, and turned on the dishwasher. I debated pouring Crystal another champagne and decided that might not be the best idea. I went out to the living room, and there she was, stretched out on the couch with her little dog, Princess, curled up on her lap. Her high heels were scattered across the floor, and she was softly snoring.

I gently shook her shoulder. She groaned and slapped my hand away, never waking. So much for a wild night. I turned off most of the lights, locked the backdoor, and made sure the front door was locked once I closed it behind me. At this time of the night, mine was the only car on the street and parked a half-block away.

Seven

I'd been up for almost an hour before Morton joined me in the kitchen. He got his morning head scratch and headed out into the backyard. I was on my laptop reading the email from Jennifer at the White House Apartments. It said she was excited to let me know that my credit had been approved and then suggested I should hurry to lease a unit because they were being inundated with rental requests.

That was pretty much what the guy moving the couch had told me would happen. Other than my name and email, oh, and my credit card, the rest of the information, starting with me earning a quarter of a million dollars, had all been false. I phoned my credit card company and told them that I was disputing the fifty-dollar charge from White House Apartments. They promised to check into the situation.

Once Morton finished breakfast, we headed down to the office. I was surprised that the coffee pot had been turned off, but then I remembered that I had done that when we left last night. I dumped the dregs down the sink and started a fresh pot. I settled in my chair and took out my binoculars. Unfortunately, neither one of the ladies in the apartment across the street appeared to be available.

Louie came in an hour later. He entered in his usual red-faced manner, huffing and puffing after climbing the steps up to the second floor. He gave me a wave, set his briefcase on the picnic table, and settled into his chair. I poured him a fresh mug of coffee, topped up my mug, and went back to my desk.

After a few minutes and a half-dozen sips, Louie asked, "So, how did things go last night?"

I filled him in and ended up telling him about my short chat with Joe Humphrey.

"Sounds like you got away with it. My advice would be to stick to your story. You don't want to tell anyone about it out of respect for the parents."

"Yeah, I'll tell you what, Crystal had that house full of people, all neighbors and friends. Actually, it put the fear of God in me about even opening my mouth. I finished the night cleaning up the place. Crystal was asleep on the couch, and I made it home at a decent hour, unfortunately."

He chuckled at that last remark just as my cell phone rang. I glanced at the screen. "Oh, here she is now. Pardon me while I take this. Hello, Crystal."

"Oh, Dev. I'm so sorry. I didn't plan to fall asleep. I woke up on the couch just after two this morning."

"Not a problem. If you'll recall, I stood you up the night before, so let's just call it even. Don't worry about it."

"That wasn't you who cleaned up and ran the dishwasher, was it?"

"As a matter of fact, it was. My folks beat it into us that you don't want to wake up to a messy house. I was happy to pick things up for you."

"Did you talk to Joe?"

"Humphrey? Yes, I did. We had a brief conversation. He seemed like a nice guy."

"Is he going to do an article?"

"No, at least I hope not. I asked him not to and didn't give him any real information, so I don't think he will. I really don't want the story out there," I said, just in case she thought she might be doing me a favor by calling Humphrey.

"Well, since I woke up on the couch, I'm guessing we probably didn't…well, you know."

"No, we didn't, but, hey, it was a fun night. You had lots of people over, you enjoyed your champagne, and—
"

"Oh, please, don't mention champagne to me this morning. My head, honest to God, I'm waiting for the aspirin to kick in."

"It's not a problem, Crystal. Listen, if you want, why not come over to my place tonight? I could do some steaks on the grill and—"

"Oh, believe me. I would love to, but I've got a meeting tonight. Well, actually, my book club. But if it would be okay, I'd like to take a rain check. I'm sorry about last night. I just—"

"Crystal, you were the hostess with the mostess. It's not a problem, so stop beating yourself up and let those aspirin do their job."

"Oh, believe me, that can't happen soon enough. All right, thanks. Chat later, Dev. Bye, bye, bye," she said and disconnected.

"So, at the end of the day, it sounds like you're left having to join me over at The Spot tonight," Louie said.

"Yeah, I'm afraid so. I thought for sure—" My phone suddenly rang. "Oh, here we go. She's come to her senses and wants to see me tonight." I picked up the phone without checking caller id and, in what one might consider a sexy voice, said, "Hello, you're speaking to hot, handsome Dev Haskell. How can I serve you?"

There was a pause, and then, unfortunately, an all too familiar voice half-shouted, "Haskell, you dumb shit. Get your worthless ass out here. Tub…err…Mr. Gustafson wants to see you now," Fat Freddy Zimmerman yelled and then disconnected.

I glanced out the window, and there was Tubby Gustafson's Cadillac Escalade double parked next to my car. My day had suddenly taken a turn for the worse.

"Something wrong?" Louie asked. "You look like the rug just got pulled out from beneath you."

"One word, Tubby Gustafson."

"That's actually two words, so it's double bad. Good luck."

"I'd better get out there. The last thing we need is Fat Freddy coming up here." I shoved the phone into my pocket and headed out. Morton hopped off his pillow and met me at the door. "Sorry, buddy. You don't want to be a part of this."

Morton stopped wagging his tail and gave a little moan as I closed the door behind me. I hurried down the stairs and outside. A muscle-bound thug in a red strappy t-shirt hopped out from behind the steering wheel and opened the rear door for me. "Have fun," he said under his breath as I climbed into the back seat.

Eight

Fat Freddy was seated in the passenger seat. "It's about damn time, Haskell," he growled and took a large bite from one of the three cheeseburgers on his lap and said, "Mmm-mmm." He chewed for a half-minute, then swallowed. "I was afraid I was going to have to send Pee Wee up to get your attention."

I glanced in the rearview mirror at the muscle-bound thug in the red strappy t-shirt sitting behind the steering wheel. His name was Pee Wee?

"Glad I came down and saved him the trouble."

"No trouble," Pee Wee said and winked at me in the mirror.

"Back home and step on it. I'm gonna have to use the can," Fat Freddy said and took another bite of his cheeseburger.

It was a short drive to Tubby's mansion on the River Boulevard. Although he wasn't speeding, Pee Wee made it there in little more than ten minutes. Incredibly, we made it through six different stoplights. Each one turned green just as we approached. Probably a half-dozen cars pulled aside as we came up behind them, and in no time at all, we were pulling into the circular drive in front of Tubby Gustafson's mansion just as Freddy finished his second cheeseburger.

We came to a stop in front of the mansion, and two of the armed guards stepped off the front porch. One of them opened the door for Fat Freddy. He grabbed his remaining cheeseburger and oozed out of the car. The other guy nodded and then jerked his head at me, signaling I could open my own door and I should hurry up. I slid across the back seat, opened the door, and got out of the car.

"Assume the position," the guy said as he spun me around and pushed me up against the Escalade.

I placed my hands on the top of the door frame, spread my legs, and assumed the position. It only took a couple of seconds, but he patted down twice, just to be sure. "Nothing, it figures. Okay, he's good to go this time," he yelled and pushed me toward the front door.

Fat Freddy had already stepped inside the mansion and closed the door. Once I stepped inside, I was patted down again by another thug who, once he was finished, shouted, "Clean." He sat back down in a chair and continued reading his comic book. I waited in the entry for another ten minutes until Fat Freddy reappeared.

"Let's go, Haskell," he said as he unwrapped his last cheeseburger. He took a large bite and headed down the hall. I followed. He slowed his pace once we passed the staircase leading to the second floor. He took another giant bite of the cheeseburger and then came to a complete stop ten feet further down. He crammed what remained of the cheeseburger into his mouth, puffing out both cheeks on his fat face. While he chewed, he folded the yellow paper wrapper and stuffed it into a back pocket. He swallowed, chewed some more, swallowed again, burped, and finally said, "Okay, you're already late, so see if you can catch up."

I walked behind him as he quickly waddled the rest of the way down the hall. His large love handles hung over his belt, and his fat rear end jiggled as we headed down the hall. I tried not to look. He stopped at Tubby's office door and knocked.

"Enter," Tubby Gustafson growled from inside his office. Fat Freddy opened the door, and we stepped in. Tubby was lying on his massage table with his eyes closed. Fortunately, a white towel was covering his massive, pink backside. Two women wearing thongs and surgical gloves stood on either side, massaging Tubby's hairy, dimpled shoulders. A layer of fat was draped over the edge of the massage table and shaking back and forth as his shoulders and upper back were massaged. Between Tubby and Fat Freddy, I was probably observing at least seven hundred pounds.

"Haskell here to see you, sir," Fat Freddy said.

Tubby appeared to take a deep breath as if my presence was suddenly interrupting some pleasurable activity. The more I thought about it, the more that seemed to be a rather accurate description. Eventually, he opened his eyes and focused on me.

"Oh, God, Haskell," he said, not sounding happy. He signaled the women to stop and waved them off with a flip of his hand. They quickly stepped away, walking backward and bowing for six or seven steps before turning and hurrying toward the door in the far corner.

Tubby groaned as he raised himself to a sitting position. He sat on the side of the massage table, breathing heavily as if he'd just run a mile. He reached for a large, white, terrycloth robe. He pulled it on and slowly slid off the massage table. Unfortunately, he exposed himself in the process, and I quickly stared in another direction. He cinched the robe closed, slipped his feet into fluffy white fur slippers, and stepped over to his desk. He picked up the remnants of a cigar from the ashtray and eventually managed to light it, sending a cloud of blue-gray smoke up toward the ceiling.

"So, Haskell. I have a little project for you."

"Oh, thank you, sir. But, unfortunately, at the moment, I'm actually working on a real estate investigation and the death of—"

"Well, put that aside. This is important to me."

"I'm sure it is, sir. But this investigation that I'm working on is important to the daughter of a family friend, and I really—"

"Wait a moment. Did I just hear you suggest that I'm not a family friend? After all I've done for you. Covering up all the mistakes you make on a daily basis. Protecting you from the likes of the Minnesota Department of Revenue, the mayor's office, the State Licensing Bureau, and the Sheriff's Department, just to name a few. Shall I go on?"

"I'm not exactly sure what you're talking about, sir. To my knowledge, I've never been under an investigation by any of—"

"Exactly, Haskell. That's because I've been protecting you. Now, as far as I'm concerned, you can continue with whatever you're investigating. Let me just ask, does it have anything to do with me?"

"No sir, at least not that I'm aware of."

"Perfect. I'd like you to spend the next week allowing my nephew to observe you in your work mode. Look at it as a mentoring project. He recently graduated from college and is considering a career in some form of law enforcement."

"But, sir, I'm not actually in law enforcement. As a private investigator, I—"

"Exactly, Haskell. Hard to believe, but you may be catching on. After spending a week with the likes of you, I suspect he'll run as fast as he can in another direction. Medicine, technical engineering, computer programing, industrial engineer, just about anything as long as he doesn't have to associate with individuals such as you."

"But if he's already graduated from college, what does he have a degree in?"

Tubby shook his head. "God only knows why, but a double major, prelaw and computer programing."

"Well, I suppose, if you want me to talk to him, I'd be happy to meet him for lunch someday. Now I—"

"Were you listening, Haskell?" Tubby said. He took a long drag on his cigar, leaned forward, and blew a cloud of smoke directly at me. "I believe I just told you. I want him to spend the next week with you, observing how you spend your days. It should serve as just the incentive he'll need to get this desire for law enforcement out of his system."

"Well, if I could have a day, or actually, two would be even better, to put a hold on things and—"

"Not going to happen. Just a minute while I send for him," Tubby said and picked up his phone. He pushed two buttons and a moment later said, "Yes, if you would bring Erik into my office. No, now, please," he said and hung up.

"Sir, as much as I'd like to help, I really don't have the time for this at the moment. If we could possibly schedule something in a few days, or actually, a week or two later would be even better—"

"No, Haskell. I'll expect you to simply carry on in your normal fashion, making mistakes, bumbling, attempting to cover up your bad decisions, and—Oh, well, that was quick. Thank you, James. Erik, please come in. This is Detective Haskell. The individual," Tubby gave me a look, "that I mentioned over dinner last night."

"Detective Haskell, my nephew, Erik Gustafson."

Erik was a nice-looking guy. I guessed early to mid-twenties. He had neatly combed blonde hair and was about my height. Contrary to his uncle, he appeared to be in very good shape as he hurried toward me. He nodded as he passed Tubby and extended his hand.

"Pleased to meet you, sir. My uncle has told me a lot about you." He winked as we shook hands.

"Nice to meet you, Erik. I was just suggesting to your uncle that it might be better if we postponed this for a week or two, and I could line some things up that would be of a little more interest to you."

"I'm sure whatever you're working on would be of interest to me, sir," he said and then mouthed the word 'please.'

"As I mentioned, Haskell, it's important for Erik to see all aspects of your occupation."

Erik nodded and shot me another pleading look.

"Well then, there's no time like the present. We might as well get started. I was chauffeured over this morning, sir. Might there be someone available to give us a ride back to my office?"

I heard Erik let off a sigh of relief.

"Frederick, if you would, please transport Erik and Haskell back to that, err, office. We'll let them get down to work. Mind yourself, Haskell. Erik, pay attention. You'll have a bird's eye view of how you will be spending your time for the next four or five decades, should you so decide."

Fat Freddy opened the office door. Erik shook hands with Tubby, thanked him, and we headed down the hall and out the front door. Freddy gave a wave to muscle-bound Pee Wee in the red strappy t-shirt. He was leaning against the back of the Escalade, looking at his cell phone, and didn't notice Freddy.

Fat Freddy suddenly gave a sharp whistle. Pee Wee glanced up, nodded, and hurried into the Escalade. Once he stopped in front of us, I climbed into the back seat. Erik was about to join me, but Fat Freddy ushered him into the front passenger seat. Just before we drove off, Fat Freddy wagged an index finger at me in a warning manner. Pee Wee accelerated, and we headed back to my office. No one said a word during the ten-minute drive.

Nine

Once we climbed out of the Escalade and Pee Wee drove off, Erik said, "So this is where your office is?"

"Look, Erik. First, let me say I appreciate you not saying anything in front of your uncle."

Erik nodded. "Not a problem. How do you know him? He's never mentioned you before, not that I see him all that often. My dad never really mentioned him. Of course, they never seemed to get along."

"What does your dad do?"

"He passed away a few years back, cancer. He had a little contracting firm with a handful of employees. They would redo your kitchen, build an addition on your house, or build you a new garage, that kind of thing."

"Did he work for your uncle?"

Erik shook his head. "No, like I said, they didn't really get along. My dad was a really straight arrow. Everything he did was aboveboard, and that's the way I was raised. He worked hard his entire life with not a lot of money to show for it. So, when I wanted to go to college, my uncle stepped up and said wherever I wanted to go, he'd write the check. At first, Dad was against it, but the reality of the cost of tuition brought him around. My uncle paid my tuition, and I'm in that minority of kids that graduated and don't have any debt."

"Wow, awfully nice of your uncle to do that."

"Yeah, I know, it comes as a surprise. I can see it in your face, but he does do nice things every once in a while. Are you going to show me your office?"

"Yeah, come on up. It will give you a taste of the real world. Although, if your dad was a contractor, you've probably already got a pretty good idea of what it's like."

"You kidding? Every summer for the past six years, I was on a roofing crew. Three guys tearing off shingles and putting a new roof on. It's one of the things that made me determined to get two degrees and good grades. I made the Dean's List all four years."

"Might have been an incentive from your dad. Where'd you go?"

"Here in town, the U. My mom needed help, and I didn't want to leave her on her own."

"Is she okay?"

"Mom? Oh yeah, it's just that, you know, left to her own devices, she'd forget about cutting the grass. She'll never know how to change the oil in the car or fix anything mechanical."

"Come on upstairs, and you can get an idea of what I go through on any given day."

Louie was out when we entered the office. Morton was up off his pillow in a half-second. He ignored me and headed for Erik, who must have had experience with dogs because he gave him a good scratch behind the ears, causing Morton's tail to wag back and forth. "You've got a friend for life now, Erik. That's Morton. Morton, meet Erik."

Erik took a couple of steps further into the office, stopped, and looked around. "You've got a picnic table for a desk?"

"Yeah, I know what you're thinking. Actually, that's not my desk. It belongs to my officemate. He's a lawyer."

"And that's his desk?"

"It is. He used to be with the city attorney's office. He's been on his own, and we've shared an office for a number of years now."

"And you're a PI, right? A private investigator?"

"Yeah, come on, take a seat at my desk. You want some coffee? It's reasonably fresh, I think."

"No thanks, but help yourself if you want," he said as he sat down in one of the client chairs in front of my desk.

I grabbed my coffee mug, filled it up, and turned off the burner. "So," I said, settling into my desk chair, "your uncle said you're thinking of something in law en-forcement."

"Well, not exactly. That's his version. I got a degree in prelaw and a degree in computer programing. What

I'm really interested in is joining some government security organization."

"You mean like the CIA?"

"Possibly, or the National Security Agency, Defense Intelligence, Homeland Security, National Intelligence. Something on that level. It's why I got the prelaw degree, although now I'm sort of toying with the idea of law school. Of course, that would take another three years."

"So why did your uncle stick us together? He may be a character, but he's not stupid."

"Yeah, I know, or I think I know. Questions about him and what he does were forbidden in our house. If someone asked my dad if he was related, he would always shake his head and say no."

"And yet you had dinner with him last night?"

"I've spent the last two days at his place, basically twiddling my thumbs. My mom doesn't know I'm there, and my uncle took it as a feather in his cap that I wanted his assistance. But after forty-eight hours of getting nothing accomplished, I just had to get out of there."

"And so you got stuck with me," I said and laughed.

"Works both ways." Erik grinned. "But I'd be interested in what you do. If and when I apply to one or even all of those agencies, it would be great if I had some experience. I don't mean taking pictures of some married guy having an affair or anything like that. But maybe you've got something you're working on, something where you could use my expertise. I know some law basics. Of course, you probably know more than me, but if I could just watch what you're doing. I promise not to get in your way."

I nodded and thought for a moment. "Here's the deal. You know all the stuff you see on TV? The guy stopping a bank robbery, arresting some jerk who was threatening a gorgeous woman, or shooting three bad guys at close range, that's all bullshit. Most of what I do is boring. I check out job applications where people list their work history, and I check to see if it's accurate. Do they have an arrest record? That sort of thing. But as you're saying this, I am just starting to look at another case, and I'm wondering if you might be able to help."

"Yeah, sure. I don't know what I can do, but I'll help you in any way I can."

I handed Melissa's file on the White House Apartments over to him. "Read this and tell me what you think. A woman I've known since she was a little girl gave me this. Her father is mentioned in there, but he and his wife were killed in a car accident a while back, and his business shares were turned over to his partner, a guy named Odell Dankworth."

Erik took the file, then opened up his laptop bag, took out his laptop, and turned it on. When he lifted the screen on the laptop, it set off a musical tone. He tapped some keys on the computer, studied the screen for a moment, typed something in, and then began reading the manuscript.

"You want our password?"

"Not necessary. I already have it."

"Already have it?"

"LouieHaskellDevLaufen, right?"

"Yeah, that's it, but how did you get that?"

"Your access is pretty much unsecured. Looks like the password is your officemate's first name and your surname and your first name and his surname, correct?"

"Well, yeah, but it's supposed to be secured. Top secret. Known only to Louie and me."

"Yeah, well, that's probably accurate for 90% of the population, but for that other 10 percent, myself included, we have a program that can usually pick the password up in a couple of seconds. It works on most personal and small business sites. Corporations and certain businesses are a different case. Anyway, thanks, but I've already got access."

"Mmm, I might ask you to tighten up our security."

"Happy to do so. It would only take a minute."

Erik read through Melissa's file for the next ninety minutes. He went back and forth from the file to typing on his laptop. At one point, he asked, "Would you mind if I highlighted some items in this report?"

"Not a problem, Erik, go ahead. Do whatever you want."

I was on my desktop computer. I had the sound turned off and was looking at some risqué online pictures. Erik set the file on the desk and seemed to stare at the ceiling for a long minute. I clicked off the XXX site and brought up a local news site on YouTube.

"Have you been out to this White House place?" he asked

"Yeah, it's out in Woodbury, just along I-94. You've probably been past it. I stopped out there yesterday," I said, and then gave him a quick synopsis of my visit and my conversation with the two guys loading the couch onto the trailer.

"I'd be interested in seeing the place."

"We can head out there now. I was going to call Melissa back. She's the woman who gave me the file. But I'd be interested in getting your perspective on the place before I call her."

Ten

On our way out to the White House Apartments, Erik gave me his opinion of the file.

"Without going into any detail, my first thought is that it would seem unusual for someone to sign a contract that automatically, upon their death, turns over all interest to a partner. But having said that, I obviously don't know the circumstances. What if the partner funded the guy? Does the agreement allow that, had this Dankworth guy been killed in a car accident, Mr. Carter would automatically obtain his percentage of ownership? It would seem to be one of the things you'd want to find out. The way you described the place, five buildings with a hundred units in each building, that's a lot of people."

"Five hundred units total, I would think a good percentage of them would be two people. I don't know, thirty or forty percent might have a child or even two kids. We'll tour a two-bedroom unit. You can see for yourself."

We exited the Interstate and took the frontage road to the White House Apartments. I headed into a different parking lot this time, but the layout was the same. There was a door in the center of the building. A small gable roof hung above the door with the sign 'Leasing Office' in blue letters. There were seven empty parking spaces next to the entrance, and I parked in the one closest to the door.

"Obviously, not a busy day," Erik said.

"I think it depends on who you talk to. The woman I dealt with yesterday sent me an email saying I was approved and I should let her know as soon as possible because they had a lot of people wanting to rent a unit. The guy I talked to who was moving out told me there were empty units available on every floor. In fact, when I was in the office filling out that application, someone called complaining that they'd moved but were still being charged rent, which suggests there are empty units and not enough people to fill them."

We entered the building. It was a carbon copy of the building I'd been in yesterday. The security door was straight ahead, with the phone on the wall next to the door. The entrance to the leasing office was just over on the right.

We stepped into the leasing office. A repeat of where I'd been yesterday, with the brown leather couch to the right of the door and the framed poster of the White House Apartments hanging on the wall above the couch. There was a marble-topped counter and a credenza with a stack of clipboards. Last but not least, a woman was on the phone. At the moment, she was saying, "Your lease was for twelve months. It will expire in August. Until then, if no one rents the unit, you are responsible for the rent. We can't send our crew in to repaint the unit and make it available to rent until you move out."

"No, ma'am, I realize you're going to move at the end of the month. Once you move, we will send a crew in to repaint the walls and deal with any damage that may have happened in the course of your day-to-day activity. Yes, thank you. Goodbye."

At least she didn't mouth some colorful term before turning toward us.

"Good morning. Are you here to learn about leasing one of our units?"

"Hopefully," Erik replied. "I'd like to look at a two-bedroom unit if that's possible."

"Certainly, that won't be a problem. Let me just have you fill out one of our application forms. Would you like one or two application forms?" she said, reaching back to the stack of clipboards on the credenza behind her.

"Just one," Erik answered.

We settled in on the couch, and Erik quickly filled out the form. The office phone rang, but after two rings, it stopped, and I guessed it automatically transferred the caller to a message center.

Erik got off the couch and handed the clipboard back to the woman. "Would it be possible to see a two-bedroom unit today?"

"Yes, of course, Mr. Gustafson. If you'll follow me, please," the woman said, setting the clipboard on the marble-topped counter. She locked the door once we stepped out of the office and then led us in through the security door. Just like yesterday, the unit was the second door on the right. As we stepped inside, the walls and ceilings and the furnishings were exactly the same, which made sense. One bedroom had a double bed, the other had a bunk bed with the same double chest of drawers, three drawers high, and the dining area had the same table and four chairs. The window on the living room wall looked out onto the poured concrete area with the tables and benches attached to the concrete. There seemed to be fewer people out there today, and I didn't notice any children.

Erik turned on the kitchen sink. He ran the sink in the bathroom for a half-minute, and he flushed the toilet. He knocked on the walls in the rooms and asked if he would be responsible for the energy bill.

"Oh, yes, energy, internet, and the water," the woman responded.

It took no more than five minutes to view the place. The woman asked if we had any other questions. Erik shook his head no. She repeated the standard line about getting the credit rating back in forty-eight hours and that, if he was interested, Erik should let her know immediately because the units were filling up quickly. She handed him a business card and led us out to the lobby. We said our goodbyes and left. There was no one loading up a trailer with furniture, so we climbed into the car.

"Well, what did you think?" I asked as I headed out of the parking lot.

"You ever do any construction work, painting, framing, that sort of thing?"

"No, never. I had odd jobs in high school, went into the army, came out, and got my PI License."

"Well, like I told you, I did a bunch for my dad over the summers and vacation weeks. That place is a dive. The walls and ceilings are painted the same color, sprayed an off-white. I don't know if you noticed, but there was spray paint residue all along the carpet next to the mopboard. When we were in that master bedroom, and all the rooms for that matter, I knocked on the walls. The place was all quarter-inch sheetrock. I'm not even sure that's legal. It means you're going to hear noise from the units on either side of you, and they'll hear just about everything you say or do. Oh, and by the way, I think the exterior walls are hardly insulated. The power bills for one of those units would be a couple hundred a month, easy. The water pressure sucked. I'm guessing you're going to have to wait a couple of minutes for hot water to arrive. The toilets will plug on a regular basis. I'm pretty sure the place is plumbed using plastic pipes. The veneer on the kitchen cabinets was warped, so sooner or later, that's going to come off, and this is in the model unit that's not even being lived in. Can you imagine what the units look like where a couple of kids or some heavy-drinking guy has been living? My first thought is the place is a rip-off. They cut corners during construction, and things went downhill from there. When did you say this place was built?"

"The five buildings were built over the course of two years from 2019 to 2020."

"Oh, man. So the place isn't even five years old, and it's falling apart. Did you smell cigarette smoke in the hallway? It's supposed to be non-smoking, but I could smell cigarettes. If they're having trouble keeping the place full, and I suspect they are, I would guess they're turning a blind eye to a lot of problems or potential problems."

I turned onto the Interstate and headed back to town. "So nothing you're telling me matches up with my friend, Jack Carter. He was a quality kind of guy. Did everything to perfection. I can't believe he'd cut corners the way you're saying things were done back there."

"What if he didn't? What if he didn't know that was being done? You said his daughter thinks he was killed?"

"Yeah, he and his wife. Damn good people."

"What if he was just funding the construction or part of it? What if he signed loans and got a percentage but never really looked at what was being done? Maybe he found out too late about all the corners they were cutting, and then when he brought it up, crash bang. Problem solved. You know anything about his partner?"

I shook my head. "Odell Dankworth? No, not really. Other than reading that file and seeing his name, I think that's the first time I've ever heard of him."

"Might be interesting to see what else he's involved in. Would you mind if I checked him out? It would be interesting to see what I can find online."

"I think that would be great, Erik. Thank you. You're a hell of a good apprentice."

He laughed. Five minutes later, we parked behind Louie's faded Ford Fiesta. The upper half of the taillight on the right side was missing. You could see the light bulb.

"Man, that thing looks like a piece of shit," Erik said.

"I have to agree with you. It belongs to my office mate, Louie. The owner of the picnic table. He probably had a court appearance this morning, or he was interviewing a new client. I think I told you he was in the city attorney's office for a while. Apparently, he didn't get along, and they let him go. Actually, he's become the go-to guy in town if you happen to be charged with a DUI. Those are pretty much the only cases he handles now, and he's damn good at it."

"So, he drives that car to try and fit in with his clients?"

"He deals with lots of upper-level folks who, for one reason or another, got nailed. Come on up and meet him.

He's a good guy, a good friend, and in his own way, he's always got my back. Oh, and he usually spends a good deal of any night at that bar behind us. The Spot. It's the neighborhood local."

"Never heard of it."

"See, Erik, that's because you travel with nice people. You want to do my business, you've got to mix with a certain crowd. Come on. I'll introduce you to Louie."

We climbed out of the car and hurried across the street. Once up on the second floor, Erik took a long moment to stare at two women sitting in chairs in the hairdressers across the way.

"Forget it, Erik. You'll only get into trouble."

"Just looking."

"Yeah, take my word for it, that's exactly how it starts."

Eleven

s we stepped into the office, Louie peeked around his laptop. Morton hopped off his pillow and hurried over to lick Erik's hand. "Louie, how did your court appearance go this morning?"

"About what I expected. My client's driver's license is suspended to limited use for six months, travel to and from work, the grocery store, and weekly AA meetings. How's your day?" he asked, eyeing Erik.

"Louie, this is Erik Gustafson. Erik, my office mate, Louie Laufen. Erik's going to be working with me on a case. He'll be looking into some things online."

"Nice to meet you, Erik. Are you, by any chance, related to Tub…err…Mr. Gustafson?"

"Yeah, he's my uncle. It's okay with me if you call him Tubby. I get it."

"Erik's dad was a brother. Erik's got a degree in prelaw and computer programing from the U."

Louie smiled. "Well, that automatically makes him the smartest guy in this office. Nice to meet you, Erik," Louie said, and they shook hands.

"Erik, you want to fire up your laptop and check out that guy at the White House Apartments? I better take Morton for a walk before he leaves an unpleasant reminder."

Erik nodded and settled into one of the client chairs in front of my desk. I grabbed Morton's leash, clipped it on his collar, and we headed out the door. We were back in the office fifteen minutes later. Louie and Erik were involved in some technical conversation.

"So you're telling me we have an ineffective security system here?" Louie asked as Morton headed over to Erik for another head scratch.

"Not exactly," Erik said. "It's just that I was able to automatically search and obtain your password in about twenty seconds. All that means is you should set up your system a little differently. I can do it for you in a couple of minutes. But wait until you're done with whatever you're working on. We can do it at the end of the day."

"What do you think, Dev?" Louie asked.

"Why wouldn't we? Then I can just write the new password down, tape it onto my computer, and I won't have to remember it."

Erik gave me a long, surprised look.

"He's kidding you, Erik. He won't do that."

"Yeah, I'll just write it on my calendar, and I'll always know where to find it. Hey, I'm going up to Roosters and grabbing some BBQ pork sandwiches. That sound all right with you, Erik?"

"Yeah, that would be great."

"Louie?"

"My usual, if you don't mind. You need some cash?"

"No, I'm good. I'll be back in fifteen minutes." I grabbed the leash, and Morton and I headed up to Roosters. It was close to 1:30, and there was only one person in line ahead of us. I ordered three BBQ pork sandwiches and got a beef marrow bone for Morton. When we left Roosters, he ignored me all the way back to the office and gave his undivided attention to the bag with the sandwiches and the bone.

Once in the office, I unclipped his leash and gave him the bone before he tried to tear the entire bag from my hands. I handed Erik his sandwich and two napkins. I placed my sandwich and two napkins on my desk and handed Louie his sandwich and four napkins.

"Oh, man, these are really good," Erik said. "Where'd you say you got these?"

"Just up the block. A place called Roosters. These are their BBQ smoked pork shoulder sandwiches. We probably grab something up there at least twice a week."

"Mmm-mmm, at least twice. I could eat sandwiches from there every day," Louie said and took a gigantic bite. Of course, a couple pieces of BBQ pork tumbled down the side of his light blue shirt.

"Oh yeah, and that's how we can tell where Louie got his lunch. Every time he eats something from Roosters, it leaves a trail of BBQ sauce down the front of his shirt."

"Which is why I wear a suit coat," Louie said. He attacked the BBQ stains with a couple of napkins but only succeeded in making things worse. After lunch, Louie worked on whatever he was dealing with, and Erik began searching anything and everything he could find on Odell Dankworth, the former partner of Jack Carter and the current owner of the White House Apartments.

Toward the end of the day, Erik reviewed the volumes of online information with me regarding Dankworth. After a couple of hours of checking the guy out, it was pretty clear it was mostly happy thoughts sorts of things online. Dankworth hosted a Christmas party fundraiser for homeless people. He hosted fundraisers for a number of political candidates. Interestingly, the candidates were from both parties, two Democrats and two Republicans, so he was playing both sides of the fence, which somehow didn't seem all that surprising.

At exactly 5:00, Louie turned off his computer and said, "Who's up for The Spot?"

"I was just thinking—"

"What if I update your password before you guys go over there? It will just take a minute," Erik said.

I nodded. "Yeah, that sounds like a good idea. Can you hang on for a minute before you rush over, Louie?"

"Sure, what do you need me to do?"

"If both of you would turn off your computers," Erik said.

Louie turned his off. My computer kept going through a half-dozen sites and then returned me to the

XXX video site I apparently never logged off from earlier in the day. After a long fifteen seconds, it finally shut down. "Okay, at long last, my computer is off."

"All right, just hang on for a moment. Let me enter your email addresses here." He typed for a couple of seconds. I had to say, he was awfully fast. His fingers were a blur flying across the keyboard. A moment later, he said, "Okay, new password?"

"What if we just use the old one?" I asked.

"That will work, but if anyone hacked into your site earlier, they'd still have access using that password."

"I say we change it," Louie said and spun his Rolodex. "You got one you want to use, Dev?"

"Not really. Go ahead if you got one there on the Rolodex."

Louie read it off, "PeekABoo.Iseeyou."

"No, I'm not doing that. Besides, I'd never remember. How 'bout this one, ElementaryMyDearWatson."

"Sherlock Holmes?" Louie said. "Yeah, that works for me."

"You want to stick with that one, Dev?"

"Yeah, Erik, change it to that for us."

Erik typed for a second or two and then glanced up at us and said, "Okay, see if you can log on."

Louie ran his fingers across the keyboard. "Yeah, okay, I'm in."

I typed the password and hit enter. I was rejected immediately. "Damn it." I typed it in again and was rejected a second time. "Something must be wrong. It's not accepting me."

"Are you typing it all as one word?" Erik asked.

"Of course I am. I'm the one who gave you the…wait a minute. I think I caught it." I typed it in again, carefully, and a moment later, I had access to our internet. "Yeah, now I've got it." I grabbed my pen and wrote the password on my calendar so that the next time I was rejected, I could just look it up."

Erik appeared about to say something then shook his head. "All right, you're both set, and your system is about a thousand times more secure."

"I'm heading over to The Spot," Louie said. "You two going to join me?"

"What time do you have to be back at your uncle's?" I asked.

"He never said anything. I can grab an Uber if you want to head over with Louie."

"No way. I don't need your uncle even more pissed off at me than usual. Let me take Morton for a walk, and we'll get you back."

"Would you mind if I went on the walk with you? I usually run a couple of miles every day. Unless you and Morton were planning to have some private conversation, I could use the exercise."

"Morton wouldn't put up with a private conversation. He always wants a witness when he's dealing with Dev," Louie said.

Louie headed over to The Spot. Erik packed up his laptop, and we took Morton on our usual three-block walk. Along the way, I thanked Erik for all his help. Not only the password and tighter control on the office internet but his suspicions on the subpar construction of the White House Apartments as well.

"I've got some other thoughts I want to check out," he said.

"Oh, great, just don't forget to spend some time with your uncle. I don't want him thinking I buried you with all sorts of work you have to do."

"Not a problem. I'll just grab a sandwich in the kitchen, tell him goodnight, and head up to the guest room. He'll be happy to get me out of his hair. I think he'd much rather interact with those two masseuse ladies."

"Oh, so you know about them?"

"Yeah, I walked in on him yesterday morning. I'm pretty sure that's why I report to James, his secretary, every morning now. It's kind of funny. I mean, both those women are really nice looking, and can you imagine what it's like for the two of them to have to give my fat uncle a massage?"

"No thanks," I said. I gave Erik my cell phone number and told him to call me in the morning.

Twelve

Morton and I drove Erik back to Tubby's mansion. When I pulled up in front of the place, two guys stepped off the front porch with the idea of telling me to move into the parking area. One of them gave me the finger. He called out a colorful term and was about to add something else to whatever he'd said when Erik opened the passenger door and climbed out.

"Oh, Mr. Gustafson. Nice to see you, sir. Everything okay?" the other guy asked.

"Yeah, fine, thank you. Just getting dropped off," he said, then turned to face me and grinned.

"Oh, I love it. Should we stay here and chat for twenty minutes and really piss them off?" I asked.

"How about I give you a call around 8:00 tomorrow morning," Erik laughed. "Hey, thanks for the day. I really enjoyed it, and I've got your file to go through at least one more time." He held up his leather computer bag, gave a nod, and headed for the front door. The security guys smiled, passed on a joke, and opened the door for him.

I watched until the front door closed behind him and then drove around the circular drive and out the gate. I headed back down to the office, parked, and Morton and I headed into The Spot. Morton was charging along the bar on a tight leash. I gave a nod to Louie, seated on his stool, and he called to Mike, the bartender for another round. As we stepped around the bar, Louie emptied half the bag of pork rinds into his hand, dropping two or three toward the floor. Morton lapped one of them up in mid-air before it even hit the floor. He licked up the other two and then cleaned off Louie's hand in about a half-second as Louie bent down.

"You give your apprentice, Erik a ride back to Tubby's?" Louie asked.

"Yeah. I would have been okay with him joining us here, but after the first day being with me, that would have sent all the wrong messages to Tubby."

"Not to worry, Tubby probably got the wrong message anyway."

"Yeah, no doubt," I said just as Mike stepped up with my beer and Louie's drink. "I'll pay for these, Mike. You've had a tough enough night just having to keep Louie in line." I tossed a twenty, my last one, onto the bar.

"There isn't enough money in the world," Mike said as he grabbed my twenty and headed back down the bar.

"How'd your day go with Erik?"

"Surprisingly well. I think he's the type of person who is going to do his absolute best on whatever project he's involved with. Whether it's creating some new computer program or shoveling snow off the sidewalk. He told me he was going to grab a sandwich in Tubby's kitchen and then go over Melissa's file yet again up in the guest room. I gave him my number, and he's going to give me a call tomorrow morning when he wants to be picked up."

"Be careful. You might get that call early tomorrow morning."

"That's what I'm afraid of." We chatted over the course of two beers, and then Morton and I headed home. I ate a bowl of leftover pasta for dinner after heating it up in the microwave. We headed up to bed after the news, and I slept until the alarm woke me the following morning.

I'd finished breakfast and was checking out the news on YouTube when Morton finally came down-stairs. I let him out into the backyard and filled his food and water dishes. He was back inside and had just fin-ished breakfast when my phone rang.

"Hi Erik, you all set to go?"

"Whenever you are. It's a nice morning, Dev, so I'm going to step outside, and I'll see you whenever you get here."

"We'll head out in just a second. See you in about fifteen minutes," I said. I got Morton into the back seat, and we headed over to Tubby's. I was halfway up the circular drive when Erik stepped off the front porch, gave a wave to the two guys by the door, and watched me pull up. He climbed in, gave Morton a scratch behind the ears, and buckled up.

"How'd your night go?" he asked as I drove back onto the street

I had the feeling he was expecting me to give him explicit details about an affair with a couple of gorgeous women. He looked a little disappointed when I told him I had a beer with Louie, went home, and climbed into bed after the news.

"So, Erik. How did your night go? Did those two good-looking women knock on the guest room door and offer to give you an intimate massage to help you sleep?"

"Oh, man, I only wish. No, my night was just a version of yours. I grabbed a sandwich, ate in the kitchen, and went over your file for the umpteenth time."

"You learn anything?"

"That might be too strong a term, but I came up with a couple of possibly good ideas."

"Such as?"

"Well, in her file, she mentions some contractors who were doing work on the White House Apartments project. Karlson Plumbing and Honey Johns, I know, or at least knew, a couple of guys who worked for those companies. Of course, that was three years ago, and I don't know if they still work there or not."

"I get the plumbing company. In fact, I've heard of them before. They work on big projects like the White House Apartments. I don't think they do home stuff, do they?"

"No, I think it's all large construction."

"And Honey Johns, it rings a bell, but I can't tell you what they do. It sounds like a bakery. Did they bring lunch to the work crews or something?"

Erik chuckled and shook his head. "They're popular on the construction sites. They're the porta-potty company."

"How'd you meet them?"

"Not the way you're thinking. It's the family business of one of my high school pals."

"Oh, I'm sure no one ever gave him a hard time about that."

"Actually, the family is highly successful, as you might imagine. A business where there is a constant need for their product. I never worked for them, but a couple of pals had summer jobs servicing the things, and they were on a truck that, you know, emptied the toilets. My pals would clean and scrub the things down, charge the toilet with fresh blue liquid, and replace paper towels and toilet paper. We'd give them a hard time, and they'd respond by reminding us of their hourly wage, which would usually be about five bucks an hour more than we were making."

"And this Honey Johns company was on the White House Apartments site?"

"Yeah, based on that file, the entire time the place was under construction. My dad's company worked at a couple of sites with Karlson, the plumbing company. I got to know a couple of the plumbers there, nice guys."

"Why don't you give those companies a ring? See if we could talk to them."

"I'll give them a call right now," Erik said.

"So, did your uncle ask you how your day went yesterday?"

"Not in so many words. He asked me what I did. I kept it vague and told him everything went fine. He nodded, said good, and said if there were any problems, I should let him know right away."

"Let him know? I better watch out and be on my best behavior."

"Yeah, well, a BBQ sandwich from Roosters every day would go a long way toward getting you on my good side."

"We'll see about that," I said.

Thirteen

Erik lined up a meeting with one of the plumbers, a guy named T.J. McKnight, at 4:00 that afternoon. We met him at a bar named Dirty Frank's. I'd heard about the place from time to time but had never been there before. The bar was over on the East side, a section of town I, more or less, know my way around but an area I'm not in regularly.

Dirty Frank's looked like your typical neighborhood bar, about the size of The Spot. A two-story building with an apartment on the second floor. A large painted sign was above the door, and a red neon sign in the window next to the door said 'OPEN.'

I parked on the street almost directly in front of the place, which, at 4:00 on a weekday afternoon, suggested it wasn't all that busy. When we stepped into the bar, I looked around and counted five people. A couple sat at a table in a corner, and three guys were seated at the bar. The youngest of the three, T.J. McKnight, gave a wave. Erik waved back as we headed over. Introductions were made, and we ordered beers.

T.J. shook his head when I offered to buy him another round. "Thanks, but one's my limit. Otherwise, the wife will make my life miserable. Besides, we got three kids I pick up at after-school daycare. I gotta be on my toes dealing with them," he said.

He and Erik exchanged updates. T.J. expressed his condolences on Erik's dad's passing and then asked what our interest was in the White House Apartments.

"Dev has a case that might have some connection to that project. You worked there, didn't you? I kind of remember some of your stories."

"Yeah, we worked there. But I'm not proud to say we did. It was shit we were hooking up, and it went against any and all advice we were giving the owner, but of course, he knew better. The company pulled out after about ninety days. I'm sure the owner figured we just wanted to jack the price up, but we had some real concerns about the place. Five stories, and it was all going to be plastic pipe? Come on. The stuff was brand new, and it wasn't able to work properly back then. I can't imagine what it's like now."

"I applied for an apartment there yesterday," Erik said and went on to tell T.J. about the water pressure and the noise.

"That doesn't surprise me. You're not thinking of moving in there, are you? If you are, don't. It's literally not safe."

"I was knocking on the walls and checking things out. It sounded like quarter-inch sheetrock on the interior walls, and I don't think the exterior walls were very well insulated," Erik said.

"Unfortunately, you're right on both counts. We warned them more than once, but they wouldn't listen. Finally got the word from our boss we were pulling out of the contract. I wouldn't want anyone I know living in that place. I'm sure we're not the only trade they cut corners on."

"Well, at the end of the day, it was approved by the city inspectors," I said.

"Yeah, I heard rumors there was something not right there, but just rumors. Like I said, we were just glad to finish the building and get onto the next project. Hey, Erik, great to see you. Thanks for the phone call. Dev, nice to meet you. I hate to drink and run, but I gotta pick up the kids in twenty minutes. If you want to talk with our foreman on that project, he's still with us and kicking everyone's ass every day. Just let me know. Good luck on whatever you're checking out."

We shook hands, and all three of us headed out to the parking lot. T.J. climbed into an SUV with a car seat in the back. Once we were settled into my car, I asked, "How do you think that went?"

Erik seemed to think for a moment and said, "Well, two things. While they're working on the place, they're telling the White House folks that they're going to have problems in the future based on the materials being used. White House didn't bother to upgrade, and I picked up on it immediately as we went through that two-bedroom unit. The second thing, and this may be a little more important, is he said the city didn't object to anything. He never said it wasn't up to code, but you'd think a city inspector somewhere along the way would question something, somewhere. Not just plumbing, but the place is poorly insulated, for God's sake, and this is Minnesota. Something's definitely not right." He glanced at his watch. "You in any hurry to get back to the office?"

"Why? Do you want to stop at McDonald's?"

"Not funny. No, I was thinking of calling Paulie again at Honey Johns to see if he's got some time."

"Oh, yeah. Give him a call."

He took out his phone, brought up his recent calls, and pressed a number. "Hi, I'm calling for Paul Kramer. Thank you," he said, then glanced over and nodded. A half-minute later, he said, "Hi Paul, Erik Gustafson calling. Fine, just fine. How about you? Good. Hey, the reason I'm calling is I'm looking into a project your company was mentioned in. No, this was three or four years ago, a place called White House Apartments. Yeah, that's it out on I-94. I wonder if I could stop by with a friend. We're just trying to get some feedback on what they were like to work with, and—No, we won't be working with them. Yeah, that's what we're hearing. We could be there in the next half-hour. Okay, thanks, Paulie. See you shortly," he said and disconnected.

"Please tell me you know where his office is," I said.

"He's out in Bloomington, just off of 494. We take the Nicollet exit and head north for half a block. I'll know the building when I see it."

It was the beginning of rush hour, and the traffic was picking up but still moving. We drove through town, crossed the river on the Fort Snelling Bridge, and drove past the airport. Five minutes later, I took the Nicollet Street exit, and sure enough, half a block later, Erik pointed at a brick building with big blue letters that said, Honey Johns.

I turned into the parking lot and parked in front of the building. Other than the name and knowing what it referred to, the place looked normal. Two guys in blue jeans and navy-blue short-sleeve shirts with 'HONEY JOHNS' embroidered in light blue over their left breast stepped out the office door. They gave us a nod, and one of them held the door for us as we stepped inside.

The woman at the front desk looked to be around fifty with hair dyed a flaming orange color. She looked up and said, "Are you here to see Paul?"

"Yes, we are, Erik Gustafson and Dev Haskell," Erik said.

"I'll let him know you're here," she punched in two numbers on the phone. "Yes, sir, your guests have arrived. Will do," she said and hung up. "If you'll just head through those double doors, he'll meet you on the other side." She pointed to a set of doors in the far corner.

"Thank you," we both said and headed toward the doors. We stepped into a warehouse of sorts with pallets stacked with blue panels and porta-potty doors.

"Back here, Erik," a voice called from the rear of the building as a heavy-set guy waved. We headed toward him.

"That's Paulie," Erik said under his breath.

A moment later, we were shaking hands, and I was being introduced. Paulie probably weighed in at 250 pounds. He was dressed in jeans and a navy-blue Honey Johns shirt. We chatted for a moment, and then he gave us a five-minute tour, such as it was, of the assembly line construction of the porta-potties. When he finished, he sat down on the closest pallet stacked with blue plastic sides and said, "So, what did you want to know about the White House Apartments project?"

Erik gave him a brief description of what we'd been looking at over the past two days.

"Humf, interesting. I don't recognize that plumber named T.J., but I know a number of the Karlson guys. They're a good group. When we did the White House site, I was on the cleaning crew. We'd place a hose down the toilet and suck everything up, and then I'd don rubber gloves and a mask and scrub the inside of the potties. I know we had to really battle with them, the White House folks, to get enough units out there. I think I heard they only wanted two, and the city code specifically states they need a minimum of six. We had to explain to them that not only was it against code, but with only two units, they were going to be paying a lot of money to guys who were standing in line for an hour or more a day. It really didn't make sense, but then that was kind of their reputation."

"Do you recall the name of the guy you were dealing with out there?" I asked.

He shook his head. "I probably heard it, but I can't recall. Like I said, it was above my pay grade."

"The name Jack Carter ring a bell?" I asked. He shook his head. "What about Odell Dankworth?"

He seemed to think for a moment and slowly nodded. "Yeah, that could have been the guy. My brother Tom would know. He's not in right now, but if you wanted to call tomorrow, he could tell you."

"Thanks, I'll give him a call. Nice to meet you, Paulie. Hey, we'll get out of your hair. I'm sure you got things to do at the end of the day."

"Not so fast. It isn't often we get people in here to visit," he laughed. "Follow me."

We followed him into a room off to the side. He opened a couple of sliding doors and said, "You take a large size, right, not extra-large?"

We looked at each other, and Erik said, "Yeah, large."

"Everyone wants one of these," Paulie said as he handed each of us a navy-blue t-shirt with a powder blue porta-potty and the name Honey Johns just above it.

We laughed, thanked him, and headed out to the car.

Fourteen

As we climbed in the car and headed back to the office, Erik asked, "So, what'd you think?"

"Well, for starters, I plan to wear that t-shirt with pride. Interesting information this afternoon, but although this may be a bit of an extreme, there's nothing unusual about keeping your costs down."

Erik glanced over for a second and said, "Yeah, but there's keeping your costs down, and then there's cutting corners to the point that you're not building a reputable place. Based on what we saw going through the tour of that two-bedroom unit, the place, and I'm talking the entire building, is an absolute dive. I'm guessing that apartment has never had anyone living in it. It's probably the best two-bedroom unit in the building, and it's an absolute disaster. It will be cold in the winter. The electricity and water bills have to be huge. They're charging market-rate rents. We didn't check it out, but my sense would be the appliances are probably second-rate. And one of the owners and his wife are killed in a car crash. I don't know, Dev. It might be coincidence, but it's feeling less and less like it."

"Well, from what I know of Jack Carter, he would never, ever be involved in a project like that. And yet, apparently, he was. I don't get it."

We parked across the street from the office and behind Louie's car. Morton turned out to be the only one in the office, which meant Louie was over at The Spot. I turned off the coffee pot and poured the remnants down the sink. I clipped the leash onto Morton's collar. Erik grabbed his computer bag, and we went back out to the car. I drove Erik back to Tubby's. Apparently, someone had passed the word that I would be dropping Erik off because, when I stopped in front of the mansion, no one moved off the front porch. I gave Erik a wave and drove off the grounds once he stepped inside.

I parked in my driveway and took Morton on a walk through the neighborhood. He got up close and personal with a couple of trees and a fire hydrant, and we headed back home. I dined on leftover French toast for dinner and ran the dishwasher. I settled onto the couch in the den and phoned Crystal. She answered on the fourth ring.

"Well, I was beginning to wonder if I'd ever hear from you again."

"Lucky you, here I am. Hopefully, you're fully recovered after the other night."

"Thanks for asking, but not a problem. Once again, I've relearned the lesson about not mixing beverages."

"I thought you were just drinking champagne. That's all I poured for you."

"That's right, but I'd had two or three martinis before you arrived. At some point, someone mixed me an old fashion, and I had something else later on, but I can't remember what it was. Just that it tasted good at the time."

"Well, glad you survived, and you're back to normal. I was calling to see if you were available tomorrow night."

"What did you have in mind?"

"Nothing crazy. Dinner out somewhere if you're in the mood."

"I've got a better idea. What if you came over here for dinner and thought about spending the night?"

"I would love to do that."

"Good, and before you even ask, let me tell you that you can bring the wine. But just one bottle. I don't want to end up falling asleep on the couch again."

"I think I can handle that. What time works for you?"

"I'll have dinner going in the crock pot, so whenever you arrive, 6:00, 7:00, it doesn't matter. If it's going to be later than that, just give a call and let me know."

"I'm looking forward to it. Thank you."

"Me too, see you tomorrow," she said and disconnected.

I went upstairs and set some clothes out for tomorrow night. I debated for a brief moment about wearing the Honey Johns t-shirt and decided that wouldn't be the best idea. I settled in to watch a movie and turned it off halfway through. I ended up watching the news, then went upstairs to bed.

I woke before the alarm went off, showered, shaved, and was eating a breakfast of oatmeal when Morton wandered in and posed for his daily head scratch. I let him out into the backyard. I was back in the kitchen finishing breakfast when Erik called.

"Hi, Dev. I hope I'm not calling too early."

"No, this is fine. You ready to be picked up?"

"Yeah, another gorgeous morning. I'm standing outside now."

"We'll see you in fifteen minutes, Erik."

It was more like twenty-five minutes by the time I loaded the dishwasher, got Morton in the car, and drove through rush hour traffic. As I approached Tubby's corner, Erik was standing outside the eight-foot-high brick wall surrounding Tubby's lot. He gave me a wave as I stopped, and he climbed in.

"Your uncle didn't kick you out, did he?"

"No, he'd never do that. In fact, we had breakfast together. He was trying to give me the third degree on what we were up to."

"What'd you tell him?"

"Not much, other than we were looking into an apartment building. I didn't mention the White House Apartments. He seemed content to leave things alone as long as we weren't checking into him or any of his business concerns."

"Well, I appreciate you keeping things private, not that your uncle is involved in this, but at the end of the day, this is the country's biggest small town. He'll know people who were involved, possibly the Karlson Plumbing or Happy Johns folks."

Erik looked over and laughed.

"I'm serious. You'd be surprised, and your uncle has been involved in a number of projects over the years and a lot of companies in one way or another."

"I suppose you're right. Anyway, I didn't tell him anything. But as he was talking, I was wondering how you'd feel about me contacting Odell Dankworth and trying to set up a meeting."

"What would you want to meet with him about?"

"Just to check him out as an individual. I also did some more checking online and looked up your friend, Jack Carter. I've come up with a theory."

"What's your theory?"

"From what I've been able to find online, there is no mention of Jack Carter being involved in the White House project. But the stuff I've been going through is more of the day-to-day sort of things. You know, interacting with Karlson Plumbing or Honey Johns. What this suggests to me is that your friend, Jack Carter, may have financed a percentage of the project and, in return, would get a percentage of the profits. I'm thinking he acted as a silent partner."

"Yeah, until he died, in which case whatever his percentage was reverted back to Dankworth. Which is exactly what happened."

"Does that strike you as odd?"

I shook my head. "Yes and no. Without seeing the actual agreement, it strikes me as something the guy I knew would never ever sign. That said, what if he was offered a percentage that was too good to pass up?"

"Yeah, from the little I've read about the man, I have to agree. Now, this is just my thought, but what about this? Somehow, Jack Carter is involved in a portion of the financing. He gets wind of what Dankworth is doing, the lousy materials, the cutting corners, not enough insulation, all of that. So he tells Dankworth he wants out. Dankworth can't convince him otherwise and views his next option, his only option, as having to take Carter out. I mean, he's cutting all the corners on the building. It doesn't seem like that big of a jump to eliminate Carter. What if Carter was going to contact the city? Or what if Carter got wind of Dankworth trying to pull this off, cheat the city and essentially anyone who's going to live in the place, and he's going to blow the whistle? He could have even given Dankworth an ultimatum and—"

"And we can hypothesize about this all day, Erik. But that's all it is. It's not facts. I'm not disagreeing with you. As a matter of fact, I'm more or less of the same mindset. But until we have actual incontrovertible evidence, it's all fiction. That's one of the things we seek in this line of work, evidence," I said as I parked.

Fifteen

I was on my second cup of fresh coffee when Louie parked behind my car. When I heard the stairs creaking as he climbed up to the second floor, I said, "Erik, Louie's going to step into the office in just a second. Sit back and enjoy his morning routine."

I stood just as red-faced Louie opened the office door. "Hey, good morning, Louie."

"Morning, Louie," Erik said and covered his mouth with a fake cough to hide his smile.

Louie gave a short wave, set his briefcase on the picnic table, stumbled around to the far side, and lowered himself into his chair.

I grabbed his mug off the picnic table, dumped yesterday's remnants down the sink, refilled it, and set it in front of him. He nodded and took a slurpy sip. After about a half-dozen sips, he cleared his throat and said, "What time did you guys get in?"

"Oh, a while back, did you meet with a client first thing?"

He nodded and said, "Just an appearance to get a continuance. My client didn't have to be there, but he wanted to show, hoping the judge might go easier on him a few weeks from now.”

“How do you think that will work?” Erik asked.

“Well, I don’t believe it did any harm. It may have even done some good.”

Erik’s phone rang. He glanced at the screen and said, “Oh, wow, that was fast. Erik Rossi,” was how he answered, and then looked over at me and nodded. “Oh, thank you for returning my call, sir. Yes, just a general interview for the paper. Our readers are interested in you and your business endeavors. Some of the projects you’ve done. Perhaps some history, how you initially got into the construction business. What you like or don’t like about it. Yes, sir. No, not a problem, sir. I’ll adjust my schedule to be there. Yes, sir, 11:30. I look forward to meeting you, sir. Yes, thank you,” he said, discon-nected, and gave me a thumbs-up.

“Who was that? And what’s the deal with Ricci as a last name?”

“The name I used was Rossi, and that was none other than Mr. Odell Dankworth calling to invite me to join him for lunch.”

“Dankworth? Calling to invite you to lunch. What did you do, Erik?”

“I called him yesterday and left a message. Told him I was working on the newspaper, and I wanted to do an article on him.”

“What newspaper? The St. Paul Pioneer Press?”

"Relax. I've got it figured out. I'm going to tell him they're looking to offer me a job, and they're letting me do an article of my choosing. I've chosen to do an article on him. I'll tout all the good things he's done. I'll present him as a standard for people to measure themselves against and see how they compare to someone working to make the world better."

"Oh, I don't know, man. He's going to check you out. Did you give him an address?"

"You mean here?" He shook his head. "I don't know what your address even is, Dev. Look, we're meeting in a public place, a restaurant."

"Which restaurant?"

"A place called Meritage. Have you ever been there?"

"Yeah, Erik. Once, it cost me an arm and a leg. I was stupid and let my date choose the place. At the end of dinner, when the server handed me the bill, I figured we were going back to her place. Instead, she stood, kissed me on the cheek, and told me she never wanted to see me again, ever. With that, she walked out and grabbed a taxi."

"Mmm, well, was the food good?"

"Yeah, excellent, and that's not the point. You're playing with fire here. I think you should call him back and tell him you've just taken a COVID test and you're infected."

"I'm not going to do that, Dev. Besides, he picked the place."

"Oh, God," I said and tried to think. "Okay, I tell you what. If you're going to do this, let's do it right. Do you have a coat and tie anywhere?"

"Yeah, back at my uncle's, but I don't have to dress up to do—"

"Erik, you're going to try and impress the guy. You're trying to get a job with the city paper. The least you can do is look the part."

"You mean kind of like a disguise?"

"Yeah, exactly. Come on, I'll take you back to your uncle's, and you can grab the coat and tie. You got a clean shirt there? Somehow I don't think a t-shirt touting the U is the thing to wear into the Meritage. They'd probably ask you to leave. Come on, we don't have much time," I said and headed for the door. Erik was right behind me.

I stopped in front of Tubby's mansion fifteen minutes later. "Get the shirt, the tie, and coat, and come back out. We've got another stop to make."

"Okay, back in a minute," Erik said and opened the passenger door.

"Oh, Erik, you got some better shoes than those Nikes?"

"Yeah, I'll grab them," he shouted as he hurried toward the front door. He said something to the guys at the door. They nodded and then glanced over at me.

I drummed my hands on the steering wheel and tried not to look too hyper. Erik hurried out the front door five minutes later, wearing a white t-shirt. I felt like I had been parked in front of Tubby's mansion for an hour. He had his sport coat and a light blue shirt draped over his right arm. He carried a pair of black loafers in his left hand.

He opened the rear door to place the clothes in the back seat, and I half-shouted, "Don't put your clothes back there. Bring them into the front seat. You don't want to get dog hair all over them."

He nodded, climbed into the front seat, dropped the shoes on the floor, and carefully folded the coat and shirt on his lap.

"All right, good job. That'll look great. We've got one more stop just to add some legitimacy to your appearance." We headed down Summit Ave. As I drove, we reviewed the background information Erik would provide if asked. "Tell the truth about everything. If he asks what your major was, tell him pre-law and computer programing. You just had a wild idea about being a journalist, and you're going to give it a try."

"What if he asks about family?"

"Tell him your dad passed away. But don't mention he owned a contracting firm. Keep returning to Dankworth, his background, education, family, and projects. How did he get involved in doing that Easter fundraiser for the homeless?"

"It was a Christmas fundraiser."

"Whatever. See if he has any other things like that going on. Do not, under any circumstance, mention the White House Apartments. Okay? Just get a sense of the guy. Also, be cautious. If he has someone else in attendance, understand that their sole task in life today is to make an assessment of you. So be extremely cautious of them."

We passed the St. Paul Cathedral, and I put my blinker on to make a right-hand turn onto Kellogg Boulevard. Halfway down the hill, I took the first left. It led into the Minnesota History Center parking lot.

"I don't think I have time to look at any exhibits, Dev."

"Just wait for me. I'll be right back," I said and hopped out of the car. I hurried into the building and headed for the souvenir store. Fortunately, it was just inside the entrance. I walked over to the bookshelves, found the two items I was looking for, and luckily had seven dollars cash. I hurried back out to the car, tossed the bag onto Erik's lap, and backed out of my parking place. I headed down the hill, turned onto 35-E, and drove a mile and a half to the Victoria Street exit. I drove down Victoria to the Spot Bar, turned right, and parked behind Louie's car.

I carried the History Center bag and Erik's shoes up to the office.

"Everything go okay?" Louie asked when we stepped in.

"Yeah, we're getting there. Erik, why don't you slip into that shirt and tie. You know how to tie a tie?"

"Yeah, Dev. I think I can handle that."

He set the coat, tie, and shirt on one of the client chairs and gave Morton a long head scratch. Once Morton returned to his pillow, Erik pulled on the shirt, buttoned it up, and then tied his tie. He slipped on the coat and then held his arms out. "So what do you think?"

"Much better. Here," I said and handed him the bag from the History Center. "That should give you some credibility."

He opened the bag and took out the top bound Spiral notebook labeled Pioneer Press and a pen that said the same thing. "Oh, this is great. Now he's got to believe me."

"Good, you've seen his picture online?" Erik nodded. "What time are you meeting him?"

"Supposedly at 11:30. He said the reservation would be in his name and to just grab a table if he wasn't there."

"It's a little after 11:00 now. Let's get you down there. If this was legit, you'd show up early just to be sure you didn't keep him waiting."

"Okay, let's go," Erik said and headed for the door.

"Might be a good idea to take off the Nikes and slip into the black shoes," I said.

"What? Oh yeah, sorry," he kicked off his Nikes and slipped into the loafers.

We headed downtown. I stopped at the corner of Fifth Street and St. Peter, right next to the St. Paul Hotel. "Okay, when you get out of the car, cross the street. The Meritage is two blocks up St. Peter on the right-hand side. If you get to West Seventh Place, you've gone a half block too far. The restaurant is easy to see. Have a great lunch and stay safe. Call me when you're finished. Don't let him give you a ride. If he insists, tell him you have another appointment at the courthouse. You know where that is?"

"Yeah, of course, I do. Who doesn't?"

"You'd be surprised. Let's do this. When you're finished, walk down to the courthouse. Go inside and call me. I'll pick you up at the Kellogg Boulevard entrance but stay inside the courthouse until I call you and tell you that I'm outside waiting. I'm purposely going to take my time just in case someone followed you. I don't think they will, but let's just play it safe. Okay?"

He nodded, slid out of the car, gave a quick wave, and hurried across the street before the light changed. I watched him head up the street toward the Meritage until some jerk behind me leaned on the horn. I ran the yellow light and drove back to the office.

Sixteen

When I got back, Louie was gone, and there was a note on my desk saying that a BBQ pork shoulder sandwich from Roosters was in my top drawer for safekeeping. Probably a good idea since Morton was sniffing around my desk when I walked in.

I settled into my chair, turned on my computer, and checked the time. It was 11:25. I brought up the police report site on my computer and then worked my way through the BBQ while checking for reports of shots fired or a physical assault at the Meritage. By 12:30, I figured they should be finishing up. I had to work to keep myself in my chair rather than get in the car and drive down to the courthouse. At 12:45, I took my phone out just to make sure it was on and charged. It was at 95%. I began pacing the office at 1:00. At 1:15, I left the office and sat in the car, arguing with myself about whether or not it was a good idea to drive past the Meritage. I went back up to the office five minutes later, just in case Erik had sent me an email. At 1:25, my phone rang. Erik. I waited for three rings, so I didn't sound anxious before I answered.

"Hello."

"Hi, Dev, Erik. We're all finished, and I'm in the lobby of the courthouse looking out on Kellogg Boulevard."

"Everything go okay?"

"Yeah, everything was fine. He had a secretary with him. Nice lady, didn't say much. Dankworth did all the talking. It was tough to even get a word in. I took notes just to look legit. I'll tell you all about it when you pick me up."

"Okay, great. I'm going to wait five minutes before I leave just so it looks like you're meeting up with someone in case he's checking you out."

"That's fine, but he said he had an appointment up near the capitol at 1:30, so they both left. I stood there and watched as they climbed into a taxi and took off toward the capitol."

"Okay, good. Just play it safe and stay in the lobby until you see me pull up."

"I'll see you when I see you," Erik said and disconnected.

Just to prove to myself I wasn't anxious, I waited five and a half minutes and then ran out to my car. I screamed twice at the cars in front of me, shouting at them to move. I ignored the 'No U-Turn' sign and made a U-turn onto Kellogg Boulevard just past the courthouse. Luckily there wasn't a police car nearby.

As I pulled to a stop in front of the courthouse, Erik stepped out of the building. He looked both ways then hurried to my car and climbed in. "Hi, Dev, thanks for coming to get me."

"How'd it go? What did he want to know? Did he mention Jack Carter? What was his secretary like? Did he suggest that you—."

"Take a deep breath, Dev. Everything went just fine."

"Yeah, okay. So tell me what happened. It seemed to go longer than I thought it would."

He nodded. "Yeah, same with me. Not that we were ever deeply involved in any conversation. He must have spent a good half-hour telling me about the different fundraisers he's involved in, helping kids in school, the homeless, wounded veterans, and any other group you can think of. I'm sure it all looks good on paper, but I just had the sense he was doing something else on the side."

"Something else on the side?"

"Yeah, you know, like keeping a percentage of the cash he raised or getting people's credit card numbers, that sort of thing. At the end of the day, he was just smarmy. I took notes on all the things he told me. Most of it is about what a wonderful guy he is. He never mentioned your friend Jack Carter or The White House Apartments, and I didn't bring up either one."

"And his secretary was there?"

"Yeah, at least that was who he said she was. She didn't say much, and in fact, she was the one who told him we should order and then, at the end, told him it was time to leave. It was like he was a politician or something, and she was in charge of his schedule. I did notice as we left that she gave a nod to a guy a couple of tables away. He was eating alone. She just nodded and didn't say anything to him."

"Did he respond?"

"No. The guy was sipping a coffee and talking on his phone when we walked out of the restaurant."

"Talking on his phone? Were his lips moving?"

"Well, I mean, he was listening on his phone. I didn't notice if he was actually talking."

"What did he look like?"

"An average guy. He was wearing a coat, no tie. He looked, I don't know, right around forty-five years old. A large guy, but not fat. Dark hair, crew cut, clean shaved."

"Rings, tattoos, anything like that?"

Erik shook his head. "I just saw him for a split second, and then we were out of the place. They climbed into the taxi, and I walked down to the courthouse. I checked behind me a couple of times. I don't think anyone was following me if that's what you're thinking."

We were coming up to our street, and I kept going straight.

"You got someplace else we're going?" Erik asked when we didn't turn.

"I just want to be sure we're not being followed. I'm not doing this because of what you just told me. It's just a standard precaution." I took a right at the next stoplight and looped back through a residential neighborhood to the office. No one followed, and I relaxed.

"You never told me what you had for lunch, Erik."

He chuckled and said, "There were more than a few things on the menu I'd never heard of. Of course, a lot of the meals were listed in French, and I don't speak it. Anyway, I had a honey-glazed duck breast, and then for dessert, I had puff pastries stuffed with ice cream and covered with chocolate sauce. What'd you have?"

"While I ran you down to the Meritage, Louie went up to Roosters and got me a BBQ sandwich. When I stepped into the office, Morton was busy sniffing around the desk drawer where Louie had put my sandwich."

"Poor Morton," Erik laughed.

I parked across the street from the office. Checked the street just to be double sure we hadn't been followed and, fortunately, didn't see anyone. We headed up to the office. My wastebasket was tipped over, and the remnants of the paper wrapping from my sandwich were scattered around the floor. Morton opened one eye as we stepped in, then turned his head in the opposite direction and pretended to be asleep.

"Now you can see why Louie stashed my sandwich in the desk drawer," I groaned and began to pick up the bits of paper wrapping.

Louie was back in the office an hour later. Erik had been going over his notes from the luncheon meeting with me. He had lots of general information that basically reinforced my view that Odell Dankworth was a self-absorbed character. That said, nothing over the course of our conversation suggested anything even close to involvement in the deaths of Jack Carter and his wife. As much as I would have loved to investigate Dankworth on those grounds, it appeared for a number of reasons to be a lost cause.

Erik gave Louie a general version of his lunch meeting. Louie asked a couple of questions, all of which concerned the menu. At exactly 5:00, Louie suggested we all head over to The Spot. Erik and I took Morton on a walk. A black Mercedes GLE passed us once. Other than noticing it was a nice car, I didn't pay much attention to it. When we arrived at The Spot, I saw it parked about a block down the street. I made a mental note, and we stepped inside.

Seventeen

Louie had just fed Morton a handful of pork rinds, and Erik was checking the bar out. Mike, the bartender, arrived with beers for Erik and me and a fresh drink for Louie when it suddenly dawned on me I was scheduled to have dinner with Crystal.

"Oh, man. I completely forgot I'm supposed to meet someone for dinner tonight. Louie, you think you could give Erik a ride home?"

"Not a problem, be happy to."

"You okay risking your life in Louie's car?" I asked.

Erik nodded. "That's fine with me. Sorry to be a hassle."

"You're not a hassle, Erik. It's just that I completely forgot. I'll take Morton home and get him set up for the night. Louie, it might be a good idea if you drop Erik off just outside the front gate. You drive in there with that Ford Fiesta, and there's no telling what the security guys might do." Everyone laughed. I paid for another round for Louie and Erik, and then Morton and I headed out the side door.

When I opened the car door for Morton, I glanced down the street and didn't see the black Mercedes. I chalked my thoughts of being followed up to me being too hyper and drove home. I triple-checked along the way, but nobody was following us.

I got Morton set for the night, grabbed a shower, and dressed in the clothes I'd set out the evening before. On the way over to Crystal's, I stopped at Solo Vino and, following her directions, got one bottle of a Sean Minor Pinot Noir wine. It was 6:30 when I parked in front of her house. It was quite different from the other night. To-night, I was one of only two cars parked on the street. I grabbed the bottle of wine and headed up the sidewalk.

Crystal answered the door wearing a light blue top with spaghetti straps and white slacks. "Oh, perfect tim-ing," she said and kissed me on the lips for a long mo-ment. She took the bottle of wine from my hand, and I followed her into the kitchen. The table was set with white cloth napkins, crystal wine glasses, and two can-dles. Elegant china plates and sterling silverware topped off the table. Soft classical music played in the back-ground, and the room had a wonderful scent of whatever she had cooking.

"I don't know what you've got cooking, but it smells delicious."

She smiled as she set the wine in the Waterford bot-tle coaster. "I've had a roast going in the crock pot for six hours. Hope you're hungry. Would you mind opening the wine and filling the glasses? I'll just get the hors d'oeuvres."

Once again, I was happy to have a twist-off cap on the wine bottle. I had the glasses filled in a couple of seconds. "You want me to light the candles?"

"Oh, yeah, if you wouldn't mind. I guess I forgot."

We settled in at the table and had a nice conversation about everything and nothing. I topped up the wine glasses as Crystal dished up the dinner, a delicious beef roast with roast potatoes, carrots, and onions. She had a platter of homemade dinner rolls that were still warm from the oven and to die for. We chatted, laughed, and had homemade blueberry pie, her mother's recipe, for dessert. I cleared the table, Crystal loaded the dishwasher, and then we settled in on the couch in the den.

She poured us each a glass of white wine, then gave instructions that it would be the last alcohol for the evening. It was just after 9:00 when she turned out the lights, and we made our way into the bedroom.

She woke me at 6:00 the following morning with a cup of coffee. She was dressed in a black, knee-length silk robe. We sipped the coffee in bed, and then I hit the shower while Crystal warmed a coffee cake. I was back home a little after 7:30 and stepped into the kitchen just as Morton appeared. I let him outside and filled his food and water dishes, then hurried upstairs and changed for work. I decided it would be the perfect time to wear the

Honey Johns t-shirt. I slipped it on, stepped into my jeans, and headed downstairs.

Morton cleaned his food dish and was gnawing on what was left of his rawhide bone. I checked the clock on the stove. It was almost 8:30, and I hadn't heard from Erik. It suddenly dawned on me that I'd left him with Louie, which probably wasn't the best idea. I was tempted to call but didn't want to add any pressure in case he was having breakfast with Tubby Gustafson.

At 8:45, I still hadn't heard from him, and I wondered if it might make sense to drive over and just park outside the gate. I immediately dismissed that thought as incredibly stupid. I was thinking I might call Louie when my phone rang. Erik.

"Are you okay?" was how I answered halfway through the first ring.

"Yeah, sorry. A bit of a late night is all. A fun time, I think. It gets a little hazy toward the end."

Oh great. A late night with the likes of Louie. I decided I would kill Louie as soon as I got to the office. "I'll head over and pick you up. Why don't you meet me out by the gate," I said, hoping to avoid Tubby, Fat Freddy, and any of the thugs on the front porch who might suggest Tubby wanted a few words with me.

"Yeah, okay. I'll head out there in just a minute."

"Good, Morton and I are on our way." I got Morton into the car, backed out of the driveway, and hurried over to Tubby's. Erik was just stepping out of the front gate as I pulled up. He carried a backpack and was dressed in sweatpants and, just like me, his Honey Johns t-shirt. He tossed the backpack onto the floor of the passenger seat and climbed in. He tilted his head back against the headrest, closed his eyes, and gave a large sigh.

"Long night?" I asked.

"I think so. I kind of don't remember coming home. It must have been fun because my head is killing me."

I'm really going to kill Louie, I thought. "Well, Erik, if it's any consolation, we've all been there. Great minds apparently think alike. We're both wearing our Honey Johns t-shirts."

"We are?" he asked, still leaning back with his eyes closed.

"Did you have breakfast with your uncle?"

"No, I guess he left for some early meeting. Probably a good thing, now that I think about it. I don't know that I could have dealt with his third degree this morning."

"Let me get you down to the office, and you can take a break."

"Mmm-mmm," he replied and didn't say another word for the rest of the drive.

When I parked across from the office, Louie's car was nowhere to be seen. The Spot was still standing, so I guess that was a good thing. I gently shook Erik's arm and said, "Erik, we're here. Time to wake up."

His eyes slowly blinked awake, and he looked around for a moment before he seemed to get his bearings. "Oh, yeah. Mmm-mmm." He grabbed his backpack and climbed out. I let Morton out. We waited for a bus to pass and then crossed the street. Erik was a couple of feet behind us. I made a fresh pot of coffee while Erik settled into one of my client chairs, folded his arms on my desk, and placed his head on top.

I was tempted to engage him in a conversation, but what was the point? Let the guy sleep for an hour, and hopefully, he'd be back to some semblance of normal. I was scanning the apartment building across the street when Louie parked behind my car. He looked the same as any other day when he climbed out of his car and headed into the building. I heard him climbing the stairs as I filled his coffee mug with fresh coffee and set the mug on his desk.

When he opened the door, he looked like his usual red-faced self. I put an index finger to my lips and nodded at Erik, still sound asleep in my client chair. Louie nodded, settled in at his desk, and drank his coffee over the course of the next fifteen minutes. I moved the empty client chair over to the picnic table, refilled his mug, and sat down.

"Long night?' I asked in a hushed tone.

Louie shook his head. "Not particularly. I did follow your advice and dropped him off just outside the gate. Probably a good idea since he'd been slightly over-served."

"Slightly over-served," I half-shouted as Louie signaled with both hands to lower my voice and shook his head.

"I dropped him off just around 9:00. It's not like we were out until the wee hours. He started with a couple of beers. Although, now that I think about it, it might have been more like four or five. He did some tequila shots with a couple of girls who wandered in. They left, and he chatted up some other couple. He was quite the social butterfly. When I dropped him off, he wasn't feeling any pain."

"He told me Tubby had some early breakfast meeting or something going on, so I'm crossing my fingers and hoping he's unaware of all of it."

"By the time I caught on to his condition, it was too late, and he was saying hi to everyone and sharing drinks. We've both been there ourselves."

"Yeah, but the difference with us is we don't have Tubby Gustafson as our uncle. We don't have Tubby wanting to make everything perfect for us. We don't have Tubby—"

"I get it, Dev. Look, he made it back to Tubby's mansion last night, and apparently, Tubby did nothing to keep you from picking him up this morning. So I think you're in the clear if that's what you're worried about. Just one question. What's he doing wearing sweatpants?"

"I don't know. If you told me that's what he wore to bed last night, it wouldn't surprise me. God!"

Eighteen

It was close to noon before Erik finally woke up. I poured him a coffee and gave him two aspirin. He seemed happy to get both items. After he finished the coffee, he stretched, groaned, and asked what we had planned for the day.

"You sure you want to work? I mean, it's barely noon."

"Oh, yeah, sorry about that. If it's any consolation, I had a great time over at The Spot last night. Met some really nice people, and Mike is a great bartender."

"Yeah, well, just for my own life preservation, from here on in, The Spot is off limits to you."

"What? Come on, Dev. How about if I promise not to overdo it in the future?"

"We'll see. By the way, what's with the sweat-pants?"

"Oh, yeah, I packed my jeans in my backpack, and I was thinking, probably one of the better ways to, you know, get back to normal was to do a run for a couple of miles. That way, I could sweat out the remnants of last night. Do we have time for me to take a run?"

"Yeah, as a matter of fact, it might be a good idea. I won't run with you, but I know a section along the River Boulevard, a couple of miles from your uncle's place. You can run two miles. I can get a walk in, and then we can get back to work. Sound like a plan?"

"Yeah, I need it. Thanks, Dev."

We headed out the door. As long as I was just going to walk, I put Morton on his leash. We drove down 35-E and then turned onto Shepard Road and drove a little more than a mile over the Highway 5 bridge. I took a right on Prior Avenue and parked. The River Boulevard ran along the bluff overlooking the Mississippi River. Tubby Gustafson's mansion was about four miles from where we were at the moment. Just across the street, on the bluff side of the boulevard, there was an asphalt walking path.

I opened the console and took out my pistol in the sticky holster.

"You expecting trouble?" Erik asked.

"Just trying to be careful. You never know. I might see a bear."

"Yeah, right," he laughed.

We walked across the boulevard and onto the path.

"Okay, so if you run along this path to the entrance to Hidden Falls Park, that's a mile. Turn around and come back here, and you've done two miles. If you keep going, the Ford Parkway bridge is another mile. Obviously, you'll do four miles if you turn around at that point. Any questions?"

"I think I can figure that out. Actually, I might do the four miles if you're okay with that."

"Whatever. We've got a laid-back day. Morton and I are going to try and walk up to the Hidden Falls entrance and walk back. If you pass us on your way back, we'll turn around and head back. Just wait here and cool down. We'll be ten or fifteen minutes behind you."

"Got it, enjoy your walk."

"Have a good run," I called as he took off and headed up the path. As we walked, I kept thinking about Jack Carter and Odell Dankworth. Thus far, with the exception of the corners cut in the construction of the White House Apartments, we hadn't found anything that suggested a problem. The White House Apartments may, unfortunately, merely point to a bad business decision from both the standpoint of the quality of construction, sub-standard materials, and the contractual obligation that, upon death, the percentage of ownership reverted to the surviving partner. I didn't look forward to meeting with Melissa Carter and telling her that, unfortunately, her father had made a bad decision.

We walked along the path for a good ten minutes. I looked out over the river when I could see it through the trees and glanced down the steep forested hills and cliffs. A passing car was an occasional event. So, when the black Mercedes GLE passed us heading upriver along the curving road, it registered with me.

Morton and I picked up our pace, almost but not quite running. The road curved back and forth so that, at any one time, the farthest I could see ahead was no more than twenty-five yards. I took out my cell phone as we hurried along and called Erik. After three rings, I got dropped into his voicemail. "Erik, it's Dev. A black Mercedes GLE just passed me. It might be the same car I thought was following us yesterday. Be on the lookout or just step into the woods and wait. We're moving faster, just a few minutes behind you."

The path curved around and went up a hill, where it leveled off for forty feet and then wound down to a grassy area with a park bench. The entrance to Hidden Falls Park was just ahead. I caught the roof of the Mercedes GLE parked partway down the road leading to the river and the park below. I'd been past the area numerous times and had never seen a car parked on the road. We hurried down the park entrance toward the Mercedes. It was locked. I looked up the hill but didn't see anyone among the trees. I looked down the steep hill into the woods on the far side of the Mercedes and didn't see anyone. There was the semblance of a path and some plants that appeared to have been recently stepped on. I was just thinking Erik was probably still jogging along the boulevard path when I heard a groan, not loud, but sounding painful. Morton seemed to point in that direction. I glanced around, took out my pistol, and we headed down the path.

Another groan, this time louder. Morton replied with a soft growl and strained on the leash. The path wound around a large oak tree, and there, not ten feet in front of us, was Erik, face down on the ground. A larger dark-haired man with a crew cut was on top of him. He had Erik's arm behind his back in an armlock, and he was raising the arm in a way that applied pressure to the shoulder joint. "I'm going to ask you again, dipshit. What the hell is your real name?"

Erik groaned as Morton suddenly growled and strained on the leash. I let go just as Morton barked and charged. The guy on top of Erik looked in our direction just in time to see Morton hit him full force and knock him off Erik. Morton rolled and was immediately back on his feet. He attacked, clamping his jaws onto the calf of the guy's right leg.

The guy screamed, swore, and wrapped his hands around Morton's neck.

"Let go, or you are one dead son of a bitch," I shouted as I charged.

"He's got my fuc—" I kicked him as hard as I could on the side of his jaw. His eyes rolled back in his head, and he went out like a light. Morton jumped on his chest, barked, and growled three or four times just a couple of inches from his face.

"You okay, Erik?"

"That's the same guy from the restaurant yesterday. The Meritage. He said he needed help with his car, and then he flipped me over his shoulder and into the woods. He was trying to break my arm, the bastard."

"Let me ask again. Are you okay?"

"Yeah, yeah. My shoulder hurts like hell. God," he groaned and rolled his shoulder as I pulled out my phone. "Are you calling the cops?"

"No, this is going to require some unique attention." I tapped the number on the screen. "Now what?" was how my call was answered.

"Dev Haskell, Mr. Gustafson. We have an incident I think you're going to want to be involved in."

Nineteen

Not even five minutes later, Tubby Gustafson's Cadillac Escalade screeched to a stop behind the Mercedes. Fat Freddy and Pee Wee were in the front seat, and Erik, standing next to the Mercedes, gave them a wave.

I was still down on the path sitting on top of the guy so he wouldn't run away. His jaw, where I had kicked him, was red and swelling, and his groans suggested he seemed to be gradually regaining consciousness. I had checked him for a wallet or some form of ID, but all I found in his pockets was a set of car keys.

A black Range Rover drove past, veered in front of the Mercedes, and stopped. Four more of Tubby's thugs jumped out and walked back to the Escalade. "Where is this guy?" one of them asked Erik.

"Down that path," Erik said and pointed at the path. "Dev is keeping an eye on him."

"Get him and throw him in the back of the Range Rover," Fat Freddy said. "Are you okay, Erik?"

"Yeah, I'm just lucky Dev showed up. No telling what would have happened if he and Morton hadn't arrived."

"Arrived? You mean he wasn't with you? Wasn't keeping an eye on you?"

"With all due respect, I don't need anyone keeping an eye on me."

"Oh, my misunderstanding. I guess there must be some other reason your uncle sent six of us down here. We're going to have a little conversation with this gentleman. I think it would be a good idea if we brought you back to the mansion. You can ride with me in the Escalade and—"

"Don't take it personally, Mr. Zimmerman, but I think I should ride with Dev. I'm sure my uncle is going to want to talk to him and thank him for saving me from whatever this guy had in mind."

"It might be a better idea to keep your distance from Haskell. Your uncle isn't all that happy right now."

"I'll set that straight. If it wasn't for Dev, I would be in pretty bad shape right about now."

Fat Freddy lowered his voice and said something, but I couldn't understand what he said. The four thugs suddenly appeared around the large oak tree. The guy I was sitting on struggled to move, but my weight on his shoulders and the fact that he was just coming back to the here and now kept him pinned down. Not only that, but Morton was still eager to go at him again. Once he growled and barked, the guy remained still.

"Looks like you did a pretty good job on him," one of the thugs said.

"He was gonna hurt my dog, Morton, and I won't allow that."

All four of them laughed, and another thug said, "You can get off him. We're going to take him back and have a little chat."

"Wait, just wait a minute, please," the guy beneath me groaned. "You should call the cops on me. I should be arrested."

"Since we're already here, we might as well save them the trouble. Do our civic duty, as it were. Go on, put his dumb ass in the back of the Range Rover," a thug said.

"No, wait, wait. You can't take me. You should call the cops. Hey, listen," he said to me as two of Tubby's guys yanked him up off the ground. "Don't let them do this. Please call the cops. I should be arrested."

"You should have thought of that fifteen minutes ago. If I were you, I'd be on my absolute best behavior. Might be a good idea to tell them whatever they want to know."

"But I told you, I—ouff!" he half-shouted as one of the thugs gave him a solid punch in his solar plexus, knocking the wind out of him. They began to lead him up the path, but his limp from Morton biting his leg was so severe that they grabbed him by his arms and dragged him the rest of the way up to the cars. Morton and I fol-lowed.

The two thugs holding onto his arms and the back of his collar threw him, none too gently, into the back of the Range Rover. The thug, who, a moment ago, had punched him, climbed in right behind him. The other three quickly opened the doors and settled in. The Range Rover moved ahead ten feet and then quickly backed up the hill, past the other two vehicles, into the street, and headed toward Tubby's mansion.

"Where's your car, Haskell?" Fat Freddy asked.

"About a mile down the road. I've got the keys to that guy's Mercedes, so we can drive down to my car, and Erik can drive the Mercedes back to the mansion."

"I was just suggesting to Erik that he ride with us in the Escalade. His uncle is very worried, and the sooner Erik gets back, the better it will be for *everyone*," Freddy said, emphasizing that last word to let me know he meant me.

"I'll ride down with Dev to his car and then drive the Mercedes up to my uncle's. We'll be right behind you. Besides, there might be something in that car we'll want to see."

Freddy seemed to think about that for a moment and then nodded. "Okay, but once you drop Haskell off, you head right back to your uncle's. He's gonna want to see you and make sure you're all right."

"I'll head right back. I promise," Erik said.

Fat Freddy stared at the three of us, Erik, Morton, and me, for a long moment and apparently decided there was nothing else he could do, so he climbed back into the Escalade. Pee Wee backed up the hill into the street and sped off toward Tubby's.

"Oh, Dev. I'm so sorry. Thank you for coming when you did. I was thinking that creep was going to break both my arms and then kill me."

"And you're sure that was the same guy that was a table or two away from you at the Meritage?"

"Absolutely. In fact, he even mentioned it. Said he knew I was full of shit the moment he saw me at the restaurant."

"Interesting. Okay, let's get out of here just in case someone called the police with all the commotion going on." I pulled the guy's keys out of my pocket and clicked the fob. The lights flashed, and the doors on the Mercedes unlocked. "I'll drive, and then you can take it up to your uncle's."

"Are you going up there?"

"Yeah, not to worry."

I put Morton in the back seat. We climbed into the Mercedes, and rather than reverse up the hill and into the street, I headed down the hill, turned around in the parking lot, and drove back up the hill. On the way to my car, I said, "Open that glove compartment and see what's in there."

"Oh, boy," Erik said as the door to the glove compartment dropped open. "He's got a gun, a bottle of pills. Oh, and it looks like, yeah, his wallet."

"Check his ID and see what his name is."

Erik opened the wallet and said, "Driver's license says his name is Louis LePew."

"You're kidding. That's his name?"

"That's what the driver's license says, and it's got his picture." He rustled through some papers in the glove compartment. "Same name on the car insurance form."

"Okay, leave the insurance papers, take the pistol and the wallet. What's in the pill bottle?"

"They're actually gummies. The label says King Cobra Gummies. You know what they're for?"

"No idea. Okay, we'll toss that stuff in my car. I was thinking we'd give that driver's license to your uncle, but on second thought, hang onto it. When we get to my car, let's check the trunk and see if anything is in there." We stopped at a stop sign, drove two more blocks, turned left, and pulled alongside my car. I parked, pushed the button to open the trunk, and turned off the Mercedes. Erik handed me the wallet and the pistol, and we climbed out.

I unlocked my car, tossed the wallet and pistol onto the passenger seat, then let Morton out of the Mercedes and put him in the back seat of my car.

Erik was staring into the open trunk. "Wow. Check this out, Dev," he said as I stepped to the back of the Mercedes. Two rifles were lying on top of black nylon cases. An AK47 and an M110 with a scope, a sniper rifle. The AK47 had what appeared to be a fully loaded magazine. Next to the weapons was a small black briefcase or perhaps a computer bag.

I opened the passenger door, grabbed the pistol, and handed it to Erik. "Put this in that briefcase. We can check it out later. I'm wondering if these were loaded and ready to go so he could deal with us."

"You think?" Erik asked and looked at me.

"Right now, I'm thinking just about anything is possible with this LePew guy. Let me open my trunk and put these in. We better get up to your uncles before we're missed. I'm sure he's anxious to see you and make sure you're all right," I said and opened the trunk of my car.

"You think there's enough evidence to turn this guy over to the police?" Erik asked as he tossed the black bag into my trunk.

"Don't worry about that. Right about now, Mr. LePew is probably offering to call them himself." I glanced up and down the street to make sure no one was around and then grabbed the AK47, the case beneath it, and placed them in my trunk. I did the same with the sniper rifle.

"I think it would be a good idea if we didn't mention these weapons to your uncle or any of his staff. Okay?" Erik nodded. I handed him the keys to the Mercedes and said, "I'll be following right behind you. You know how to get there, don't you?"

"Yeah, just follow the River Boulevard until I see his place, and then drive through the gate."

"Yeah, it might be a good idea to lower your passenger window so the guys can see it's you. You don't want them getting upset with an unfamiliar car. Slow down, so they get a good look at you, and then pull ahead and park in that parking area. Hang onto the car keys. It looks like there's a house key on it, and if we have time later this afternoon or tomorrow, I'm thinking we should go through the place."

He nodded, climbed in the Mercedes, and pulled away from the curb. I was right behind him all the way up to Tubby's mansion. Erik slowed as he drove up the circular drive. There happened to be three guys standing on the front porch, no doubt a result of Fat Freddy and company arriving with Louis LePew. They spread apart as Erik slowed, and then one of them said something and gave a friendly wave. Erik tooted the horn and drove ahead to the parking area.

I slowed down and lowered the passenger window. One of the guys frowned and gave me the finger. At least they recognized me. I followed Erik and parked.

Twenty

The Escalade and the Range Rover were off to the side of the parking area. They were parked in a somewhat haphazard manner, which was more than a little unusual at Tubby's. As we parked and walked toward the mansion, I spotted traces of blood on the pavement but didn't mention it to Erik.

Someone must have gotten word of our arrival to Tubby because, as we approached the mansion, the front door swung open, and Tubby waddled outside. He was wearing his furry white slippers and his white terrycloth robe, which suggested to me that he'd been in the middle of getting a massage by those two beautiful women when he'd been alerted to our arrival.

As we walked toward him, he shook his head and said to Erik, "It looks like Haskell had you playing in the mud."

For the first time, I noticed the dirt all over Erik's sweatpants and his Honey Johns t-shirt.

"Yes, sir, I was on the ground, but I wasn't exactly playing."

"So I heard. Why don't both of you come on back to my office and fill me in on the details? No need to pat Haskell down. He's okay this time," Tubby said as we followed him into the house and down the hall to his office. He held the door for us as we stepped inside, closed it quietly, and then in a not-so-subtle voice, said, "Just what in the hell is going on?"

The massage table was set up behind his desk, and a towel was crumpled up in the middle of the table. Apparently, I'd been correct in guessing that our arrival had interrupted Tubby's therapeutic session. Not the most positive note on which to begin a conversation with him.

Erik cleared his throat. "I was out on a run, and that guy called over to me. Told me he had a car problem and asked if I could help him. The next thing I know, he's got me in some kind of chokehold. He dragged me into the woods, flipped me onto the ground, and was going to break my arm. The only thing that saved me was Dev and Morton showing up."

"Who the hell is Morton, and why isn't he here?" Tubby half-shouted.

"That's my—"

"I didn't ask you, Haskell."

"He's Dev's dog, sir. He knocked the guy off me and then bit him in the leg and wouldn't let go. Dev kicked the guy in the head, knocked him out, and then called you right away. I'm not kidding, sir. If it hadn't been for Dev and Morton, I don't think I'd be here right now."

Tubby took a deep breath and then reluctantly said, "Okay, Haskell. Thank you for being there, I guess. But this shouldn't have happened in the first place. Who in the hell is this guy? What did he want?"

"His name is LePew," Erik said. "Louis LePew."

"What kind of name is that? I've never heard of him. Do you know him, Haskell?"

I shook my head. "I don't think I've ever heard of him, sir."

"Well, what was he doing? Trying to rob you, Erik? He's driving a Mercedes, for God's sake. Does he really need ten bucks?"

"I've only got about three bucks in my wallet, sir, and I didn't have it with me when I was running."

Tubby turned and glared as his face grew even redder. "What in the bloody hell have you gotten him involved in, Haskell?"

"All we've been doing, sir, is looking into the building of an apartment complex a few years ago called the White House Apartments. There are some questions regarding the death of one of the owners. We haven't accused anyone or investigated any individual. We just went through the process of filling out an application and taking a tour of one of the units," I said. "We haven't talked to the police or the city attorney. In fact, other than the woman who gave us a tour of the model apartment, we haven't talked to anyone."

"The place was a dump, and its been that way since it was built. Poor insulation, plastic plumbing, cheap veneer cabinets in the kitchen, and quarter-inch sheetrock on the walls. You never would have built a building like that or ever been involved in a contract like that," Erik said.

"And the name of that place is the White House Apartments?" Tubby asked as he headed for his desk.

"Yes, sir. Out on I-94 in Woodbury. You can't miss it if you're driving east."

Tubby picked up the receiver on his desk phone and punched in a couple of numbers. "Yes, Frederick. What have you found out?" He nodded two or three times and then said, "Ask him about an apartment complex out in Woodbury called Work House Apartments."

"White House Apartments, sir," Erik said.

"Oh, yeah. What in the world did I say? They're the White House Apartments. Like the building in Washington, only they're in Woodbury. Yes, let me know. Be gentle," he said in a tone that suggested otherwise and hung up. "They're in the midst of a discussion. I'm sure if this LePew character knows anything, he'll be only too happy to bring us up to date."

"Where is he?" Erik asked.

"He's in a meeting down in Mr. Zimmerman's office."

A 'meeting' in Fat Freddy's office. Does he even have an office? I guessed right about now LePew was probably tied to a chair and getting the hell knocked out of him in between begging for mercy and answering any and all questions Fat Freddy and his crew asked.

"Well, I guess I should go upstairs and get changed, and we should get back to work, Dev," Erik said and flashed his eyes a couple of times toward the door.

"Do you even have a plan for the rest of the day, Haskell?" Tubby asked.

"Yes, sir, we were going to review the legal procedures for mergers and acquisitions in Minnesota."

Tubby looked at me, not exactly sure what to say.

"It's an area I'm interested in, sir," Erik added.

Tubby nodded and said, "All right, go on, get cleaned up. You're done checking out this White House thing. I don't want you involved in any aspect of that. Am I clear?"

"Yes, sir," Erik said.

"Did you hear me, Haskell?"

"Oh, yes, sir. Couldn't agree more." Tubby shot me a look as Erik hurried out of the room.

Once Erik was out of the office, Tubby reached into his desk drawer, took out a bottle of Irish Whiskey labeled 'Very Rare', and poured a good inch into a crystal glass. He took a sip, settled into his desk chair with a groan, and said, "All right, Haskell. Tell me everything you know about this LePew bastard."

"Honestly, sir, I've told you everything. I've never dealt with him. I've never even heard of him before. I intend to find out everything I can about the guy. This wasn't some random assault, and he certainly wasn't attempting to rob Erik. I'm pretty sure whatever information he was after has something to do with the White House Apartments. That's the only thing we've been looking into. But Erik wasn't kidding. Other than taking a walk through the model apartment, we haven't really done anything out there."

Tubby took a large sip. "Why are you even looking into the place?"

"A woman I know, actually, her father was a friend and a mentor of mine. I hadn't seen her in years. Her folks were killed a year or so ago in a hit-and-run car accident. Her father was one of two principles in the White House Apartment construction. The contract stipulated that should one of the principles die, the deceased's percentage immediately transferred over to the surviving partner."

"What the hell kind of contract is that?"

"Not a very good one, for starters. It goes contrary to everything the guy I knew would do. At least, I think that's the case. So anyway, we were looking into it, and up until today, we weren't finding anything that aroused suspicion other than the place is a dump, and I didn't think my friend would have been involved in a contract like that. Now, this happened, and I don't know what to make of it."

Tubby shook his head. I read his lips as he silently swore. "Let me be perfectly clear, Haskell. No one assaults a member of my family. No one. Erik will be down in a minute. I expect you to keep a very watchful eye on him. Let me be even more clear. If anything should happen to him, if he sprains an ankle, bumps his knee, or, God forbid, is assaulted again, I'm going to take it very personally, and you, Haskell, you will pay the price. Do I make myself clear?"

"Yes, sir. Very clear."

"Good. Now, if you will excuse me." He drained his glass, refilled it with a similar amount, and placed the bottle of Irish Whiskey back in his desk drawer. "I'm beginning to feel some back pain and think it might be a good idea if you depart and wait for Erik out in the hall. You can wait by the staircase. He should be down shortly."

"Happy to do so, sir. Thank you for being so understanding."

"Keep me informed, Haskell." Tubby picked up the phone and punched in two numbers. I figured he was calling Fat Freddy, but instead, he said, "Yes, I'd like the both of you back here. I think it would be best if we started from the beginning." He hung up the phone and said, "What the hell are you waiting for, Haskell? You're dismissed. Go on, get out of my sight."

I hurried to the office door, opened it, and turned just as the two women in thongs hurried out of the door in the far corner of the room. Tubby was in the process of slipping off his terrycloth robe. I quickly closed the door behind me and tried to erase that final image of Tubby from my mind.

Twenty-one

I stood at the base of the staircase for a couple of minutes until Erik came down.

"Oh, where's my uncle?" he asked and looked around.

"He's back in his office in a meeting with some people. He told me to pass on his goodbye, and he'll see you tonight."

"What do you want to do?"

"You've still got the keys to the Mercedes?"

"Yeah." Erik pulled the keys from his pocket. The car fob and what looked like the house key dangled in front of me.

"Let's leave the Mercedes here. We'll take Morton back to the office, and then let's see if that key fits LePew's front door."

"Does my uncle know we're going there?"

"I didn't want to bother him with the details. I'm sure he has more than enough on his mind."

"Are those guys still talking to LePew?"

"Yeah, probably taking notes and recording the conversation," I lied. We headed out the door and over to my car. As we approached, Morton's head popped up in the back seat. "Mmm-mmm, it might be a good idea to take him on a walk when we get down to the office."

We took Morton on our standard three-block walk, then took him up to the office. Louie wasn't there. I tossed Morton a biscuit, we turned our cell phones off, and hurried back to my car. Louis LePew's driver's license listed his address as being on Warbler Lane in the Battle Creek area of the city. I drove east on I-94 to the Ruth Street exit and headed south on Ruth to Valleyside Drive and Warbler Lane. The address was in a neighborhood of nice-looking homes, probably forty or fifty years old. LePew's place was a two-story structure with light blue aluminum siding, white trim, black shutters on either side of the front windows, and an attached double garage. An asphalt driveway ran from the street up to the garage.

I turned into the driveway as Erik took LePew's keys out of his pocket.

"Put those keys back in your pocket. Let's see if anyone's home. If someone answers the door, we'll ask for Louis and then leave." I opened the console box, pulled two pairs of latex gloves from the box, and handed a pair to Erik. "Put these on once we're up at the front door and after we've rung the doorbell." We climbed out of the car and headed for the front door. We walked past the living room picture window, and I gave a casual glance. It didn't look like anyone was home, but they could be in another room, upstairs, or in the basement.

We rang the doorbell three separate times, waiting twenty or thirty seconds between each ring. No one answered, and we didn't hear a dog bark.

"Okay, pull on those gloves, and let's give the key a try. If we hear an alarm, we'll close the door, calmly walk to the car, and drive away."

The door handle set was brass, with a single key cylinder just above the handle. With the latex gloves on, Erik inserted the key in the lock and turned it. We heard the deadbolt click inside, and he looked over at me.

"Okay, like I said, open the door slowly. If we hear an alarm, just close the door, and we'll walk back to the car."

He nodded, took a deep breath, took hold of the handle set, pressed down, and opened the door six inches. We didn't hear anything.

"Okay, let's step inside," I said.

We stepped inside. Erik closed the door, and I quickly looked around for an alarm keypad but didn't see one anywhere. "I think we're in the clear. Amazing, there isn't an alarm." I looked again for a keypad and quickly scanned the ceiling for a camera or some kind of motion detector, but never saw anything. A staircase off to the left ran up the wall to the second floor. Off to the right was a living room with a large flatscreen hanging over the fireplace. A coffee table was positioned in front of the fireplace. A black leather couch was on either side of the coffee table. Straight ahead was a wide hall leading back to what appeared to be the kitchen.

"Let's check the kitchen first. Don't touch anything. We're looking for something that would suggest two people live here. A glass or cup with lipstick, two coffee mugs, anything."

We headed down the wide hall into the kitchen. There was a door off to the left as we entered. The kitchen looked very nice and had white marble-topped counters, white cabinets, and white ceramic subway tile on the wall between the upper and lower cabinets. At the other end of the room was a dining area with a table and six chairs. The kitchen sink held a small white plate with a white bowl on top of it and a coffee mug resting in the bowl. The coffee mug and the bowl were filled with water, and a spoon was in the coffee mug.

"These look like LePew's breakfast dishes. Breakfast for one. Check out those envelopes on the dining table."

Erik stepped over to the dining table and moved the three items with a gloved finger. "Two are addressed to occupant, and one is addressed to Louis LePew. "

"Peek in the living room. I'm going to check the garage." I walked back to the kitchen entrance, opened the door, and peeked into an empty garage. Nothing seemed unusual. A lawnmower, snowblower, and bicycle were lined up against the far wall. A number of basic tools, hammer, saw, wrenches, and screwdrivers, were neatly hanging on a pegboard, and in front of that was a small workbench with a metal vice.

I stepped back into the kitchen and called to Erik, "You find anything?"

"Nothing unusual. Just a Sunday newspaper, and a book on sailboats."

"Let's check out the second floor," I called and walked back down the hall to the staircase.

The second floor was pretty standard. Three bedrooms, with the master bedroom en suite. What I guessed was a guest bedroom was just across from a bathroom. The closet in the bedroom was empty, and the room and bathroom across the hall appeared to be unused. The master bedroom had a king-sized bed with an oak headboard and a matching double chest of drawers, four drawers high. A large mirror the length of the chest of drawers was attached to the wall. We quickly checked the drawers. They only contained men's clothing. The walk-in closet featured the same, men's sports coats, shirts, trousers, and shoes. There was nothing that suggested a woman lived in or even visited the place.

The other bedroom was where things began to get interesting. It was an office. A framed black and white photo displayed the image of a younger, shirtless LePew in camouflage trousers, a helmet, and holding an M16. I guessed it had been taken somewhere in the Mideast, maybe Iraq or Afghanistan. A high school diploma from St. Paul Central High School, 1993, was framed and hanging next to the photo. The 1993 graduation date would make LePew around forty-seven years old.

There was a pair of matching wooden client chairs in front of the Formica-topped desk. I settled in behind the desk and started going through the various drawers while Erik went through the two wooden file cabinets. Other than pens and pencils, a box of 9-millimeter ammunition, and a stun gun, there was nothing of interest in the 'L' shaped desk. Nothing suggested any form of employment. There wasn't a Private Investigator's license, nothing from a company like a paycheck stub or a business card. Nothing like tax information, insurance information, bank statements, or credit card statements were in the desk drawers. Nothing.

I noticed Erik had taken a couple of files from the drawers and set them on top of one of the wooden file cabinets. He was working his way through the drawers and was now kneeling next to one of the cabinets and going through the bottom drawer.

"You find anything? I see you got those two files."

"Might be something. I just gave a quick look at them and haven't really checked them out yet."

I turned and faced the desktop computer. It was a MAC, and the button to turn it on was in the back of the lower left-hand corner. I pressed the button, and a second later, a tone sounded, alerting that the computer had been turned on. The screen lit up. The word 'Password' appeared with an empty line next to it. I quickly checked the side of the computer for a post-it note with the password. No such luck. I checked LePew's desk calendar, but there was nothing that might suggest a password. In fact, there was nothing written on the calendar. The entire thing, all twelve pages, was blank.

There was a narrow table behind the desk chair. A round, silver tray held an empty wine bottle. Dusty crystal wine glasses stood on either side of the wine bottle. The label was French, Chateau Lafite. I'd heard of the stuff before but couldn't remember if I'd ever had a glass. Just the fact it was French put it out of my league. I'd bring a ten-dollar bottle to a date's house and hope she'd drink the entire thing just to get her in the mood. Otherwise, beer was my poison of choice.

On a guess, I typed in 'Chateau Lafite.' The password line wiggled back and forth a couple of times and then didn't move, denying access. I typed in 'LePew' and 'Warbler' the street name, and got the same result. I thought about the wine bottle again. I typed in the name all in lowercase. Between the two words, I placed the underscore symbol, tapped the return key, and suddenly, I had access to the computer.

"Oh, man, check this out. I can't believe I got access to the guy's computer."

"You're kidding. Really? You?"

"Yeah, I just guessed and tried the name on this wine bottle, and it let me in. Some of your computer skills must be rubbing off on me."

"Oh, that's great. No offense, but would you mind if I took a look? I might be a little more up to date on computer files, options, and programs."

"No offense taken, Erik. I'd be the first to admit any five-year-old is probably way more savvier than me. Let's trade places. You sit here, and I'll go over those two files you got sitting on top of the file cabinet."

Twenty-two

An hour and a half later, Erik was still going through the computer printing off dozens of pages. I was halfway through the second file he'd set aside. Both files were labeled ODU, which I assumed referred to Old Dominion University out in Norfolk, Virginia. As it turned out, they referred to Odell Dankworth, although I couldn't figure out what the 'U' stood for. Still, there was plenty of information, not the least of which was what appeared to be an original signed contract between Jack Carter and Odell Dankworth. The difference was the initials and signatures were in blue ink, and there was no mention that the percentage belonging to the deceased would be immediately transferred over to the surviving partner in the event of death.

"Did you have a chance to look at these contracts?" I asked as Erik was running his fingers over the keyboard.

He stopped typing. "No, I never got to them. Why? Did you find something?"

"I can't be sure, but this contract appears to be original. It's signed, initialed in places, and dated in ink, so it's not a copy, but the paragraph about one of the partners dying and their percentage of investment automatically transferring over to the surviving partner isn't in the contract. Here, it's even been stamped by a notary public. I'll have to check, but I think the date on the thing is the same as the copy Melissa had attached to her file," I said and handed the contract to him.

He glanced at the front page and then glanced at every page until he got to the back page. "I don't know. I've never really seen a contract like this. I mean all the pages and the legal descriptions. You know who would probably know?"

"You mean Louie, my officemate?"

"Oh, yeah, he probably would, but I was actually thinking of my uncle. Say what you will about him, but if something changed, if the version you have was adjusted in some way, he'd probably be able to pick it out."

"Hmmm. Interesting. Which reminds me, if I gave you an address, could you send some files from that computer to me?"

"Yeah, sure. What's your email address?"

"It's so easy even I can remember it. Dev Haskell, all one word at yahoo dot—"

"You have an address that's a little harder to trace? There's going to be a history left on this computer. Even if I delete the history, a tech person will be able to access it in a couple of seconds."

"That's the only email address I have."

Erik seemed to think for a moment. "Okay, I've got a couple of addresses I can send this stuff to. Let me check and see what else I can find as far as online files regarding Dankworth, too. It's possible LePew might have some things online that we haven't seen."

"Good idea. Do you think we can be out of here in the next thirty minutes? I'm worried LePew might make his way back here."

Erik gave me a quick look after that last statement but didn't say anything. It turned out to be closer to an hour before we left. I brought the two ODU files on Odell Dankworth, along with all the pages Erik had printed off from LePew's desktop computer. I wiped down everything except the keyboard while Erik continued to transfer files. Once he turned off the computer, even though we were wearing gloves I wiped it down along with the keyboard, just to play it safe. We looked out the window for any neighbors working in their yards but thankfully didn't see anyone. We locked the door behind us. As we walked to the car, Erik gave a friendly wave to the empty living room.

We backed out of the driveway, and I took Erik back to Tubby's. Along the way, we stopped at a hardware store and had a copy made of the key to LePew's front door. There was a mist in the air, and it threatened to sprinkle as I stopped in front of Tubby's mansion, and Erik slid out. "Thanks, Erik. Glad you're safe. Give me a call tomorrow morning, and I'll pick you up."

"Thank you, Dev. Check out those files tonight. Oh, I'm thinking I should give my uncle the keys to that Mercedes. Is that okay with you?"

"Yeah, good idea. See you in the morning." I watched until Erik stepped inside the mansion. Perfect timing, as the first drop of rain hit the windshield. I drove down to the office and parked behind Louie's Ford Fiesta. I glanced across the street to the second floor. The lights were off up in our office, so I decided to step over to The Spot. A light rain was just beginning to fall, and I picked up my step.

Louie was seated on his stool at the end of the bar. Morton was curled up on the floor next to Louie's stool. Two empty pork rind bags were crumpled up next to Louie's empty glass.

"Well, finally," Louie said as I rounded the corner of the bar.

Morton raised his head as his tail began to bounce off the floor, but he didn't make an effort to stand. I bent over, gave him a scratch behind the ears, then signaled Mike for a beer and a refill for Louie. "How'd your day go?"

"Oh, the usual craziness. I picked up a new client."

"Someone driving under the influence?"

"Yeah, until she crashed through the 'Construction Ahead, Right Lane Closed' sign and ended up eight feet below in the trench dug for a sewer line replacement."

"She okay?"

"Well, other than bumps and bruises, yeah. Of course, emergency services had to cut a hole in the roof of her totaled car. Fortunately, she'd fallen asleep and didn't wake up until they strapped a belt around her and lifted her out."

"Oh, man, how much did she have to drink?"

"Not sure on the exact figure, but I think the term 'Way too much' would be an accurate description."

"Was she at some party, or was some guy buying her drinks?"

"She was at one of those hen parties, you know, a girlfriend getting married and all the ladies get together. She'll spend the next forty-eight hours in the drunk tank. Her father gave me a call. He wasn't a happy camper."

"Does she have a job?"

"Oh, yeah, a schoolteacher, third grade in a parochial school. I'm sure they'll be thrilled with the information."

Mike arrived with my beer and Louie's drink. For a half-second, I wondered about drinking, then remembered it was my first drink.

"Anything up with you and your apprentice, Erik? I thought he might be joining us tonight."

"Bit of an eventful day." I went on to tell Louie about LePew's involvement. I left out any details regarding the weapons, the arrival of Tubby Gustafson's thugs, and Erik and I going through LePew's house.

"I'm guessing Erik's uncle wasn't too happy."

"Not the guy you'd want mad at you. I'm purposely not getting involved with dealing with LePew. I'm sure the police are asking him what in the world he was thinking."

"What was he after?"

"Not really sure at this point, but I suspect it has something to do with the White House Apartments and Odell Dankworth. I think I asked you before, but let me try a second time. Are you aware of him? Dankworth."

"Only what I read in the paper or see on the news. Seems a nice enough guy, always working a fundraiser for some worthy cause. I think he hosted one for the homeless last year, right around Christmas. He did another one on the Fourth of July for wounded veterans. I'm pretty sure he did something for poor kids at the start of the school year, buying them computers or something last September. He does some political stuff too, but I can't remember which party," Louie chuckled.

"Yeah, I read that he did fundraisers for candidates in both parties, apparently just covering his bets."

"Probably a good move," Louie said.

I had a second beer and then left. We walked out into a steady rain and ran to the car. I let Morton into the back seat, then hurried in behind the steering wheel. No sooner did I get inside and close the door than Morton shook himself, essentially shaking water all over the interior. I grabbed a handful of Kleenex from the console and wiped off the inside of the windshield, then started the car, and we headed home.

It was raining even harder as I stopped next to the gate in the backyard. I opened the door for Morton, and he was up on the back porch in about two seconds. He shook himself off just as I stepped onto the porch and out of the rain. I slipped my shoes off in the kitchen and went down into the basement. I took my clothes off and tossed them into the washing machine. I tossed the laundry basket of dark clothes on top of them, started the washer, then went up to the second floor and took a long, hot shower.

I settled in front of the TV, started to watch a comedy series, and woke up in the middle of the third episode just after midnight. We headed up to bed and were asleep in a minute or two.

Twenty-three

I was up before my alarm went off. I was down in the kitchen and had just started the coffee when I remembered that I had the two rifles from Louis LePew's car still in my car trunk. I stepped outside. There wasn't a cloud in the sky, and the air smelled and felt fresh after last night's rain. I opened the trunk, slipped both weapons into the black nylon cases we'd taken out of LePew's car, and noticed LePew's black briefcase or computer bag or whatever it was that I'd tossed in the trunk. I grabbed it along with the weapon cases and went back inside.

I stood the two gun cases in a corner next to the radiator and placed the black case on the kitchen counter. There was a zipper around the top, and I unzipped the thing and lifted the lid. The first thing I saw was a leather pocket that held a laptop computer. I pulled out the laptop, set it on the counter, and then raised the leather pocket. Staring back at me were five bundles of neatly wrapped hundred-dollar bills with standard mustard-colored bundle straps that were labeled $10,000. Fifty thousand bucks. I just stood and stared. My cell phone ringing snapped me out of the fog.

"Hello."

"Hi, Dev, it's Erik," long pause. "Dev, are you okay? Hello?"

"Oh, yeah, Erik. Sorry, I was just checking Morton. You ready to go to work?"

"Yeah, gorgeous morning. I'm already outside the gate enjoying the sunshine."

"We'll be there in fifteen minutes. See you shortly."

"Okay, I'll be waiting right by—"

Apparently, I'd hung up before he'd finished. I stood and stared at the bundles of cash. I picked one up and quickly fanned through it. All the bills appeared to be hundreds. I started counting the bills. I made it up to sixty and, based on the uncounted bills, figured there were most likely a hundred in each bundle. I thought for a minute, grabbed the bundles, and hurried upstairs. I got a screwdriver out of my dresser and went into the back bedroom. Inside the closet was an access panel to the shut-off valve and the shower drain. I undid the four screws, placed the cash up against the cast iron tub, and replaced the access panel.

I hurried back down to the kitchen and quickly went through the briefcase. There were two zipped pockets on the inside. Both were empty. A zipped pocket was on the outside of the lid, and that held the pistol that Erik had placed in there. I clicked Morton's leash onto his collar, grabbed the briefcase and the laptop, and hurried out to the car. Morton hopped into the back seat, and I placed the briefcase and the laptop on the passenger seat.

On the way to pick up Erik, I debated stopping at a local grocery store that had a pair of donation bins for used clothing. I thought about tossing the empty briefcase into one of the bins, decided against it, and drove on to Tubby's.

Erik was just where he said he'd be, leaning against the wall outside the gate to his uncle's mansion. Today, he was wearing the same jeans as yesterday and a t-shirt that touted the U of M Hockey team. He grabbed the laptop and the briefcase from the passenger seat and climbed into the car.

"This was in the briefcase?" he asked, setting the case on his lap and opening up the laptop. It gave off a tone, and a moment later, the screen lit up with a login box. He looked at it for a couple of seconds, closed it, and set it inside the briefcase.

"Yeah. Given my computer skills, I thought it might be best if I didn't attempt to open that thing up."

He nodded and said, "If it's okay, I'll check it out this morning."

"I was hoping you'd do that. How'd your evening go?"

"Wonderfully dull. I was in bed around 9:00. Did some things on my laptop for an hour or so and then slept through the night."

"Any news on LePew?"

He shook his head. "No, I gave his car keys to my uncle last night. LePew's name never came up at breakfast. When I stepped outside this morning, his Mercedes was gone, so I figured they probably sent him home once they were done talking to him."

I gave a quick glance over at Erik. He was looking out the window at a woman waiting for a bus and clearly oblivious to the fact that Louis LePew was probably wrapped in chains and at the bottom of the Mississippi river. I saw no point in suggesting this to him.

We parked behind Louie's car and headed up to the office. Louie was on the phone as we stepped inside. "Yes, Michelle, I do understand, but their policy is that you remain there for forty-eight hours. There's nothing I can do to change that. Because your father posted bail, you will be released tomorrow morning at 10:00. You will need someone to pick you up. I'll be happy to do that, but I have to charge you for my time. Yes, your father can pick you up. All right. Any problems or concerns, feel free to call me. Oh, they have you in two or possibly three sessions today. Maintain a positive and respectful attitude. It will help during your court appearance. They will probably provide some sort of option for AA. Take it. It will be one more thing that will aid the final result of your trial. Yes, you too. We'll talk in a day or two," Louie said and disconnected.

I had just grabbed my coffee mug. "Was that the sewer lady?"

Louie laughed. "Yeah, she's got her father on one end, her school principal on the other, and her sentencing on the horizon. Not fun."

"Hopefully, it will be a lesson learned. Can I top up your mug?"

"Yeah, please," he said and slid his mug across the picnic table. "You get a new computer, Erik?" Louie asked as Erik opened the top of LePew's laptop, and it gave off a tone.

"Oh, just checking it out for someone."

I topped up Louie's mug, and we all settled into our business. Erik was intensely studying the contents of LePew's laptop. I was going over the stack of pages Erik had printed off yesterday in LePew's office. Louie was working on whatever he had going. He packed up and headed down to the courthouse at 10:30. Erik and I kept at it for another hour.

"You in the mood for a quick lunch?" I asked.

"Oh, you heard my stomach growling?" Erik laughed.

"No, but only because mine has been making more noise. I'm thinking a cheeseburger down at Shamrock's, and then maybe we drive past LePew's place. I'd like to check out his place once more, but for no more than an hour and only if he's not there."

"You find something in those documents?"

"I don't know, could be. He's got some information on Jack Carter, my friend that was killed in the hit-and-run. He had the White House Apartment contract with

Odell Dankworth. If I had to guess, I'd say LePew was checking Jack out. Be nice to see if I could find out why."

"I'm ready whenever you are."

We took Morton for a walk, took him back to the office then drove over to Shamrock's. We turned our phones off once I parked and then headed into the restaurant. We each inhaled their Juicy Nookie Burger, a medium fried burger stuffed with cheese. Just because I needed the sweetening, I ordered both of us a Brownie Sundae for dessert.

I said hi to folks I knew at a couple of tables on our way out the door, and we headed over to LePew's place. The driveway was empty, and I turned in. Erik pulled two sets of latex gloves from the box in the console, and we headed up to the front door. Same as yesterday, we rang the doorbell three times, waiting between each ring. No one answered, so we slipped on the gloves, and Erik took out the copy of the key we had made yesterday.

He slipped it into the key cylinder just above the brass handle and turned it. When we didn't hear the deadbolt click, Erik looked up at me.

"Try it again," I said. He turned the key again, and there still wasn't a sound. "See if the door is unlocked."

Erik took hold of the handle set, pressed down, and opened the door a couple of inches.

"Open it, and let's step inside," I said.

We stepped inside, closed the door behind us, and any questions we had were answered. The living room off to the right was in shambles. The cushions on the two leather couches were slit, and the stuffing was strewn on the floor. The flat screen that had been mounted above the fireplace was lying upside down on the floor, and bits of shattered screen covered the floor.

"What the hell happened?" Erik said.

"The place has been ransacked, is what happened. Let's get out of here before someone spots us and calls the cops."

We stepped outside, and Erik closed the door behind us. "You want me to lock the door?"

"No, let's leave it just like we found it and get out of here." We walked swiftly to the car, backed out of the driveway, and drove off. "I can only hope we're not picked up by someone's doorbell camera. Keep your phone off until we're back at the office. This is one of the reasons I turn my phone off when I'm doing something like this. It eliminates any location history of us being here." We drove back to Shamrock's, and I parked in the parking lot.

"We going back inside?" Erik asked.

"No, turn your phone back on. If, for some reason, the police check our phones, it will look like we just turned them off over a long lunch. Now they'll ping our location as here and show us heading back to the office. Hopefully, we'll never be checked out, never be suspected, but if we are, well, we were just having lunch. Same with yesterday, we just took a break."

"So what happened there? Who could have done that?" Erik asked.

"We can discuss it, but I want you to keep it to yourself. You don't mention it to anyone. Okay?"

Twenty-four

I started the car and headed up the street to the office. "Who do you think tore that place apart?"

Erik shook his head. "I don't know. I'm sure LePew wouldn't do that to his own house. It had to be someone who was pretty pissed off and—wait, you don't think my uncle did that, do you?"

"No, at least not him personally, but I'm pretty sure he gave the word. He would have told Fat Freddy to check the place out, and Freddy would have sent a few guys over. You gave your uncle the keys last night, didn't you?"

"Well, yeah, but I think LePew left. I mean, his car was gone when I stepped outside this morning. But to trash the place like that?"

"Erik, get a grip," I said as I parked across the street from the office. "This is what your uncle does. It's the business he's in. You know anyone else who has two or three armed thugs standing outside his front door twenty-four hours a day, seven days a week?"

"But they were talking to LePew yesterday and—"

I turned the car off and looked at Erik. "Hey, you're supposed to be a smart guy. Get with it. Talking to LePew yesterday? Talking? LePew was probably going to kill you. Your uncle's guys were not talking to him. They were beating the shit out of him until he told them whatever it was they wanted to hear. Whether it was the truth or not. That's the business they're in. LePew is probably dead and at the bottom of the river. I don't like it. In a way, it's not fair, although in this case… But that's the business, and that's why your parents kept you away from your uncle. Look, I know he's helped you, paid for college, and probably has done a number of things for you that you'll never know. Let me put it this way. If the shoe was on the other foot and LePew had the opportunity to question your uncle, he would be just as aggressive."

"You think they killed LePew?"

"I'd say there's a pretty good chance that happened."

Erik shook his head, seemed to think for a moment, and then said, "I better get back to that laptop and see if we can find anything else on the White House Apartments."

We'd been working for over an hour when a call came through on my cell phone. Aaron LaZelle, my pal who heads up the city's homicide unit. "Hello, Aaron. I know why you're calling, and I think you're wrong. I believe I bought dinner last time, so it's your turn."

"Hi, Dev. Hey, sorry, but this isn't about dinner. I'd like you to stop down, in, say, the next thirty minutes or so. If you've got car problems, I can have someone pick you up."

"No, Aaron. No car problems for a change. Is everything okay?"

"Just have a couple of questions and hope you might be able to help us out."

"Be happy to help. Anything we could discuss over the phone?"

"No, I think it would be better if you came down here."

"Okay, yeah, sure. Not a problem. I'll head out right now. See you in ten minutes or so."

"Thanks, Dev. I appreciate that," he said and disconnected.

"You look like you're deep in thought. Everything okay?" Erik asked.

"I'll find out in a bit. I've got to head over to the police station. Umm, stay here. I should be back in an hour or so. Louie might show up at any moment. Oh, and just in case I'm not back, would you take Morton for a walk around 3:00?"

"Yeah, I can do that. You sure you're okay? You want me to go with you?"

"Thanks for offering, but I'm fine. See you in a bit," I said and headed out of the office. I climbed into my car, wondering what Aaron's call was about. He was a busy guy on the best of days, and if he wanted me down there, something was up. I wondered if it was something about LePew. What if they found a body, but then how would they associate him with me? That info wouldn't have come from Tubby. Neither Erik nor Louie would have contacted the police. I looked up the street, and a police cruiser was parked on the other side of the street, a half-dozen lots past our building. Was he responding to a call or keeping an eye on me?

I turned on my car, waited for a woman on a bike to pass, and then made a U-turn and headed down the street. I checked my rearview mirror. The cruiser was now driving in the same direction as me, about a half-block behind. Something was up.

With heavy traffic and stop lights, it took us almost ten minutes before I turned into the gravel parking lot across the street from the police station. A moment later, the cruiser drove past the lot and disappeared around the far corner.

Some recent work must have been done in the parking lot because all the large potholes were no more, at least for the moment. I parked, walked across the street, and headed into the station.

"Well, Haskell, it's been a while. Here to turn yourself in?" Sergeant Strehlow at the front desk joked. I'd known him since we were in grade school together.

"Hey, how's it going, Sarge? No, I'm here to see Aaron. He's expecting me."

"I'll give 'em a call. Grab a seat. Good to see you, Dev," he said and picked up the phone."

I settled into a chair a bit away from the dozen or so people already waiting in the lobby. It wasn't more than a couple of minutes before the security door opened, and a guy I recognized as a detective but had forgotten his name called, "Hassle?"

I gave a wave and headed over. "Thanks for coming down, Detective. How are things going for you?"

He shook his head and said, "Same shit, different day." We took the elevator up to the third floor, walked down the hall past the entrance to the homicide department, and into a hallway with a half-dozen interview rooms. He stepped into Interview Room Three. He held the door for me and then said, "Grab a seat. They'll be in here in just a moment. You want a coffee or anything?"

"Yeah, a coffee would be nice. Black, no cream or sugar."

He closed the door behind him, and I heard the lock click. I headed over to the metal-topped table and sat down. I was pretty sure whatever the reason I was down here was, it had to have something to do with Louis LePew. I wondered if anyone was in the viewing room watching me, and I made a concerted effort not to look stressed.

Aaron and his second in charge, Detective Sergeant Norris Manning, entered the room two minutes later. Manning carried a cardboard tray with two cups of coffee.

"Coffee black?" Manning said and set the cup down in front of me.

"Thanks. How are you guys doing?" I asked and took a sip of coffee. It was dreadful, and I tried not to grimace, but I probably did. Neither Manning nor Aaron said anything.

They sat down, and Aaron said, "Thanks for coming down right away, Dev. We've got a bit of a situation and wondered if you might be able to help."

Manning read the standard introduction asking me if I was there of my own free will and did I want an attorney. As he read, my first thought was to say something along the lines of, 'Why the hell didn't you tell me you had a situation on the phone?' Instead, I said, "Happy to help in any way I can. What's this about?"

"Do you know an individual by the name of Louis LePew?" Manning asked.

"Not really. I met him for the first time yesterday afternoon. He was in the process of assaulting a young man who was working with me. Morton, my dog, and I yanked him off the young man."

"What did you do once you got him off?"

"The young man had been jogging and didn't have his phone, so I called one of his family members. He sent some friends, and that was pretty much the end of it. Everyone left and went their separate ways."

"Would you care to be a little more precise in your explanation?" Aaron said.

"Sure. The young man working for me had been jogging along the River Boulevard. This guy, Louis LePew, who I had never met before, had asked the young man for help with his car. The young man offered to help, and LePew assaulted him. He wrestled him to the ground. When I arrived, LePew was on top of him, attempting to break his arm. I told him to stop, he didn't, and my golden retriever knocked him over and then took hold of the calf of his leg with his jaw. The man then attempted to choke my dog."

"When you say your dog took hold, are you suggesting he bit LePew?"

"He grabbed onto him with his jaw and did not let go until I pulled him off LePew."

"Who is the young man working with you?"

"His name is Erik Gustafson."

Aaron and Manning flashed a half-second look at one another. "Any relation to a gentleman by the name of—"

"He's Tubby Gustafson's nephew. He's a recent college graduate with bachelor's degrees in prelaw and computer programing. He's interested in working in some aspect of law enforcement, Homeland Security, National—"

"And he's working for you?" Manning asked.

"Just to get first-hand experience at some of the things I deal with. He's only been with me a few days.

I'm not paying him. I'm looking into an apartment complex, the White House Apartments, out in Woodbury, and he's helping me."

"So, is LePew involved in that complex?"

"Not that I'm aware of. I honestly have no idea why he assaulted Erik. But having said that, I have no doubt he intended to harm the boy. Maybe even kill him. I can state for the record that Erik's father was a construction contractor. He passed away a few years ago. In no way, other than bloodline, is Erik associated with Tubby Gustafson."

"So why do you think LePew attacked him?"

"I have no idea. As far as I know, LePew didn't even know his name. Erik certainly didn't know LePew."

We chatted for another fifteen minutes, and then they brought the conversation to a halt. Manning mentioned the time, gave the standard conclusion to our conversation, and shut down the recording computer. I found it interesting that they didn't ask about Tubby's guys taking LePew.

As we all rose to leave the room, I asked, "Have you talked to LePew about this?"

"Not yet. We wanted to hear from you first. He had a note in his pocket with your name and address," Aaron said.

I shook my head. "I don't know where he would have gotten that. Other than his assault on Erik, I've had no interaction with him, and truthfully, I've never heard of him before. If I had, I'd certainly remember that last name."

"Thanks for your time, Dev," Aaron said, and they walked me to the door. Manning headed back to the Homicide office, and Aaron escorted me to the elevator. Once we stepped onto the elevator and the door closed, I asked, "What's going on, Aaron?"

"LePew was found in his car in the parking lot at Regions hospital."

"You mean he drove himself there?"

Aaron shook his head. "He was unconscious, in no way capable of driving. He had been beaten to within an inch of his life. Anyway, he's in a coma in intensive care and has been given a thirty-five percent chance of surviving. Stay tuned. We'll probably have some more questions," he said as the elevator door opened.

I stepped out. Aaron pushed a button, and the elevator door closed just as I turned to face him.

Twenty-five

When I stepped into the office Erik Asked. "That didn't take long. Everything go okay?" Morton looked up for a moment and returned to his rawhide bone.

"Yeah, interesting. I picked up some information." I grabbed the coffee mug off my desk, filled it, and then turned off the burner.

"So what'd you learn?"

"Well, it turns out that Louis LePew was found in his Mercedes last night in the parking lot at Regions Hospital. He was unconscious, and the police don't think he was able to drive himself. He's currently in a coma in the intensive care unit. They're giving him a thirty-five percent chance of surviving. No idea what condition he'll be in if and when he recovers."

Erik thought for a moment. "So my uncle's guys did this?"

"I don't know that for sure, but I would say it's a very strong possibility."

"Did you tell them what his house was like this afternoon?"

"They didn't ask, and I didn't volunteer that information. I would guess whoever went through the place was obviously looking for something. But I don't know what that would be." I immediately wondered if they were looking for fifty-thousand things. Namely, the five bundles of hundred-dollar bills. My next thought was, where did LePew get the money? All roads seemed to lead to Odell Dankworth. "What have you learned about Odell Dankworth?"

"Just some general stuff. His office is downtown in the Northwestern Building. Do you know where that is?"

"Yeah, it's just across the street from the Farmer's Market." Typical of the younger generation, Erik had a blank look on his face. "It's a nice eight-story building, built by the Northwestern Railroad, hence the name. I think it was built around 1916. Today, it's offices for small businesses and artists. The last time I was in there, pretty much the entire first floor was taken up by a business called Golden Deli. It might be interesting to pay Mr. Dankworth a visit."

"Why would you want to do that?"

"Just to let him know we're on to him. I don't think your pal LePew would have done what he did without clearing it with Dankworth first."

"Are you thinking of mentioning the difference in the contracts? The copy version with the paragraph transferring everything to the surviving member in the case of death?"

"No, I don't think so. It might upset him more if we didn't say anything, and he'd get all worked up that we would find it and bring it to court."

"So why see him if it's just going to cause a problem? I think if you asked him anything, there would be a good chance he wouldn't give you an honest answer. He may not even be aware of LePew being in the hospital."

"Yeah, and he's probably unaware of who your uncle is. I guess I just like to stir the pot."

"Would you mind if I took a pass and kept working on these files? I really don't want to get involved in any more physical situations, and I don't want my uncle thinking he has to come to the rescue in his particular fashion."

"Not to worry, I get it, Erik. I'm going to head down there and check it out. He probably won't even see me without an appointment."

"Just be careful, Dev."

"Get back to work on those files. I'll expect a full report when I return."

I headed out to the car and drove downtown. The city Farmer's Market is in operation Friday thru Sunday. During the rest of the week, it serves as a parking lot. I turned in, parked, and walked across the street to the eight-story Northwestern Building. The walls of the inside lobby were lined with large sheets of white marble an inch thick and probably original to the building. A brass sign on the wall listed the building as having been placed on the National Register of Historic Places. A set of stairs straight ahead led up to the various floors. Fortunately, there was a set of elevators just to the right. Next to the elevators was a directory with an alphabetical list of the building's residents. Dankworth Building Brokers was located in unit 613.

I took the elevator up to the sixth floor and stepped into a hallway with polished concrete floors. The walls were painted an off-white color. Doors and windows trimmed in dark-stained wood indicated the various offices. Unit 613 was four units off to the right and halfway down the hall. There were three windows next to the door. All three windows were single hung, meaning they could only open from the bottom panel. The glass in the windows and the door was frosted, so it was impossible to see into the office. A nameplate attached to the wall identified the unit, number 613, and the occupant, Dankworth Building Brokers. I could hear what sounded like classical music coming from inside the office, probably a radio.

I took hold of the doorknob and went to open the door, but it was locked. I tried it twice, definitely locked. I knocked on the wooden door three separate times, each time just a little louder. No one ever answered. The volume of the music didn't sound like it had been adjusted. I thought about dropping a card in through the mail slot in the door and quickly decided that would be stupid. I took the elevator down to the main floor and walked out to my car.

I climbed into my car and counted up six stories and then counted over to the right what I thought might be four units. There was a bald guy looking out the window. He may have been looking at me, but I couldn't be sure. He suddenly faded from view as if he stepped back a few feet. I waited for him to reappear, but it never happened, and I headed back to the office.

Twenty-six

Louie was back in the office with his feet up on the picnic table. Whatever he was saying had Erik laughing. "Well, he finally returns. You were down at the police station all this time?" Louie asked.

I shook my head and said, "No, that only took about thirty minutes. I'm just back from the Northwestern Building. I went down there hoping to meet Odell Dankworth. His office door was locked, and no one answered when I knocked."

"Erik told me about this LePew character. That doesn't sound too good."

I shook my head. "No, it doesn't. Although, based on what he probably had in mind to do to Erik, I can't say I'm too bothered. What's your latest on the sewer lady?"

"Oh, Michelle? She's all on board with whatever they're offering. She spends one more night locked up, and then she's out tomorrow at ten. I don't know, a very upset father ready to kill her and a school principal who would probably like to fire her, except they can't because they're desperate for teachers. She may just want to stay locked up. It's too bad, and like all of us, she's a nice person who did something stupid. Speaking of which, it's getting close to my nightly appointment over at The Spot. Are you two interested?"

"Will you behave if we go over, Erik?" I asked.

He hung his head and said, "I suppose if I have to," then looked up and grinned.

"You guys head on over. Morton and I will join you in about fifteen minutes."

Louie nodded and turned off his computer. Erik arranged his files in a neat stack and stood. I clipped the leash onto Morton, and we all headed out of the office. Erik and Louie walked over to The Spot. Morton and I headed in the opposite direction on our walk.

We stepped into The Spot fifteen minutes later. Morton strained on the leash as we headed down the bar. Erik was seated on a stool next to Louie, and as we rounded the corner of the bar, Erik leaned over with a large handful of pork rinds, which Morton inhaled in a half-second.

"Oh, God, Erik. Talk about making a friend for life. Morton will be forever grateful."

"Are you kidding? Believe me, I'll be forever grateful to him for knocking LePew off of me. Grateful to both of you. Thanks, Dev."

"Be interesting to see if your uncle has anything to say about it."

"I don't think it would be like him to mention it. I hesitate to say it's unfortunate that LePew is hospitalized, but if things had been left up to him, I think there's a good chance my body would be lying in the mud somewhere along the Mississippi right about now."

"Well, here's to things not working out," Louie said as he raised his glass, clearly suggesting we change the subject.

We stayed for one, and then Morton and I drove Erik back to his uncle's. He was quiet on the drive home. I slowed as we approached Tubby's mansion, stopped, and said, "Is everything all right, Erik? You seem deep in thought."

"Mmm, I guess I'm dealing with some mixed emotions. On the one hand, I'm thinking that this LePew prick got exactly what he deserved, and on the other, I guess I don't know. I might feel a little bad about it, but not too bad. As a matter of fact, I want to thank my uncle for fixing things so that I'm not looking over my shoulder every thirty seconds."

"Yeah, I get that. I've been thinking about it too, and I think he made a mistake. He was—"

"A mistake? Dev, he was going to kill me."

"Yeah, that's probably right, I'm not criticizing your uncle, but here's the mistake. We were both wearing the Honey Johns t-shirts. You were jogging by yourself, and I think he mistook you for me. Remember, he had just a second or two to react. You go over to help him, and he either thinks you're me or that he may have alerted you, and you could ID him later if he did get me, and so he proceeds to make his original bad situation even worse. Believe me, if he knew who your uncle was, there would be no way he'd do what he did."

Erik nodded. "You know, I gotta say, I'm glad he's my uncle."

"Can I give you some advice?"

"Okay," he said, drawing the word out and not sounding too sure.

"Tell him that. Tell him you're glad he's your uncle. Thank him for making sure LePew won't be out there waiting to hurt you. Sometimes in this business, things get very black and white. If LePew was arrested, there's a pretty good chance someone like Odell Dankworth would pay his bail, and to LePew's way of thinking, the best thing he could do would be to eliminate you so you couldn't testify against him."

"You mean he'd try to eliminate both of us?"

"Yeah, I suspect he would. I didn't think of that, but yeah, that's exactly what he'd do. You interested in coming in tomorrow?"

"What? Oh yeah, sure. I'm counting on it. Sorry you weren't able to meet up with Odell Dankworth this afternoon, but if we try it tomorrow morning, we might have better luck."

"Let's do that. Give me a call when you're ready to head in, and I'll pick you up."

Erik held out his hand, and as we shook, he said, "Thanks for the advice on my uncle. I'm going to go inside, try to find him, and tell him thanks."

"Just don't interrupt his massage time."

"Are you kidding? I've been trying to figure out a way to get some of that for me," Erik said and laughed.

"Go on, I'll see you in the morning." I watched until he stepped inside the mansion and then drove home.

We had just entered the kitchen, and I'd tossed Morton a biscuit when my cell phone rang. Crystal. "Hey, how are you doing?" was how I answered.

"I hadn't heard from you in a couple of days and wondered if everything was okay."

"Oh, sorry. Yeah, everything is fine. I've just been tied up with work. More importantly, how are you?"

"How am I? I'm bored. You think you could handle a visitor a little later tonight?"

"I promise I would handle you very carefully. I would love to have you come over. In fact, as soon as I'm off the phone, I'll run up to Solo Vino and get a bottle of wine, or would you prefer a bottle of champagne?"

"Really, you're giving me a choice?"

"Yeah, sure. Whatever you want."

"How about champagne? If that's not being too pushy."

"Consider it done. I'll see you when you get here. Looking forward to it."

"Oh, thank you. See you in about forty-five minutes. Bye, bye, bye," she said and disconnected.

I put my shoes on and hurried up the block to Solo Vino. Chuck was working the counter when I stepped in. "Well, Dev Haskell. I knew I should have locked the doors. How are you?"

"Hi, Chuck. I'm on a mission. I need two bottles of chilled champagne, and I really don't know what would be good."

"Perfect timing. We just put a couple of bottles in there this morning. They'll be nicely chilled. They're in the back cooler on the left-hand side, second shelf. There's a yellow label on the bottle. "

I hurried to the back of the store, and sure enough, there they were, four bottles with yellow labels. I didn't want to overdo it, so I just grabbed two bottles and hurried up to the front counter.

"Anything else you need?" Chuck asked.

"No thanks. This will be perfect."

He rang the bottles up, and I took out my debit card and looked at the price. Fifty-nine dollars a bottle, a hundred and eighteen bucks, and that was before the city and state tax.

"Is there a problem?" Chuck asked.

"Oh, no, everything is fine. I was thinking of something else," I said and inserted my debit card into the credit card machine. It asked if I wanted cash back and then told me to input my code. I input the four digits, crossed my fingers, and said a prayer. It was a miracle, my card was accepted. "Can you give me a receipt with that?"

Chuck tossed the receipt in the bag with the bottles. I thanked him, stepped out the door, and hurried home. I placed the bottles in the refrigerator, arranged Oreo cookies on a plate for hors d'oeuvres, and then ran upstairs to my bedroom.

A couple of t-shirts were on the floor, along with socks. I tossed them in the closet. I slipped on a fresh pair of jeans and a button-down shirt that wasn't too wrinkled. I took the duvet off the bed, quickly yanked off the sheets, and put a clean set on the bed. I pulled the duvet up, folded the sheet over the top, and hurried downstairs. I had just stepped out of the entryway when the doorbell rang. Good thing I'd hurried. I didn't expect Crystal for another twenty minutes. I stepped back to the front door and opened it.

"Mr. Gustafson requests your presence," Fat Freddy said.

"Now?"

"Yeah, now. Come on, let's go."

"Oh, I'd really love to, but I can't right now. I've got someone coming over. They're on the way. Look, I'll do anything to make this up, but I can't leave right now, and I've got a lot of money invested in this meeting. Could we possibly reschedule and I'll—""Put him in the car, Pee Wee," Fat Freddy said and stepped to the side.

"No, wait, wait. Please, we can work something out here and, hey, hey, wait a minute. What the hell do you think you're doing?" I shouted at Pee Wee as he wrapped a muscular arm around my waist, lifted me up, and carried me out to the Escalade.

Twenty-seven

I was lying on the floor of the back seat. Fat Freddy was seated with his feet on top of me. I'd pleaded and begged for a good five minutes and then finally gave up as we headed toward Tubby's mansion. I didn't say anything else, and despite being furious, I have to say we made very good time.

Pee Wee screeched to a stop in front of the mansion, and Fat Freddy oozed out of the back seat. "Well, come on, Haskell. You were bitching the entire time about being on the floor. Now the door is finally open, and it's time for you to get your worthless ass out of the car. So do it, for God's sake."

I pushed myself up onto the seat, gave Fat Freddy a mean look, and then climbed out.

"For the love of—would you at least straighten yourself up? Fix your shirt. You're going to meet his highness. Try to look like you know what the hell you're doing."

I tucked my shirt in as I followed Fat Freddy to the front door.

"Assume the position," one of the armed guys leaning next to the door said.

"Oh, let him by this time. We already checked him," Freddy said and opened the door. I followed him inside. He gave a nod to the guard just inside the door, and we headed down the hall toward Tubby's office. I wondered if Erik would be in the office and then wondered if Erik was in some kind of trouble with his uncle.

Fat Freddy knocked on the office door, and Tubby immediately answered, "Enter."

When we stepped inside, I fully expected to see the two women rubbing Tubby's dimpled shoulders. Instead, Tubby was seated at his desk. Soft classical music played in the background, and the two masseuses were nowhere in sight.

"Well, Haskell, how very nice of you to join us."

"I have to say, sir, I was waiting for a client to arrive for a meeting."

"Couldn't you have called them and rescheduled?"

"I wasn't given that opportunity."

Tubby glanced over at Fat Freddy, who just shrugged and said, "He was being his usual difficult self."

"Go ahead and make your phone call, Haskell."

"Oh, thank you, sir," I said, then reached into my empty pocket and realized my cell phone was still sitting on the bedroom dresser.

"Problem?" Tubby asked.

"I'm afraid my cell phone is back at my place."

Tubby shook his head. "Honest to God, all right, you can use my desk phone, but make it short," he said, then pushed the phone across the desk toward me.

I went to reach for the phone but then realized I didn't know Crystal's number. I just pushed the button for speed dial on my phone. "You know, sir, it might be a long call, going over various items on her case. I'll reach her later on."

"Suit yourself, Haskell. I've called you here because I have some information that might be helpful to a case you're apparently working on." Tubby reached inside his suit coat, brought out a number ten business envelope, and tossed it across his desk. "Go ahead and open it up."

I opened the envelope and took out a sheet of paper. A set of keys that looked like it could be for a front door and a car fell onto the desk. All that was on the sheet of paper was a West Seventh Street address address ending with, 'Unit 147.'

I looked up at Tubby. "Is this someone's address?"

"I guess you'll have to go there and see for yourself."

"I'm not quite following, sir."

"Consider it a thank you from me for your work with Erik. He's now much more focused on finding employment outside of your area. You've managed to alert him to just how dreadful your life really is, and for this, I am eternally grateful."

"Always happy to help, sir. I did have an interesting chat with the police today."

Tubby nodded. "Yes, interview room three, I believe. I hope it went well."

"How did you know where it was?"

"Haskell, my line of work requires me to be continually informed on a vast array of subjects. I advise you to look into that address. Frederick, if you would please escort Mr. Haskell home."

I stood, placed the sheet of paper back in the envelope, and stuffed the envelope in a back pocket. I held out my hand to shake, but Tubby waved it off with a flick of his hand. "Off with you, Haskell. I've work to do."

"Let's go," Freddy called as he headed toward the door.

It was misty out, and Pee Wee had the windshield wipers on. At least this time, I could sit in the back seat instead of laying on the floor with Fat Freddy's feet on top of me. Once again, we made excellent time driving back to my place. The traffic lights all turned green as we approached, and cars seemed to pull to the curb and let us pass. Fat Freddy munched on a chocolate-covered doughnut and didn't say anything until we stopped in front of my house. I was hoping Crystal's car might be waiting in the driveway, but no such luck.

I opened the car door and was only halfway out when Fat Freddy shouted, "Enjoy," and Pee Wee accelerated up the street. I fell out of the Escalade and landed on my knees on the wet boulevard lawn. I hurried up onto the porch, hoping that Crystal hadn't been here yet. The red thong hanging from the doorknob suggested otherwise.

I went to open the door, forgetting for the moment that the door automatically locked, so when Pee Wee hauled me out of the house, and Fat Freddy closed the door, I was effectively locked out of my house.

I knew where both spare keys were. One was hanging where I always kept it, in the kitchen right next to the backdoor. The other was in my desk down at the office. No one else had a key to the house. I could have broken a basement window, but I'd cleverly had them all replaced a few years back with glass blocks to stop someone from kicking them in.

It couldn't have been later than 8:00, and if I hurried, I might make it down to The Spot before Louie left for home. He would have a key to the office, and I could get the key from my desk. The office was about three miles away, and I started off at a trot.

The mist seemed to be growing a little heavier as I made my way through the various neighborhoods. I cut through someone's backyard, was chased by a dog, fortunately on a chain, hopped a fence, and landed in a hedge with branches that scraped my face and arms and ripped my jeans. I was too tired to run any further. I stumbled down a wooded hill near the freeway. I fell in the mud twice and almost got hit by a city bus. The mist had changed to drizzle, which had now increased to a pretty serious rain, and in short order, I was soaked, but

I kept going. Eventually, I could see the illuminated sign above the front door of The Spot, about six blocks ahead.

I picked up speed for a block and then simply couldn't run anymore. I continued walking as fast as my legs would allow and finally made it to the side door of The Spot. Louie's car was still parked on the street, and I stepped into the bar right where Louie's stool was. Only Louie wasn't on his stool, and an empty glass rested on the bar.

The conversational level dropped noticeably as people stared at me, muddy, soaking wet, scratched, scraped, and breathing heavily.

"Dev, Dev, what happened? Are you okay?" Mike shouted as he hurried along the bar toward me.

"Where's Louie? Is Louie here?"

"He just left out the front door. He—"

I hurried back out into the rain. Louie's Ford Fiesta was still there, but the brake lights suddenly came on, and the engine started.

"Louie, Louie, wait. Louie, please. Louie," I shouted as I ran toward him. He rolled away from the curb. "Louie, wait, Louie," I shouted, and thank God, he stopped.

I was seated on Louie's stool, on my second whiskey. Mike had given me a bar rag to dry my face. I had the house key in my left hand, and I was in the process of telling Louie, Mike, and three or four other people how I was locked out of the house and ran all the way down to The Spot to catch Louie.

I didn't mention anything regarding Fat Freddy, Pee Wee, or Tubby Gustafson. I skipped Crystal's thong hanging on the doorknob and might have embellished the bit about the dog, saying it was two German Shepherds instead of that little Corgi, but still.

Once I finished the second whiskey, Louie suggested it might be a good time to leave. I climbed into his passenger seat, and he drove me home.

"You sure you've got your house key?" he asked for the third time.

"Yeah, right here," I said, holding it up.

"You need help getting in?"

"No, but thanks for bringing me home, Louie."

"Yeah, good thing you ran all the way, or we wouldn't have linked up. You think you'll be in tomorrow?"

"Oh yeah, first thing. I'll be bringing Erik. Thanks again. I'll buy lunch tomorrow," I said and climbed out. I hurried up onto the porch, took the thong off the doorknob, inserted the key in the lock, and prayed. The door clicked open. I gave Louie a wave and stepped inside.

I took my wet clothes off down in the basement in front of the washer and went upstairs. I took a long hot shower and then crawled into bed next to Morton.

Twenty-eight

My cell phone ringing the following morning woke me. "Hell, Hello," I said and cleared my throat.

"Hi, Dev. I'm outside in the sunshine after all that rain last night. Ready to be picked up whenever you can get here."

I glanced at the clock. It was 8:20. "Oh, thanks, Erik. I've got to deal with Morton, so it might be about twenty minutes if that's okay."

"Not a problem. It's a gorgeous morning, so whenever you get here, I'll be waiting."

"See you just as soon as we can," I said and hurried out of bed. I quickly dressed, skipped shaving, and headed downstairs. Morton was in the kitchen anxiously waiting next to the backdoor. Based on the way he was moving back and forth, he'd apparently been waiting patiently for quite some time. I opened the door, and he dashed into the backyard. I picked up the remnants of Crystal's red thong that he'd chewed up and tossed it in the trash. I filled his food and water dishes and let him in a couple of minutes later. While he wolfed down his breakfast, I had a dish of sea salt caramel ice cream for breakfast. I Googled the address from Tubby on my laptop. Five minutes later, we were in the car and heading toward Erik, waiting just outside of Tubby Gustafson's mansion.

"Oh, wow, that was fast," Erik said as he climbed into the car. "I didn't expect you guys for another fifteen minutes. What the hell happened to you? Is everything all right?" he asked, looking at the scratches on my face and arms from the hedge I landed in last night.

"Yeah, just me dealing with a screw-up." I went on to tell him a light version of my previous evening. I didn't mention Pee Wee and Fat Freddy picking me up or pounding down two whiskeys at The Spot. I told him I jogged the entire way from home.

"How many miles is that?"

"I feel like it was about ten," I said, and we both laughed.

Louie wasn't in the office, and since I hadn't had any coffee yet, I made a full twelve-cup pot. I searched online for the address Tubby gave me and was on my second cup when Louie arrived. I filled his mug, and after he'd recovered from his climb up the stairs, he asked, "How'd you sleep last night?"

"Like a baby. I woke up and cried every thirty minutes."

"Really?"

"No, I was out like a light. A run like that will do it to me."

"Not to mention battling your way through the woods. Next time you might want to think about using the sidewalk."

"Yeah, but if I'd done that, you would have been gone by the time I made it to The Spot. It was just by the skin of my teeth that I caught you."

Louie glanced over at Erik and said, "I thought it was Mike yelling that I forgot to pay. That's the only reason I stopped. If I'd known it was Dev, I would have floored my car."

"And that Ford Fiesta would rev up to about five miles an hour if it didn't cut out altogether. Are you in court today?"

"Just a brief appearance this afternoon. I've got to ask for a continuance on a case. One of my clients home-tested, and he's got covid. The continuance won't be a problem. No one want's him in their courtroom with that stuff."

"Does he know where he got it?"

Louie shook his head. "He's been religious about not going out, keeping things very low-key, especially after being charged with a DUI. He offices in the Osborn building, and he thinks he may have picked it up there, on an elevator at the beginning or the end of a workday."

"Not fun. Speaking of which, I've got an address I want to check out, Erik. You want to come with?"

"Yeah, sure. Is it here in town?"

"Yeah, down on West Seventh Street, in fact, that's the name of the place, Seventh Street Storage. You going to be here for a while, Louie?"

"Yeah, not to worry."

"If it's close to the noon hour before we get back, I'll grab lunch for everyone. I really appreciate you giving me a lift home last night."

"I'm just glad you caught me."

We headed out and drove over to the storage place. I'd been past it a million times but had never stopped and been inside. Jumping on the interstate for two miles put us there in just a few minutes. There was a parking lot in the back of the building, and that's where I pulled in. We walked inside, and a woman flashed a quick smile and said, "How can I help you? Looking to rent some space?"

"Actually, no. I've got a client who's out of town. Out of the country, actually, and he asked us to check out his space. I also want to make sure that his rent payment is up to date."

"What's the unit number?" she asked as she brought up a screen on her computer.

"The unit number is one-four-seven."

She nodded. "And the renter's name?"

"It's either under Odell Dankworth or Dankworth Building Brokers."

"Mmm, that's not the name I'm seeing here."

"Oh, sorry, it might be under Louis LePew."

"Yeah, that's it, and paid in full until the first of the year."

"Glad to hear that. Can we just go out that door and get to the unit?"

"Yes, for one-four-seven, just walk down and take the first right, and it should be about halfway down on the left side."

"Thank you," I said, and we walked out the door and down a narrow corridor barely wide enough for a car. There were a series of yellow metal doors, no more than five feet apart, with red numbers on them. These would be walk-in units. Probably about the size of a walk-in closet.

"Where'd you get this information?" Erik asked.

"Checking a lot of sources. One of the guys I talked to had some recent interaction with LePew and wasn't too happy with the guy," I said, not mentioning I was describing Erik's uncle, Tubby. We walked about fifty yards. On the right was a larger corridor with a pickup truck parked further down and a guy pushing a two-wheeled dolly into a storage unit. Once again, all the doors were yellow metal, and the unit number was in large red numbers on the door. The difference now was the doors were actually single-car garage doors that rose overhead. The number on the first door was one-ninety-nine.

We walked past the guy loading the two-wheeled dolly and got a friendly nod. Number one-four-seven was another eleven doors further down. I took the set of keys out of my pocket. The lock for the door was actually a padlock attached to the garage door and a steel ring set in the concrete. I inserted the key, turned it, and the shackle on the padlock popped up. I slipped the padlock out of the steel ring, lifted the hatch, and the door rose just a quarter of an inch. I raised the door with one hand, and it quickly flew up the track. Inside was an older-looking vehicle painted bright red. Both headlights were shattered, the grill was gone, the hood was buckled, and the windshield looked like someone had hit it a couple of times with a baseball bat. The car had clearly been in some kind of major accident.

White scrape marks along the front and the driver's side suggested it had either rammed into or been hit by a white vehicle.

"What the hell is this thing?" Erik asked. "Was LePew thinking of restoring this?"

"I have no idea," I said and stepped back. There wasn't a license plate on the front, but given the damage, that wasn't a surprise. I stepped along the side of the vehicle and peered in through the driver's window. With the exception of the driver's seat, which appeared to be steel and featured a complex seatbelt, everything else had been removed. The passenger seat and the entire rear seat were gone. The interior of the vehicle was now re-inforced with two sets of steel pipes running from the rear of the vehicle to the front and then another two sets of pipes welded across to either side of the vehicle about where the rear seat would have been and then just behind the driver's seat.

"Who in the hell would do this to a car? I don't get it. You think this was in a demolition derby?" Erik asked. He walked around to the back of the vehicle. "Everything looks more or less normal back here. The taillights aren't busted. No dents."

"Is there a license plate?" I asked.

Erik stepped back and shook his head. "Nope, nothing."

I opened the driver's door and was going to check the glove compartment, only there wasn't one. I noticed for the first time that the entire dashboard had been removed, and in its place was a sheet of steel that the reinforcement bars from the back of the vehicle were welded to.

"Take your phone out and start photographing the back. I'll take pictures of the front. If you can open the passenger door, take pictures of the interior." We started taking photographs. Both of us must have taken twenty or thirty pictures. I stepped outside and photographed the front of the vehicle. Hopefully, someone who knew more about cars than me would be able to identify the make and year.

When we had finished, I asked, "Have you seen enough?"

"I'm not sure what I've seen. Is this stolen or something?"

"That's something we're going to have to figure out. Let's go," I said.

I lowered the door, locked the padlock, took a picture of the garage door, and we left. On the drive back to the office, Erik kept going through his pictures, shaking his head and saying, "Incredible."

Twenty-nine

We stopped at Roosters, and I got three BBQ pork sandwiches and a beef marrow bone for Morton. When we stepped into the office, Morton looked up from his pillow and then, a half-second later, leaped up and rubbed his nose against the Roosters bag.

Louie was typing on his keyboard, and I set his sandwich on the picnic table. His suit coat was draped over the back of his desk chair, and the sleeves on his shirt were rolled up to just below his elbows.

"Thanks, Dev," he said without looking up.

I placed our two sandwiches on my desk and pulled out the tinfoil-wrapped marrow bone. I opened the tinfoil and held the bone out for Morton. His tail was wagging and slamming against the side of my desk. He snatched the bone and hurried back to his pillow.

Louie looked up from his keyboard and slid his sandwich in front of him. "Perfect timing, Dev. Thank you." He unwrapped his sandwich, inhaled the smell of BBQ, and smiled. He loosened his tie, draped it over his shoulder, and licked his lips.

Both Erik and I unwrapped the upper third of our sandwiches and took a bite, careful not to drop BBQ sauce or, God forbid, a piece of BBQ onto our jeans or t-shirts.

Louie picked up his completely unwrapped sandwich in both hands and took a big bite. A large chunk of BBQ dropped out of the bottom of his sandwich, left a trail down his white shirt, and settled on his trousers. He mumbled something, picked up the chunk of BBQ, and continued eating as if nothing had happened.

When we were finished, Louie made his usual attempt at scrubbing the BBQ stains, which only served to make the situation worse. I was about to give him some wise-ass remark when my cell phone rang.

"Haskell Investigations," was how I answered without looking at the screen.

"Hi, Dev. It's Melissa. Just checking in. I wondered if you've had a chance to go over that file I left with you?"

"Nice to hear your voice, Melissa. Yes, we've been going over the file and have come up with some more thoughts and information. What's your schedule like in the next few days?"

"Are you suggesting we meet?"

"Yeah, I think that would be a good idea. We've come up with some interesting information, all of which leads to more questions. If you would—"

"I could stop over toward the end of the afternoon if that would work for you."

"That would be just fine. Why don't you give me a call before you leave, just in case something comes up and we have to run out? But right now, I expect that we'll be here."

"Okay, I'll call ahead. Do you have someone working with you?"

"I do, and I'll be happy to bring you up to date on that aspect when we meet."

"Okay, thank you. I'll give you a call a little after 4:00."

"I look forward to seeing you," I said and disconnected.

"That was the Carter girl?" Erik asked.

"Yeah. She's going to come over toward the end of the afternoon. That will give us some time to get things lined up for her."

Erik nodded and said, "Would you mind giving me your phone? I'll load all the photos we took of that car onto my computer, and we can show her those. Plus, it will be a file that we both will have, and I can send it to her as well."

"Yeah, that makes sense, Erik." I slid my cell phone across the desk to him. "Line them up in some order that begins with the photo of the outside of the storage unit. The one with the locked garage door."

After attempting to scrub his BBQ sauce stain, Louie had managed to pretty much spread the stain over the entire left side of his shirt. He pulled on his suit coat and buttoned it, which hid the stain on his shirt and half the stain on his trousers. He didn't seem to be upset. He picked up his briefcase, gave a wave, and headed out the door to the courthouse.

At precisely 4:00, Melissa phoned, and fifteen minutes later, I saw her park in front of my car and hurry across the street. "Melissa's coming up the stairs now," I said to Erik, and a second later, the door opened.

She stepped into the office wearing high-waisted black slacks and a white blouse, looking gorgeous. She somehow managed to resemble both her father and mother, and for a moment, I could feel a lump in my throat.

I stepped around my desk and grabbed both her hands. "Thanks for coming, Melissa. Let me introduce you to Erik Gustafson. He's been helping me look into this case, pro bono, I hasten to add."

"Hello, it's nice to meet you, Erik."

"Thank you, Melissa. It's nice to finally be able to meet you in person. I feel like I already know you based on all the files we've been going through. You're in law school?"

"Yes, night school at Mitchell Hamline. Which means I don't get much sleep. Fortunately, tonight is my night off. No classes. I just get to read and study until the wee hours," she said and laughed.

I waited for a moment, expecting one of them to say something, but they seemed to be studying one another. Finally, I said, "Why don't you take a seat next to Erik, and we'll bring you up to date."

Erik quickly pulled back a client chair, and she sat down. He settled into the other chair and moved it an inch or two closer to Melissa, then positioned his laptop on my desk so that it was between the two of them.

"Okay, so as we cover what we've been doing, feel free to ask questions at any time. Any concerns we should know about before we start?"

"No, I'm anxious to hear what you've found out."

We reviewed our experiences at the White House apartments. I told her about my experience and a little about Erik's, but he gave her the laundry list of information regarding the shabby construction, the plastic plumbing, the quarter-inch sheetrock, and the lack of insulation. He told her about his lunch with Odell Dankworth at the Meritage restaurant. I told her about the two guys who were moving and loading the couch and chairs onto the trailer and how they said people were leaving and that there were empty units throughout the building.

I asked her if she had ever heard of a man named Louis LePew, and she shook her head and said, "No, never." I went on to tell her about him assaulting Erik and how Morton attacked him, and we called for help. I did not mention Tubby Gustafson or the fact that LePew was found in a coma in his Mercedes in the hospital parking lot.

We told her about the weapons in his car and the files we found in his home. I didn't mention my suspicions that Tubby's crew was responsible for tearing LePew's house apart. All in all, it took the better part of an hour. She only had an occasional question, none of which was what you'd call probing.

Finally, I laid the stack of files and paperwork we took from LePew's office in front of her. The first two items were the partnership agreement that transferred all ownership to the surviving partner in the instance of death, and next to that was the original version of that document with the signatures and initials in ink and no mention of the ownership transfer agreement.

She looked at the original agreement with her father's and Dankworth's signatures in ink and said, "I've never seen this before. I've only seen the one with the transfer agreement. I got it from my father's office. You found this in Mr. LePew's files?"

"Yes. We suspect the version you saw was created and passed off as the real deal. Your dad didn't have a copy like this?" I asked, pointing to the original.

She shook her head. "No, the copy with the transfer agreement is what I found in Dad's office file, and I went through his files a number of times. Actually, Mr. Dankworth contacted me with his condolences and then told me about the agreement. He was the one who told me to check my father's files. So I did, and that's the copy I found. It struck me as something my dad would never agree to, but there it was, and it's bothered me ever since. Now, when you tell me about the substandard construction," she looked over at Erik, "Dad would never, ever go along with that. I just know he wouldn't."

"Tell me about the car accident," I said.

'Well, it was a hit and run. They were coming home from a dinner with friends. It was just after nine on a Tuesday night. They met at the St. Paul Grill and had dinner. I think my mom had a couple glasses of wine, and my dad drank decaf coffee. They were going to pull into the garage. You know that street that dead ends in front of the house?"

"Yeah, I do. Is it Penfield?"

She nodded and said, "Yes. They drove down that street like we always did, and a car broadsided them right at the driveway. Hit them on the driver's side. The police report said they both died instantly. There was almost nothing left of the car. It was virtually cut in half. The funny thing is, you'd think a car driving fast enough to do that damage wouldn't have been able to drive away, but somehow it did. Given the damage and what the police could determine, they insisted it was a car that struck them. But their car was so destroyed that I still think it almost had to be a truck, and I—" Tears suddenly came down both cheeks, and she couldn't talk.

Erik placed both hands over her right hand resting on the arm of the client chair, and she quickly placed her left hand over his.

I reached inside my desk drawer, took out a box of Kleenex, and set it in front of her. She sniffled, grabbed a Kleenex from the package with her left hand, and dried her eyes. After a moment, Erik removed his hands, and she blew her nose and said, "I'm sorry. It still gets to me.

Who, in God's name, would do something like that and then drive away? What kind of person does that?"

It seemed a good time to take a break.

Thirty

I phoned The Spot. Mike answered on the fourth ring. "You've reached The Spot."

"Hi, Mike, Dev Haskell. You got any frozen pizzas over there?"

"Hey, Dev. You're not locked out of your house again, are you?"

"No, thankfully, and thanks for your help last night. Much appreciated. So, do you have any frozen pizzas?"

"We got cheese, cheese and sausage, pepperoni and cheese, and pizza with everything."

"Can you heat up two of the ones with everything, and I'll be over in about twenty minutes?"

"Yeah, that'll work. See you then," he said and hung up.

We chatted, or should I say Erik and Melissa chatted, talking back and forth about where they went to school and what they were currently involved in. Erik didn't mention anything about Tubby, and Melissa casually inserted the fact that she wasn't currently seeing anyone. It was as if I was invisible. I eventually excused myself and headed over to The Spot. Lo and behold,

Louie was already at the bar. "When did you get here?" I asked.

"Just about ten minutes ago. I figured you'd be in sooner or later. Where's Erik?"

"Up in the office chatting with Melissa Carter. We were bringing her up to date, and things got a little emotional. I thought it might be best to take a break. We've got some potential information on her parent's car crash, and it might be difficult for her, so I had Mike toss a couple of pizzas in the oven. In fact, here he is now," I said as Mike stepped out of the back room where the oven and the refrigerator were kept.

"Perfect timing, Dev. All set to go. Twenty bucks each."

"Thanks, Mike. I really appreciate it. I got a client up in the office who's getting some pretty tough information and figured these pizzas would help."

"Sorry to hear it," he said and then clearly waited to be paid.

I took out my wallet and looked twice at the lonely dollar bill in there. "Oh…umm…I wonder if I could take these on credit and—"

"I'll cover them, Mike. Go ahead and get back up there, Dev," Louie said.

"Thanks, Louie, I owe you."

"Yeah, big time," Louie said.

I grabbed the two pizza boxes and hurried out the door before Louie had a chance to change his mind. I charged up the stairs and into the office. Erik and

Melissa were still chatting. Morton was on his pillow, up close and personal with the beef marrow bone from Roosters. I set both boxes on my desk and opened them. The delicious scent of pizza filled the immediate area. Morton looked up for a moment, seemed to think about it, and went back to gnawing on his marrow bone.

It was another thirty minutes of talking about everything and nothing. I told a couple of funny stories about Melissa's folks, and when it was obvious she was ready to start again, I placed the boxes, both with the remnants of half a pizza, on Louie's picnic table and settled into my chair.

"So Melissa, we would like to go over some things regarding the car crash that took your parents. Do you feel up to it?"

She nodded and said, "I do. I need to hear what you've found out."

"Okay, so first off, can you recall what kind of car your dad was driving?"

She smiled and gave a little laugh. "Oh, yeah, it was his favorite. He bragged about it to anyone who would listen. It was a 2019 Acura NSX. One of the reasons he liked it was because it had, and I'm quoting him here because I heard it so often, a hybrid electric powertrain that combined a twin-turbocharged 3.5-liter V-6 with three electric motors for a combined total of 573 horsepower. A 7.0-inch touchscreen infotainment system with integrated navigation and was hooked up to an ELS Studio nine-speaker stereo."

"I knew he liked cars, but he actually said that?" I asked.

She nodded. "Yeah, at least a million times, it drove me and my mom crazy, but he loved the thing. He, well, let's just leave it at that, okay?"

"Yeah, sure. Can you tell me what color it was?"

"Whenever I told someone it was white, if he heard me, he would correct me and say it was Casino White Pearl. It was still white, but, well, that was him. I never had the courage to look up and see what he paid for the thing."

"But it was white, or White Pearl?" I asked.

"Yeah,Casino White Pearl."

"Why don't you bring up those images, Erik?" As Erik opened his laptop and the tone sounded, I wrote down the name of the color and went on to mention that we came into possession of a set of keys that belonged to Louis LePew. As before, I didn't mention that I got the keys from Tubby. "So Melissa, along with the keys was an address, which turned out to be a storage company. Louis LePew had rented a space, actually more like a single garage, and he stored a car in there. We were able to gain access to the storage area, the car was still there, and these are the pictures we took of the vehicle."

Erik leaned toward Melissa, and she placed her right hand on his forearm. He moved the computer closer to them. I could hear as he tapped the key displaying the images one by one, starting with the picture of the out-side of the unit and the yellow metal garage door closed and locked.

I waited until I heard Erik bring up the next picture. "You'll notice on the photos that there are white scratches on the front of the vehicle. I'm pretty sure they're from a car that was struck."

"But this car is just dented, and Dad's car was al-most completely cut in half. I mean, I, I couldn't physi-cally identify my mom and dad. There was nothing to see. They were literally in little bits and pieces and, and, ohhh—"

Erik took his hands off the keyboard, wrapped his arms around Melissa, and held her for a long moment.

"Oh, God, I'm sorry," she said. "I didn't mean to—Go on, what were you going to say?"

"If you look at the pictures, you can see that every-thing in the interior has been removed, and there are just steel-reinforced bars in there. That would not only limit the damage to the red vehicle, but it would also essen-tially turn the car into a massive battering ram, and at speeds up to, I don't know sixty or seventy miles per hour, it could quite possibly do the sort of damage that killed your parents."

"Where is this LePew bastard now?"

"He's not going anywhere if that's what you're wor-ried about."

"The way you say that makes me think that he hasn't been arrested yet for the murder of Mom and Dad. Why is he out walking the street?"

"A couple of things, Melissa. You're the only one, other than Erik and me, who has the information we've given you. And as to LePew being arrested, we're going to pursue that. Not to worry, he's currently lying in a hospital in a coma."

"I hope to God the son of a bitch dies."

I signaled Erik with a nod to turn off the computer. He closed the lid, and we chatted for another twenty or thirty minutes.

Melissa turned to Erik, placed a hand on his forearm, and said, "It was a pleasure meeting you, and thank you for helping on this investigation."

"I'm awfully sorry about your parents. It was nice to meet you, Melissa, and we won't leave a stone unturned on this."

"Thanks," she said and stood.

"We had better get going, too," I said and gathered up the stack of files. I walked over to the file cabinet, where Morton was still gnawing on his bone.

"Where do you live?" Melissa asked Erik.

"Oh, I'm staying with my uncle at the moment. He's got a great big place over on the River Boulevard. It's really nice and really boring. Dev picks me up every morning."

"And drops him off every night," I said as I placed the files into the top drawer of the cabinet and pushed it closed.

"The River Boulevard? I don't live too far from there. I can give you a lift if you want."

"Oh, thanks, Melissa," I said. "But don't worry about it. I can—"

"Oh, Dev, really. It's not a problem. I'm just a couple of blocks from there, literally. I probably drive right past the place almost every day."

"It would save you the trouble, Dev, and you've got that meeting with Louie, anyway," Erik said and flashed his eyes in the direction of The Spot.

"Oh, yeah. Thanks for reminding me, Erik. Yeah, Melissa, if it wouldn't be too much trouble, you would save me some time."

"Sure, so not a problem. Are you able to go now?" she asked.

Erik stuffed his laptop in his computer bag in about a half-second and said, "All set."

"I'll see you in the morning, Erik," I said as they headed for the door.

He grinned, gave me the thumbs-up, and closed the door behind him. I watched as they stepped out of the building and hurried across the street. Erik held the driver's door open on a nondescript white car, then closed it once Melissa was behind the wheel and hurried around to the passenger side. I watched as they headed up the street, but instead of continuing, Melissa took the first left and disappeared.

I thought for a minute and was happy for both of them. I clipped Morton's leash onto his collar, and we walked over to The Spot.

Thirty-one

orton appeared upset having to leave his beef marrow bone in the office, but he quickly overcame that when we entered The Spot, and the idea of a handful of pork rinds flashed into his mind. He strained on the leash, nearly pulling my shoulder out of the socket, and rounded the corner of the bar to Louie's stool. Louie had just filled his hand and bent down. Morton inhaled the pork rinds, never knocking even one onto the floor.

"Did you already drive Erik back to his uncle's?" Louie asked, then signaled Mike for another drink and a beer for me.

"No, he seemed to hit it off with my client, Melissa. She apparently lives near Tubby's and offered to give him a ride. He jumped at the chance."

"I can just imagine after the better part of a week of dealing with you and his uncle. Poor guy! Right about now, he's probably ready to jump off a bridge."

"I can't understand it. He skips a ride with Morton and me and climbs into a car with a beautiful young woman. What's the world coming to?" I asked just as

Mike arrived with our drinks. He dropped them off and hurried back down the bar to deal with two couples who had just walked in.

"Here's to common sense," Louie said and raised his glass.

We clinked glasses, I took a sip, and my cell phone rang. I took it out and looked at the screen. Crystal. With everything going on and my getting locked out last night, I completely forgot. Well, except I did remember the thong hanging on my doorknob.

"Crystal. Oh, thank God, I've been meaning to call you, but I've been dealing with a case all day. First, let me apologize for last night. I was called away. Wait, let me rephrase that, I was dragged away at the last moment, literally. And when I finally made it back home, I was locked out and had to run in the rain all the way down to my office to get the key to my house and then run back." There was a long pause. "Crystal?"

"I'm just wondering if I should believe you or not."

"Oh, please believe me. As a matter of fact, my entire body is cut and scrapped after running through a wooded area along the freeway. It was just awful."

"Good. Would you happen to have some time for me this evening?" she asked.

"Yes, absolutely. I would love it. Can I swing by? I happen to have two bottles of champagne chilling in the refrigerator just for you. I would be more than happy to bring them over and serve your every need."

"Mmm-mmm, I so love it when you grovel. No, why don't I plan on arriving at your house an hour from now? That should give you plenty of time to finish whatever you're drinking and get home. I'll be at your door in sixty minutes."

"Oh, actually, I just stopped into The Spot to deliver a phone message to my office mate, Louie. He's working on a case and—"

"Yeah, sure you did, Dev. One hour and if you're not there, you needn't worry about ever contacting me again. Goodbye," she said and hung up.

"You have a message for me?"

"Yeah, I have to finish this beer and run. Hey, I'll bring some cash in tomorrow morning and catch up with you for the pizzas and this beer."

"That would be a pleasant surprise, Dev."

I finished my beer in about thirty seconds, Morton got another handful of pork rinds, and we hurried out the door. We parked in the driveway. I tossed Morton a biscuit once we were inside and hurried upstairs to shower and shave. I slipped into a reasonably clean sports shirt and some pretty clean jeans. I placed silk pillowcases on the pillows and hurried down to the kitchen. I dimmed the lights, lit two candles, and placed the hors d'oeuvre plate of Oreo cookies on the kitchen counter. I had just set the champagne flutes on the counter when there was a knock on the door. I crossed my fingers, prayed it wasn't Fat Freddy, and hurried out to the entryway.

Thankfully, there was Crystal in all her glory. Dressed in a short, low-cut, dark blue dress with brass buttons all the way down the front, leaving nothing to the imagination. She was carrying a matching blue hand-bag with a brass chain and the brass initials YSL. She raised her eyebrows when she smiled and gave a little wave. I opened the door, and she stepped in. I quickly looked up and down the street, praying I wouldn't see a black Cadillac Escalade. Thankfully, I didn't. I closed and double-locked the door.

Crystal was smiling as I turned to face her, but the smile quickly left her face. "Oh, my God, Dev, what in the world happened to you? You look like you got in a fight with a very angry cat."

"Like I told you earlier on the phone. I arrived home last night, and I was locked out. I had to run all the way down to my office to get a key and then run back. Rather than take the time to wind through the streets, I cut through a large, wooded area. I just kept running and running, hoping I'd make it back here in time to be with you. Unfortunately, after all the pain and suffering, I still didn't make it back in time," I said and hung my head, hoping I looked like I was about to cry.

"Oh, my poor baby. Come here," she said and wrapped her arms around me.

"I'm just so sorry, Crystal. I tried so hard to make it back. I did, honest I did."

"I know you did, Dev. I can see that, and I'm going to make it worth your while. Shame on me for thinking otherwise. I think a glass of champagne would be just the thing to start the night off right."

Bingo. Let the games begin. She smothered me with a long kiss, then took hold of my hand, and I led her into the kitchen.

"Oh my goodness, candlelight? Dev, you shouldn't have. You know what that does to me."

"I just wanted to make it right," I said, knowing exactly what effect candles had on her.

"Oh, we're going to make it very right, believe me. You'll love what I have in store for you, for us," she said and set the blue velvet handbag on the counter.

"Let me pour you a glass of champagne." We kissed, and I eventually slipped out of her arms. I took one of the bottles of champagne out of the refrigerator, undid the wired top, and slowly inched the cork up and out of the bottle. At the last moment, the cork shot across the room and bounced off the wall. Morton barked, jumped from his pillow, and sniffed the cork.

"Oh, my God, does he like champagne?" Crystal asked as she held out her champagne flute, and I filled it.

I filled my flute, we clinked glasses, and I took a sip. Crystal took a sip, grinned, and took two more healthy sips, draining her flute more than halfway.

"Mmm-mmm, I love it," she said, holding her glass out. I topped it up, and she took another healthy swallow.

"I put out some hors d'oeuvres for us," I said and pointed toward the Oreos.

"Oh, my God, you are so hilarious," she said and gave me another sexy kiss. I topped up her glass again, and we clinked glasses once more.

"To a very memorable evening," she said and took another hearty sip. "Oh my, I'd better slow down, but this is so good. Where did you get it?"

"I got it just up the block at Solo Vino. I'm friends with the owner, Chuck, and he recommended it. Not to worry, I've got another bottle waiting for us in the refrigerator."

"Oh, well, in that case," she said and took three more swallows.

We were seated in the den and on our second bottle of champagne, which had been all Crystal's doing. Her heels were off, and she had unbuttoned the top three brass buttons on her dress, exposing her wonderful cleavage. I was on my second glass, and it was still more than halfway full. Crystal had been ranting on and on about something with her book club girlfriends, and she kept repeating herself. Not that it made any difference, because she was slurring her words so much, that I had a hard time understanding whatever boring thing she was saying. The plate of Oreos was resting on her lap. There were only four left, and I hadn't had any.

I was worried we were dangerously close to the point where any bedroom activity was going to be out of the question.

"I think you better top me up here, darling," she said after taking another double gulp. Her head suddenly swayed back and forth, and I was afraid she might throw up, but she only burped again and then held out her glass. I emptied the second bottle into the glass, and it barely filled it past the halfway mark.

"I'm thinking we might be more comfortable upstairs," I said.

She smiled at me and tried to focus, then held out her glass and said, "Hold this, lover."

As she thrust the glass toward me, champagne sloshed over the edge and down my shirt. "Oh, look at what you made me do," she said and leaned forward to lick the champagne off my shirt. I grabbed her glass just before she fell to the floor, landing on all fours and laughing. "Here, help me up. I have something I have to get for you."

I set her glass on the floor next to mine and helped her up. The hors d'oeuvres plate was upside down on the floor, and the four remaining Oreos were scattered across the rug. "Kitchen," she said and began to stagger toward the door. I wrapped an arm around her waist, led her out into the hall, and turned her to the stairs. "No, my handbag, baby. I got some toys just for little old you."

I turned her around and led her into the kitchen. She picked up her handbag and draped it over her shoulder. I guided her back into the hall, and we miraculously made it upstairs. I kept my arm around her waist the entire time so she wouldn't fall. Once in the bedroom, I sat her on the bed and led Morton into the hall.

As I stepped back into the room, she had the open handbag off her shoulder and attempted to focus on me. "Here you go, lover boy, choose your weapon," she giggled and turned the handbag upside down. She dumped out no fewer than eight different sexual appliances and a bottle of lubricant. She dropped the handbag on the floor, swayed back and forth a couple of times, and fell backward onto the pillows with the silk pillowcases.

"Crystal? Hey, Crystal?" I gently shook her, but she was out cold and started to snore.

Thirty-two

At some point, Morton came downstairs and ate the Oreo cookies while I washed the champagne flutes. By the time I went upstairs, Morton was already asleep next to Crystal and her battery-operated equipment. Rather than attempt to wake either one, I stretched out in the guest room.

I heard a distant noise in my dream that slowly woke me up. It was still dark outside. Suddenly, there it was again, pounding, only not so distant and clearly not in my dream. I stuck my head into the hallway. More pounding, this time much louder and coming from the front door. I turned on the light over the stairs and hurried down. Two, unfortunately, familiar figures were on my front porch. Fat Freddy and Pee Wee.

I unlocked the door and opened it. "What's going on?"

"Where the hell is Erik? Is he here?" Fat Freddy shouted as he pushed me out of the way and stormed into the house. Pee Wee followed and shrugged. At least Pee Wee was dressed. Fat Freddy was wearing a faded blue sweatshirt that said 'Shit Show Supervisor' in white letters, a pair of red plaid boxer shorts, and black cowboy boots completed his ensemble.

"What are you talking about?"

"What am I—Listen, dumb shit, he didn't come home last night. The boss man is ready to call out the national guard. You were probably the last one to see him. So where in the hell is he?"

"He didn't come home?"

"Were you even listening? Hello. I just told you that."

"Yeah, yeah, I get it. Umm, I, or I mean, we met with a client yesterday in my office. She seemed to have a thing for Erik, and when we were finished with the meeting, she offered to give him a ride home. He looked really excited, and I figured since she was a really nice girl, yeah, that would be great."

"So she was supposed to give him a ride home? He never, ever showed up. The boss is ready to kill."

"Look, Freddy, I watched her drive up the street, and she took the first left. They're about the same age. She works in the city attorney's office, and I'm willing to bet they grabbed something to eat somewhere, and things went from there to—"

"Oh, great move, dumb ass. You lined up Erik with some woman from the city attorney's office? Are you kidding me? Come on, let's go. I'm not going to tell the boss man this shit. You are, Haskell. It's going to be your dumb ass on the line."

"Freddy, calm the hell down, man. Listen, I've known this girl since she was a little kid. In fact, Erik and I are looking into her parent's death. This is the same case that Tub, err, Mr. Gustafson gave me the keys and the address to LePew's storage unit."

"Oh great, so he gave you the keys we obtained, thinking you'd keep it quiet. And now I'm supposed to tell him his nephew is spending the night with a woman in the city attorney's office. Are you f'ing kidding me?"

"Come on, man. She's not even an attorney. Yeah, she works in the office, but she's still going to law school."

"What better way to get ahead in the world than to get inside information on the boss. She'll get Erik to the point where he'll say and do whatever she wants."

"That doesn't always happen," I said, thinking back on my night.

"Oh, really? Good. I think we'll just let you explain that to the boss."

"Freddy, it's the middle of the damn night, man. I'm sure he's sound asleep and—"

"That's right, it is the middle of the night, and if you ever want to see daylight, you'll get your dumb ass out into the car."

"You gotta be kidding me."

"Pee Wee, drag his worthless ass out of here."

"Okay, okay. Just give me a minute to get my keys so I can get back in, okay? Besides, it would be nice to get some shoes on."

"You got sixty seconds, so you better hurry."

I hurried into the kitchen, took my keys off the hook, slipped my Nikes on, and hurried back to the entry. "Let's go, dipshit," Fat Freddy said, and I followed him out the door. At least I was allowed to sit in the back seat instead of lying on the floor. At this hour of the day, early morning and still dark out, we sped through town. I think we only saw three other cars, and each one was headed in the opposite direction. Pew Wee drove onto Tubby's circular drive about seven minutes later. A record-fast trip to Tubby's. Fat Freddy climbed out of the passenger seat and headed for the door.

The two armed individuals on either side of the front door were drinking steaming mugs of coffee. I was hurrying to catch up to Fat Freddy when he said, "You'd better give Haskell a thorough pat down. I don't trust him."

One of the thugs grabbed me by my t-shirt and swung me up against the brick wall. As my chin bounced off the wall, I bit my bottom lip. He kicked my legs back and then kicked my feet apart. I slapped my hands against the wall in case they tried to bounce my head off the bricks. One of them aggressively patted me down, causing me to jump, and his partner to laugh. "I guess this idiot's okay. Let him in."

Freddy chuckled and stepped inside. The usual thug reading a comic book just inside the door wasn't around at this hour, and I followed Freddy down the hall. I touched my index finger to my throbbing lower lip, and blood showed up on my finger.

Freddy knocked on Tubby's office door as he opened it.

"Get the hell in here," Tubby shouted as we stepped into the office.

He was seated at his desk, wearing what appeared to be a very large, black silk robe and sipping a glass of whiskey. I noticed the open bottle on the desk but was more focused on the woman clad in a black lace negligée standing behind Tubby and massaging his shoulders. Tonight, or I guess, this morning, she wasn't wearing latex gloves, and her usual partner was nowhere around. I found it interesting that Tubby didn't even blink at Fat Freddy in boxers.

"So, where in the hell is my nephew, Haskell? Since you're here, I'm presuming he's not asleep at your place. God help your sorry ass if you've got him staked out someplace alone. You will live to regret it in very short order. Well? Where the hell is he?"

"He's with a client, sir. A young woman by the name of Melissa Carter. And—"

"Carter? Melissa Carter. Why is that ringing a bell?"

"If you'll recall, we were investigating a company by the name of Dankworth Building Brokers. You had provided me with the keys to the storage unit owned by Louis LePew, who had been working for Odell Dankworth. LePew was the individual that attempted to assault Erik the other day. We checked out his storage unit and found a vehicle that had been involved in an accident. We suspect the accident led to the death of Jack Carter and his wife. We informed their daughter of our suspicions. Erik assembled a series of images to reinforce our belief. Melissa, the daughter, was moved by the excellent job Erik had done and offered to give him a ride home. This would have been just after 5:00 last night. It was clear to me that the two of them had hit it off, and because I've known Melissa since she was a little girl, I decided that the two of them spending some time together would be acceptable. I suspect they had dinner, talked, and one thing led to another. I believe you would—"

"What he's failed to mention, sir, is that the woman in question works in the City Attorney's office," Fat Freddy interrupted.

"Is that right, Haskell?"

"Yes, sir, it is. However, she is currently enrolled in law school. So, she is not, at this stage, a practicing attorney, and our thoughts were that, what better way for you to possibly have someone with intimate knowledge of whatever the City Attorney's office may have plans to do."

Tubby took a sip and seemed to think for a moment.

"And Erik was willing to extend a friendly offer? You didn't force him?"

"No sir, this was strictly his idea. As a matter of fact, he went out of his way to offer some gentle support when she became emotionally overwhelmed regarding the death of her parents."

Tubby nodded. "Might there be a way to link Dankworth to the death of the parents?"

"I think there is a real possibility, sir. I hasten to add, this could benefit a number of people. Erik would have the experience of solving a cold case, if you will. Miss Carter would be able to finally begin to put the passing of her parents to rest."

I suspected Tubby had some ideas about Dankworth. He quite possibly might know of the falsified contract, but I didn't want to stir the pot.

"Will Erik be working with you today?"

"I expect to hear from him, yes. I think he may arrive here shortly, compliments of Miss Carter, and will call me in a couple of hours for a ride. Of course, I would never mention this early morning conversation to him."

"That would be wise of you, Haskell. Very well, the sooner you're out of my sight, the better for all involved. Frederick, If you'd see to Haskell's return."

"Happy to do so, sir," Fat Freddy said and headed toward the door.

He opened the door and stepped into the hall. I took hold of the door and turned to give Tubby a 'Thank you' just as another woman without a negligée climbed out from beneath Tubby's desk, bent over, and gave him a long kiss.

"Come on, Haskell, get your ass in gear," Fat Freddy said, and I closed the door behind me.

Pee Wee came to a stop in front of my driveway eight minutes later. Once again, I was amazed at how fast we'd gone from Tubby's mansion to my place. I opened the door and then waited for a second just in case he tried to take off and make me fall to the ground. The two of them, Pee Wee and Fat Freddy, just sat staring out the windshield as the sun threatened to come up. I quickly jumped out, closed the door, and walked over to the steps leading into my front yard. I thought it would be funny to turn and give them a wave or, better yet, the finger. As I turned, I noticed the flashing red lights on the grill of the Escalade. Essentially making it appear to be a police vehicle, which explained why the traffic lights always turned green as we approached and cars pulled to the side so we could pass. As I stared, Pee Wee drove away at a normal speed, and once again, I felt like an idiot.

Thirty-three

I climbed the front porch, unlocked the door, and stepped inside. It was a quarter after five, and I saw no point in attempting to go back to bed. I went into the kitchen and made a pot of coffee. I put last night's champagne flutes back in the cabinet, put the two empty champagne bottles in recycling, and quietly headed up-stairs.

I slowly opened the bedroom door. Crystal's blue dress with the brass buttons was now crumpled and lying on the floor at the foot of the bed. Next to it were the remnants of a flowered thong that Morton had apparently chewed up. She was naked on the bed. Various personal appliances were scattered across the end of the bed or down on the floor. Her arm was over Morton's shoulder, and they were both sound asleep. I was tempted to take a picture but didn't.

Instead, being the thoughtful individual I am, I went downstairs and placed a bottle of aspirin and a glass on the kitchen counter. I poured myself a coffee and had a couple of pieces of toast with blueberry jelly.

I'd been on my laptop for almost two hours before Morton wandered downstairs. I gave him the standard head scratch and had to laugh because, after the over hundred bucks I'd paid for champagne, at least he got to sleep with Crystal. I let him outside and filled his food and water dishes.

Morton had been back inside for almost an hour. He'd finished his breakfast and was closely involved with his rawhide bone when I heard the shower upstairs. I put two pieces of bread in the toaster but didn't turn it on and then mixed up a little dish of cinnamon and sugar. Once the shower went off, I waited another ten minutes, and when I heard Crystal making her way downstairs, I filled the glass with orange juice, turned on the toaster, and took the eggs out of the refrigerator.

She stepped into the kitchen with all the buttons done up on her dress. "Oh, hey. Been up long?"

"Good morning, lady. How did you sleep?"

"Umm, okay, I guess. Would you happen to know where I left my shoes?"

"Yeah, they're in the den. I'll get them for you. It would probably be a good idea if you had a couple of aspirin and drank that glass of orange juice. Toast will be ready in a minute, and I'll scramble up some eggs for us."

"Oh, I'm not sure I should have anything to eat. Did we, umm, well, you know?"

"Yeah, I do know, and no, we didn't. As a matter of fact, you slept with Morton."

"Morton? Where were you?"

"In the guest room. You sort of passed out after you emptied your handbag on the bed."

"Oh, yeah, sorry about that. I might have had one glass too many."

"Or even one bottle too many. I had a glass and a half, and you finished both bottles."

"Ewee, that explains the headache. Sorry about that. It was very good champagne."

"Humor me, drink this orange juice, take a couple aspirin, and let me get some food in you. It will do a lot to eliminate that headache and get you back on track."

"Sorry that you ended up in the guest room, and we didn't, you know."

"Relax, it was great to have you over, no pressure. Let me get your shoes." I went into the den, grabbed her shoes, glanced around for anything else she may have left behind, and stepped back into the kitchen. The toast popped up just as I set her shoes in front of her. I quickly buttered both pieces, sprinkled cinnamon sugar on them, and pushed the plate in front of her.

"Oh, I don't think I'm ready to—"

"Trust me, Champagne Queen. Your system is craving sugar right now. Eat that, it will help to get rid of that headache, and I'll make some breakfast for you."

She gradually began to come around. She ate the second piece of toast faster than the first, drank some more orange juice, and inhaled the scrambled eggs. "Oh, thanks, Dev. You were right. I almost feel good after all that."

"Just remember to hydrate today, and you'll be fine. Can I grab a rain check on last night?"

"Yes, absolutely. I know I owe you. I'm sorry."

"No, you don't owe me. Remember, it wasn't that long ago that you came over, and I had locked myself out."

"How could I forget? Thanks for reminding me. Gee, I'm feeling better already," she said and laughed. She gave me a kiss on the cheek, and I walked her to the door. Her blue handbag, apparently filled with her devices, was hanging from the newel post. She grabbed it and draped it on her shoulder. "God, and I had such plans. Okay, champagne is off-limits the next time we're together."

"I'll leave it up to you to give me a call when you're ready."

"Don't take it personally, but I'm going to need at least twenty-four hours. Thanks again for putting up with me."

"Relax, I just loved your story about the girls in your book club."

"Oh, my God. Don't tell me I went on about that."

"Oh, yeah, on and on."

"Okay, no champagne for a month. Goodbye, and thanks for putting up with me." I got another peck on the cheek, and she hurried out the door. She started her car, gave me a wave, tooted the horn as she backed out of the driveway, and drove off. My phone rang before I was back in the kitchen.

Thirty-four

I answered the phone with, "Could this be Erik Gustafson?"

"Oh, God, Dev. Can you come and get me? My uncle read me the riot act this morning. I'm waiting outside the gate right now. I guess he's already talked to you."

"Yeah, not a happy camper. Listen, we'll head out right now and see you shortly."

"Thanks. I'm afraid he's going to send a couple of his goons out here just to teach me a lesson."

"Well, then, we better hurry. See you shortly," I said and disconnected. I stepped into the kitchen, rinsed off the breakfast dishes, and placed them in the dishwasher. I unplugged the toaster, turned off the coffee pot, and wiped down the kitchen counter.

I went upstairs and unscrewed the access panel in the closet of the back bedroom. I took two hundred dollar bills from one of the bundles, reattached the access panel, and then loaded Morton into the back seat.

We headed over to Tubby's, but I drove the speed limit the entire way and lost count of the number of cars that passed us. From a block away, I could see Erik waiting outside the entrance gate to Tubby's. He apparently recognized my car because he hurried down the street toward me. I pulled alongside him, and he quickly hopped in.

"Everything okay?"

"Are you kidding? He was really pissed off. I should have called him, but well, I had other things on my mind, and all of a sudden, it was 7:00, and we were waking up."

"So you had a fun evening?"

He looked at me and shook his head. "Not funny, Dev. He was really pissed off."

"Do you have his phone number?"

"Yeah, sure, of course."

"So, next time, give him a call. That's all you have to do. He gets it, and that way, when you call, instead of tearing you a new one, he can brag about you being out with a very pretty girl. Oh, excuse me, I meant to say a very gorgeous woman."

"Yeah, that's a good idea."

"Let me ask you something. Did you know your uncle's Escalade has flashing police lights on the grill? It never has to stop for a red light, and folks pull to the side so it can pass."

"Yeah, he said because of his position with the city, he gets that benefit."

"Benefit? Erik, he—never mind. It's not important. So you and Melissa got on okay? You don't have to give me specific details."

"Yeah, it was great. We had a really nice time. We grabbed dinner at a place called The Nook. Are you familiar with it?"

I nodded. "Yeah, it's owned by the same two guys who own Shamrock's, Mike and Ted. Nice guys."

"Yeah, it was really nice. We had dinner, talked over a beer, then ended up at the Groveland Tap. Melissa wasn't kidding. Her apartment is just two or three blocks from my uncle's. I'm just glad she dropped me off in front of the gate. I went inside, showered, and was changing clothes when he came in and read me the riot act. He was really pissed off. You wouldn't believe it."

"Actually, I probably would believe it. I may have seen him like that once or twice. Did he kick you out?"

"No, nothing like that, but for a while, I was afraid I might end up sharing a hospital room with LePew."

"Say, speaking of which, have you had a chance to go through his laptop?"

"Funny you should mention that. Melissa and I talked quite a bit about LePew, and I got to thinking about his computer. All I really did was print off a bunch of those files from his desktop computer when we were upstairs in his office. I haven't gone through them yet, and there's gotta be more stuff on that laptop that I haven't had a chance to look into."

"I'll go through those files we printed off if you'll see what might be on his laptop," I said as I parked behind Louie's car.

"Good. It'll be interesting to see what we can come up with." We crossed the street and headed up to the office. Morton hurried over to his pillow and the beef marrow bone. He curled up in a way that sent the message he wasn't interested in sharing with either one of us.

"Well, I was beginning to wonder," Louie said, looking past his computer screen. The coffee was on, and it appeared to be a fresh pot. The pizza boxes were closed and sitting on my desk.

"Can I top up your coffee, Louie? Hey, sorry, I didn't mean to leave the pizza boxes on your desk."

"Not a problem. I just had a bunch of forms and contracts I had to spread out and arrange. I'll eat some of that pizza for lunch."

"Oh, which reminds me. I stopped at the bank this morning," I lied and handed him one of the hundred dollar bills I took from the bundle.

"Oh, thanks, but this is way more than you owe me," he said.

"Yeah, well, consider it a payment in advance. God only knows I'll probably need it at some point."

I topped up Louie's mug, then filled the other two mugs and turned off the burner. I started reading the printed files while Erik began working his way through LePew's laptop.

About a half-hour later, Erik's phone rang. He answered by saying, "Hey, how are you?" Then smiled and stepped out of the office.

Louie glanced over with a questioning look on his face.

"I'm guessing it's Melissa Carter. They seemed to hit it off yesterday."

"Oh, that's nice," Louie said.

Erik was back on the laptop a few minutes later. We ate the leftover pizza for lunch, and Louie went down to the courthouse just before 2:00.

After a half-hour, Erik said, "Dev, I think I've got a file here with emails between Dankworth and LePew. It looks like this file goes back three years."

"Three years, that puts them well before Jack Carter's death."

"I'm going to duplicate the file and send a copy to both of us. There might be something in here."

"I'll start going through it right away. You keep going through the rest of that stuff and see what else you can find."

It was almost 4:00 when Erik said, "Hey, Dev. Does the name Bobby Kelly mean anything to you?"

"Bobby Kelly? It rings a distant bell, but I can't recall why. What did you find?"

"There's an email here from Dankworth dated March 20 back in 2020. Dankworth sends him one sentence, 'Need you to deal with Bobby Kelly.' LePew replies, 'Make him an offer.' Dankworth replies back,

'Said he's not going to cooperate. Deal with him NOW.' And the word now is in capital letters."

I got out of my desk chair and walked around to Erik. He moved the laptop toward me as I leaned over and read the emails on the screen. "Anything else with this Kelly name?"

Erik shook his head. "I went back for two months previous and didn't find anything. I did a search on the full name and just the last name, and this is all that came up. You said you never heard of him?"

"No, I said it rang a distant bell. But Kelly is a pretty common name. I'll check him out. Keep reading through those emails and see what else pops up." I settled back into my desk chair and did a search on Bobby Kelly. I came across a comedian with a shaved head, a high school baseball player, an insurance agent, and a number of other people, but no one who was likely to have any interaction with Odell Dankworth.

I did a search on Robert Kelly and came up with pages of individuals, a poet, a professor, the comedian again, doctors, lawyers, more insurance agents, and then there, on the sixth page, an obituary.

Thirty-five

Robert Kelly lived in Woodbury and died on March twenty-second, back in 2020. He was forty-nine years old and had three children, two girls and a boy. No wife was mentioned, and no cause of death was listed. According to the Woodbury police statistics, there were two murders in the city, and Robert Kelly was one of them. The fact that the cause of death wasn't mentioned in the obituary wasn't unusual. But the emails between Dankworth and LePew, with Kelly dying forty-eight hours later, gave me pause.

I searched for news articles regarding Kelly and found three articles spanning two weeks in late March and early April of 2020. Kelly was found murdered in his home on the afternoon of March twenty-second, 2020. He was a Building Inspector for the city of Woodbury and didn't report for work that day. Phone calls to him went unanswered. Standard procedure was to conduct a safety check at the individual's home, and that was where police found him in his bed, the victim of a gunshot wound to the head. Based on evidence, police presumed the murder was a botched home robbery attempt.

I debated for about five seconds and then called Aaron LaZelle on his cell phone.

'Hi, you've reached Aaron LaZelle. I'm unable to take your call at the moment. Please leave your name and number, and I'll get back to you as soon as possible. Thank you, and enjoy your day.' A beep sounded a moment later.

"Hi, Aaron. Hey, working on my Jack Carter case, which involves Louis LePew, and we've come across some emails between LePew and Odell Dankworth. Would you call me when you have a chance? These emails may point to a 2020 case in Woodbury, the murder of an individual named Robert Kelly."

"He wasn't in?" Erik asked.

"He probably is, but it's not like he doesn't have anything going on. They've been seriously short-staffed ever since the George Floyd disaster over in Minneapolis a couple of years ago. You finding anything else?"

"No, which makes me think the email is even more of a direct order. You must have found something if you called your cop pal."

"Yeah, that email is dated the twentieth of March, and a guy named Robert Kelly was found shot in his bed on the twenty-second. Get this, he was a building inspector for the city of Woodbury."

"Woodbury, where The White House Apartments are located?"

"Yeah, and Jack Carter and his wife are killed in the car accident not long after that. It's pretty far-fetched at the moment, but they could be tied together. Those emails certainly begin to suggest a link between Dankworth, LePew, and this Kelly murder. It suddenly isn't that big of a jump to tie Carter's hit and run into some sort of a connection to this Kelly murder, especially given that battering ram of a car we found yesterday."

"It would be great if we could tie that Kelly murder to LePew. You said Kelly was shot?"

"Yeah, no mention in the three articles of anything actually stolen. I'm just surmising, but it doesn't seem too far-fetched that LePew broke into the house for the sole purpose of killing Kelly. He sneaks into the bedroom, kills the guy, and then maybe grabs sterling silver or something to make it look like a robbery. I wish we had—holy shit—wait a minute."

"What?" Erik said.

I reached over between my desk and the wall and grabbed the computer briefcase we took from LePew's car. The pistol was still in the large, zipped pocket on the lid of the case. "We may just have the murder weapon here," I said and set the case next to my wastebasket.

"The gun from LePew's glove compartment?" Erik asked.

"It just might be the murder weapon. Hanging on to it is exactly the kind of stupid thing someone would do. Which reminds me, let me make a call to a guy I know. He's a car nut, and I'd like to have him take a look at our pictures of that battering ram vehicle of LePew's."

I picked up my cell phone, searched my contact list, and called Donnie Grogan. He answered on the second ring.

"No, Dev, I'm busy, and I won't have time to fix whatever is wrong with the lousy car you're currently driving."

"How's it going, Donnie?"

"No complaints. All I gotta do is look out the window, and there's always someone out there that has it worse than me. What's up?"

"I'm working a case, and we've run into a vehicle that's been reinforced with steel rods. The case we're looking at is a hit-and-run. Two people were killed pulling into their driveway. I'm thinking we may have found the vehicle, but as you know, I'm not a car guy. Would you be interested in taking a look at a bunch of pictures we took of the vehicle?"

"Oh, yeah, you know I would. Just off the top of my head, the steel rods would have to be done in a certain way. On one level, it's a pretty standard project. Not that many folks do it. I can think of one guy I sort of know, and he was working in the movie biz. In fact, as far as I know, he still is, doing things for stuntmen and stuff. The car he worked on was for some movie. I forget what the name was. The car wasn't in the movie for more than thirty seconds, but it took my pal the better part of a week to get all the work done, and that was with him working overtime and all that. Anyway, yeah, I'd be interested in taking a look."

"You doing anything tonight?"

"I got a hot date. I'm taking dinner over to my mom. But I could meet you after that, probably be around 8:00, if that would work for you."

"Let's do it. You know where my office is?"

"You in the same place as before? Across the street from The Joint?"

"Yeah, it's actually called The Spot, but I'm just kitty corner from there. I'll see you around 8:00, Donnie, and thanks."

"My pleasure, Dude," he said and hung up.

"So, he's coming over tonight?"

"Yeah, you want to hang around, or I can take you back to your uncle's? Whatever works."

"Sorry to be a downer, but I should probably head back to my uncle's. I'm going to meet up with Melissa tonight."

"Oh, great. Congratulations. If I might give you just a word of advice. Keep your uncle informed. Please. For both our sakes."

"Yeah, I'll tell him I've got a date tonight as soon as you drop me off."

"We'll all be happy for you and will want to hear all the intimate details."

"That might be a stretch," he said.

I clipped the leash onto Morton's collar, and we headed out the door. Fortunately, Erik had me drop him off at the front gate, so I was able to avoid the possibility of having to interact with either Fat Freddy or Tubby. I took Morton home, tossed him a biscuit, and headed back down to the office. I had parked behind Louie's car, and the lights were off up in the office, so I headed into The Spot.

Louie was seated on his stool, and he gave me a wave as I headed in his direction. I kept thinking there was something different about the place tonight, and then I realized it was because Morton wasn't straining on his leash trying to get to Louie and the pork rinds.

"No Morton or Erik?" Louis said as I rounded the corner.

"Erik's got a date with Melissa. I dropped him off at Tubby's with strict instructions to keep his uncle informed. As long as I was dropping Erik off, I took Morton home. I got someone coming over to the office in about an hour. You remember Donnie Grogan?"

"Grogan? Was he the car nut? Got a couple of those old beaters you were driving to last another year or two?"

"Yeah. Anyway, he's coming over to look at the pictures we took of that car in LePew's storage unit. I want to get his opinion, see if he thinks that vehicle was capable of basically cutting Jack Carter's car in half."

"Wasn't he a heavyset guy with a blonde mohawk and a lot of ink on his arms?"

"Yeah, you got him. That's the guy."

Louie nodded and grinned. "Well, he just stepped in and is headed this way."

Thirty-six

I turned just as Donnie Grogan came around the corner of the bar and gave me a bear hug. "Hey, Dev. I thought I might find you in here. Hi, we've met before, but in my old age, I'm blanking on your name, my name's Donnie," he said and held out his hand.

"Louie Laufen, Donnie. Nice to see you again. Dev was just telling me you're going to be looking at some pictures later tonight."

"Well, that kind of depends on whether or not he buys me a beer."

We all laughed at that, and I signaled Mike, standing down at the far end of the bar, for two beers and a fresh drink for Louie. "How you been, Donnie? It's good to see you, and I appreciate you making the time to come over."

"My pleasure, and thanks for buying all the beer tonight. Actually, the way you described this vehicle, you've got me more than a little curious. I know a guy. In fact, I mentioned him on the phone. Jamie Donovan. He does that sort of thing, reinforcing a vehicle. He used to do it for guys who were into that whole demolition derby stuff, but that became a thing of the past. Now he does the occasional movie stunt vehicle and, once in a while, turns cars into work vehicles. You know, for hauling stones or timber. I think there's one guy who hauls firewood around. Brings him an old beater, and Jamie removes the roof and seats, reinforces the thing with some steel pipe like you described, and for about fifteen hundred bucks, the guy gets a vehicle that works for another twenty-four months."

Mike appeared with two beers and Louie's drink. We all raised our glasses and took a sip.

"So, it sounds like you're still doing all that secret agent kind of stuff," Donnie said.

"Yeah, you know how it is. Either I'm so busy I don't have enough time to sleep, or things are so quiet I'm thinking of committing a crime myself just so I'd have something to investigate."

"Mmm, I doubt that's the case. You still pals with that gangster guy? Guy's got a funny name."

"Oh, you mean Tubby Gustafson, or are you thinking Fat Freddy Zimmerman?"

"Both of them, I guess, and I think you just answered my question."

We talked for another ten minutes until we finished our beer, and then Donnie said, "Why don't you show me those pictures? You got 'em with you?"

"No, they're on my computer over in the office. Thought you might want to see them. That way, you can enlarge the image, possibly get a closeup to check some things.”

“Let’s do it,” Donnie said. “Louie, nice to see you again. We’ll be back when we finish up. If you’re still here, I know Dev would love to buy you another drink.”

“Well, if that’s the case, I’ll be waiting,” Louie said as Donnie and I headed out the side door.

There was some kind of souped-up orange thing with flames across the hood and along the sides of the vehicle parked on the street in front of Louie’s car. I asked Donnie if it was his. He said it was and then proceeded to list the engine size, the type of tires it had, and the model. The only thing that stuck with me was it was his car.

We headed up the stairs, and Donnie gave a wave at two women sitting in the lobby of the hairdressers across from my office. One of them waved back, and for a moment, I was afraid I might lose him, but he followed me into the office.

The first thing he did was look at Louie’s picnic table desk and say, “Oh, man. I’m digging that idea. I may just have to do something like that.”

“I can’t take any credit. That’s Louie’s. I’m at that boring old wooden desk every day.”

“No surprise,” Donnie said.

I settled into my desk chair, turned on my computer, and then moved it so Donnie would be able to see the screen better. “Pull one of those chairs over here and make yourself comfortable. We got fifty or sixty pictures to look at," I said as I brought the file up.

Donnie settled into the client chair and gazed out the window at the apartment across the street. "Is that the building you told me about with all the naked women?"

"There used to be a number of them. Now there's just two sharing the same apartment, and it's only once in a great while."

"That's a shame," he said as the first image, the yellow metal garage door with the number one-four-seven, appeared on the screen.

"So this is the door on the storage unit. It's in Seventh Street Storage down on West Seventh Street. You familiar with the place?"

Donnie nodded and said, "Never been in there, but it's near the candy company, isn't it?"

"Yeah, Pearson Candy, they make Nut Goodies and some other stuff. Anyway, the vehicle was backed into the unit. I've no idea how long it's been there. The accident we suspect it was involved in happened back in 2020," I said and clicked my mouse, bringing up the next image, the front view of the vehicle showing the damaged headlights, buckled hood, smashed windshield, no grill, and red streaks from the vehicle it crashed into.

Donnie leaned forward and studied the image for a long minute. "That's a 1970 Dodge Charger, and I'm almost positive that Jamie Donovan did the work on it. Based on the damage to the front, that thing could probably hit another vehicle at up to a hundred and twenty miles per hour and survive. He'd have it set up so the driver would survive but no one else in the vehicle. Damn, another one of Jamie's works of genius. Let's see what else you got."

I started going through the pictures. Donnie had me stop more than once and enlarge the image, although, in short order, the picture would become too blurry to allow any close-up study. Still, after a good hour and a half, Donnie was even more sure than before that he wanted to check out the vehicle in person.

"This thing is still right here in town, isn't it?" Donnie asked.

"Yeah, it's in that storage unit down on West Seventh. You want to take a look tomorrow? I'd be happy to meet you down there."

"Let me make a phone call right now. I want to have Jamie Donovan there too. He's got a pretty flexible schedule, and when I tell him why we're checking the vehicle out, I think he'll jump at the chance. He's done some things for the cops in the past, and he would love to get in on this."

"Please give him a call."

"I'll do it now," he said and took out his cell phone. At no surprise, his phone was in a case with a red race car. He pressed a speed dial button and, a moment later, gave me a nod and said, "How's it going, douche? Hey, listen, I'm going to be checking out a 1970 Dodge Charger tomorrow morning. It's all reinforced and looks like your work. It's suspected of being involved in a hit-

and-run back in 2020. No, the cops aren't involved, yet. That's one of the reasons we were hoping you might want to tag along and take a look. Yeah, my P.I. pal, Haskell. Yeah, that's the one," Donnie said and laughed at whatever Jamie Donovan had just said.

"We're thinking first thing tomorrow morning, 9:00 down on West Seventh." Donnie lifted his phone and said, "What's the name of that place again?"

"Seventh Street Storage," I said.

He repeated that to Donovan and disconnected thirty seconds later. "He'll meet us down there. He's going to love checking it out."

"Thanks for making the call, Donnie. Any questions I can answer for you?"

"Yeah, where's my next beer?"

"Waiting for you over at The Spot," I said.

We headed over and actually had two beers. In the old days, we probably would have closed the place. Tonight, I was home before 10:00. I let Morton out, made a grilled cheese, and we went up to bed at 11:00.

Thirty-seven

It was just after 7:00, and I'd been down in the kitchen for an hour. Morton was out in the backyard, and I sent Erik a text message. 'Let me know when you're ready. I've got to meet two guys at 9:00 to inspect LePew's vehicle.'

I got an immediate reply, 'See you at 8:00.'

He didn't mention if he was at Melissa's or Tubby's, so it would be interesting to hear how his night had gone. Morton was back in the kitchen eating while I washed my dishes, took a pork chop out of the freezer, and set it in the refrigerator for dinner tonight. I checked a couple of things on my laptop, and then we headed over to Tubby's. Erik was waiting outside the gate. He looked a lot happier than yesterday.

"Morning, Dev," he said as he climbed in, then reached into the back seat and gave Morton a head scratch.

"Hi, Erik. How did your night go?"

"Oh, fine. Melissa grabbed some sandwiches at a deli. She drove over, we ate in her car, and then she took off about fifteen minutes later. I forget what classes she had last night, but there were two of them."

"Yeah, I've had some friends go through night law school. It's really tough. If she can't see you, it's not that she doesn't want to. It's just that they really crack the whip at those places."

"Yeah, she's told me that a couple of times. It's nice she's doing it, but I sure wouldn't want to."

I told him about meeting Donnie and Jamie at Seventh Street Storage. "You're welcome to join us, but if you don't want to, that's fine, too. You can go through the rest of LePew's laptop."

"Actually, I'd like to hear what those guys have to say about that vehicle. Especially the one who's supposed to have done all that work on the thing."

"These guys are both gearheads. Without meaning to, they'll be talking way over my head right from the start."

Once in the office, Morton settled onto his pillow and went after what remained of his beef marrow bone. I started a fresh pot of coffee, left Louie a note that we were out for a couple of hours, and we headed over to Seventh Street Storage. I wanted to get there before Donnie and Jamie arrived. We beat them by about two minutes. After making introductions, we headed out the door, down the corridor, and took a right into the section of larger units with the garage doors.

I unlocked the door, and before I had it completely raised, Jamie said, "Yeah, that's the one I worked on. It's a 1970 Dodge Charger. The guy wanted it painted Hemi Orange number 2186. Given the reinforcement I put in, whoever was driving had to be doing upwards of eighty miles per hour. This should have been able to reach that speed from a standstill in about three seconds.”

Erik and I looked at one another.

“Are these white streaks from the vehicle it hit?” Donnie asked.

“That’s what we’re thinking,” I said. “My client’s parents were driving a white—”

Jamie bent down and did a close-up examination of the white streaks on the front of the vehicle. “Technically, this isn’t white. It’s called Casino White Pearl. Do you know, was the car an Acura?”

“Yeah, a 2019 Acura NXS,” I said.

“I think you mean an Acura NSX,” Donnie replied, and Jamie nodded.

“That’s it. I haven’t seen any pictures, but I guess the car was pretty much cut in half. My client said she couldn’t identify her parents. They were all in bits and pieces.”

“Yeah, it would be like getting hit with a sledgehammer, only a hundred times worse,” Jamie said as they both stepped along opposite sides of the vehicle, looking inside at the steel reinforcement and the metal driver’s seat.

“I did this work for a guy named LePew, Louis LePew. I’ll never forget his name. He told me he wanted to get involved in the whole Demolition Derby world, not that there was much going on there. I didn't care as long as I got paid. As a matter of fact, he paid me in advance. Damn it, and this is what he did with the vehicle? Killed two people?"

"Would you be willing to testify to that?" I asked.

"You bet I would. Hell, I'll pull the damn switch on the guy when he's strapped into the electric chair."

"We don't do that in this state, Jamie," Donnie said.

"Yeah, well, case in point. We sure as hell should."

"You got that right," I said, and everyone nodded.

I was going to mention the fact that LePew was in a coma in the hospital but decided against it with Erik here. Donnie and Jamie took a number of photos and discussed materials used that went way over my head. I traded business cards with Jamie, and the two of them took off in Donnie's flame-enhanced sports car. Erik and I headed back to the office.

Louie was at his desk typing away on his computer. I topped up his coffee mug and filled two for Erik and me.

"How did things go with the car guys?" Louie asked and took a noisy sip.

"Better than I expected. Not only did the one guy do all the work on the vehicle, but he confirmed who his customer was and volunteered to testify."

"Doesn't get much better than that," Louie said.

Erik began to tell him some specifics on the damage to Melissa's father's car just as my phone rang. Aaron LaZelle.

"Hi, Aaron. Thanks for returning my call."

"What do you have?" His tone suggested he had about eight different things up in the air.

I cut to the chase and gave him the update on the Carter hit and run out in Woodbury and finished up with, "This guy Donovan did the work on the vehicle, and he's willing to testify against Louis LePew. He even identified the paint on the vehicle that was struck as Casino White Pearl. That's the same color that was on the car that Jack Carter was driving when he and his wife were killed."

"That's good, Dev. But it will be viewed as circumstantial at this point."

"Okay, so how about this? In March of 2020, Odell Dankworth sent an email to LePew telling him to deal with Bobby Kelly. LePew replies to Dankworth, telling him to make an offer to Kelly. Dankworth sends back an email saying Kelly won't accept an offer and LePew needs to deal with Kelly now, and the word now is all in capital letters."

"Who is Bobby Kelly?"

"He is, or rather was, the building inspector in Woodbury. Forty-eight hours after Dankworth's email, Kelly is found dead in his house, shot in bed."

"Where did you get this information?"

"LePew's laptop. It's got a ton of information we're still going through and—"

"Dev, you need to stop that right now. Turn the computer off, and we will be over to pick it up."

"Aaron, there's a ton of stuff that connects Odell Dankworth to some major crimes. We've got the vehicle LePew used to kill Jack and Kate Carter. We haven't found it yet, but I'm sure we'll be able to prove that Dankworth told LePew to kill Carter. If I can—"

"Dev, what you're doing is making this evidence inadmissible. Please don't mention anything else. I'll have our team go through the files."

"But Aaron. Everything I've told you—"

"Dev, everything you've told me suggests you are responsible for ransacking the home of Louis LePew and—"

"I didn't ransack LePew's home."

"Well, someone did. The desktop computer is missing from his office. The furniture was destroyed. Pillows were slit, chair legs broken, bathroom mirrors broken, dresser drawers dumped onto the floor, and clothing in closets ripped and torn. There's easily over a hundred thousand dollars' worth of damage and destruction. Are you suggesting to me that you are responsible?"

"No, I'm not. I had nothing to do with anything like that. And while you're suggesting that I have unlawfully obtained these items, I should tell you that I intervened and stopped Louis LePew from assaulting an individual. As a result of my intervention, I feel I stopped a potential murder and confiscated not only LePew's laptop but a pistol and two long guns as well. You can certainly send someone to pick up these items. They're stored at my home, and I'll be happy to meet you or anyone from the department there in forty-five minutes. Oh, and by the way. I would think there just might be a pretty good chance that LePew's pistol is the same weapon that was used to murder Robert Kelly in 2020."

"You're probably in your office, Dev. Which means you're only five minutes from your home. So I'll see you there in—"

"I'm not in my damn office, Aaron," I half-shouted.

Louie and Erik stared at me wide-eyed.

"You had better be telling me the truth," Aaron said and hung up.

"Everything okay?" Louie asked.

"Aaron's on his high horse and being a pain in the ass. I've got to run home for a bit. Erik, I have to take that computer," I said, placing LePew's case on my desk. I set the laptop inside and zipped the top closed. The bulge in the pocket confirmed the pistol was still there, and I hurried out the door.

Thirty-eight

Just in case Aaron checked to see if I was home, I drove into the parking lot across the street from my house. I grabbed LePew's briefcase and hurried over to my place. I set the briefcase on the kitchen table and laid the two long guns next to it. I hurried upstairs into the guest room and waited to see if Aaron would show up. He eventually did, but it was an hour after I had arrived. A squad car parked behind him, and together, the two of them walked up to the front door and knocked.

I hurried downstairs and opened the door.

"Oh, didn't see your car in the driveway, so I wasn't sure if you'd made it home yet," Aaron said.

I ignored his comment. "Come on in. I just laid everything out in the kitchen." We walked back to the kitchen, and I pointed at everything on the table. "Those two long guns were in the trunk of LePew's car. They were out of the cases, and I put them back in and confiscated them along with that briefcase that has his laptop. LePew's pistol is in that pocket on the exterior of the briefcase. I touched the laptop and had a computer guy I know go through the files stored on the thing, so both our fingerprints will be on the computer."

"Did you fire any of the weapons?" Aaron asked.

I shook my head. "No, I did not."

The officer took out a form and began filling it out.

"You said the emails back and forth regarding the building inspector—"

"Robert Kelly," I added.

"The emails mentioning him are on the laptop?"

"Yes, they were sent back in March of 2020."

Aaron nodded and said, "Thanks for these, Dev. I've got a call in to the head of homicide over in Woodbury."

The officer handed me the form and said, "If you just sign this, sir. I'll give you a copy and be out of your hair." I signed the form, and he tore off the back sheet. It was yellow paper, and I set it on the kitchen table. He picked up the two long gun cases and draped them over his shoulder, then picked up the briefcase.

"You can see where that pistol is in the pocket. I can't recall if I handled the pistol. If I did, I just held it for a moment. I did not fire it. My computer guy may have picked it up too. Obviously, you have my prints on file. I'm not sure about my computer guy. I'll see him later today, ask if he's on file and let you know."

"I'll run these out to the car. You need me for anything else, LT?"

"No, you can head back to the station. I'll be right behind you."

Once he left the room, Aaron said, "Sorry about the phone call earlier, Dev. It's been a tough couple of months with no sign of letting up."

"Not a problem, Aaron. I'd offer to help in any way I can, but as you know, I would probably just screw things up even more for you."

"Yeah, no doubt," he said and smiled. "But I appreciate the offer. You mentioned these two guys who viewed the vehicle you suspect was involved in a hit and run."

"Yeah, Donnie Grogan and Jamie Donovan. Jack Carter and his wife were killed. Do you remember him? He was a mentor of mine, used to give me some very good information and direction, not that I ever followed it."

"Yeah, I remember you mentioning him. Are we okay?"

"Yeah, we're good. Thanks for being patient with me, and like I said, if there's anything I can help you with, let me know."

"You wouldn't happen to know a hundred and twenty people who'd want to join the force, would you?"

"I wish I did."

We shook hands, and I walked Aaron to the door. I watched him walk out to his car, climb in, and drive off. Hopefully, they'd act sooner rather than later on Louis LePew. I'd keep my fingers crossed.

I waited ten minutes and then went across the street and climbed into my car. I stepped into the office ten minutes later. Both Erik and Louie stopped what they were doing and watched me as I walked to my desk and picked up my coffee mug.

Finally, Louie said, "Everything go okay?"

I nodded and said, "Yeah, it did. Aaron is really overworked, and it's not going to get any better. They're short-handed. He told me they need a hundred and twenty officers, what with people retiring or just quitting. The good news is he took possession of the briefcase with LePew's laptop and pistol and the two long guns. We're back on speaking terms and friends, well, until the next thing goes crazy. What are you working on, Erik?"

"I'm going over the files Melissa sent. She mentioned something the other night, and with the murder of Kelly, the building inspector, I wanted to go through and check things out."

"You find anything?"

"Not yet, but I'm not even halfway through. There are a number of different inspection reports. The foundation is poured concrete, and then the upper floors are timber, which is standard up to a certain height. I still can't figure out how the place even passed inspection."

"Things must have gotten crazy on the city's end with the murder of Robert Kelly, the building inspector. They may have had unqualified people filling in, doing their best, but at the end of the day, they were still unqualified."

"I'm sure that's possible. I'll just keep going through and seeing what I can find. I wish we still had LePew's laptop."

"Yeah, no doubt there was more on that thing. Still, we got the emails from Dankworth telling him to deal with the problem, and we had Donnie Grogan and Jamie Donovan examine that vehicle in storage."

"I still can't believe Jamie was able to identify exactly the color of the Acura."

I nodded. "Yeah, what is it, White Pearl?"

"Casino White Pearl," Erik said.

"I can't even tell you what colors are on the walls of my house, and I painted all of them. I guess Donovan has served as an expert for the police during occasional trials. I just hope my homicide pal Aaron gets in touch with him. Well, don't let me hold you up. I'm going to fire up my computer. Stand by."

I proceeded to go through Melissa's files. Fortunately, there was some coffee left, so I didn't fall asleep. I was at the point where things were beginning to run together. I had a legal pad out in front of me, and I'd been making notes, but I couldn't read half of them because I'd either been writing too fast or I'd made abbreviations that I couldn't translate now.

"Hey, Dev," Erik said. "Can you remember off the top of your head when Robert Kelly, the building inspector, was murdered?"

"Toward the end of March, but hang on, I've got it here," I said and paged three pages back on the legal pad, and there it was next to a star I'd drawn out in the margin. "Robert Kelly died March 22nd, 2020. I don't have a time of death, but do you need an address?"

"No, it's not that, but check this out. He signed off on this building inspection," Erik said and handed the document over to me. It was a twelve-page copy of the original, listing all sorts of technical stuff and stamped approved. I guessed the original was probably filed somewhere with the City of Woodbury.

"Well, there you go, you saw first-hand what a lousy job they did, using substandard materials, and they went ahead and approved it. Incredible."

"That's not what caught my attention. It's the date on the document, April fourth. That's two weeks after Kelly was murdered, and he somehow came back and signed off on the document."

"Perhaps this was the date it was approved, but it was actually submitted back in March before he was killed."

"No, the approval stamp is dated April eleventh, a week after Kelly supposedly signed the inspection form. But he'd already been dead for two weeks."

"You're right," I said, looking at the dated approval stamp and then the date next to Kelly's signature. "I think it might make sense to check with someone who knows what they're talking about. Who was the guy we met at Dirty Frank's?"

"Oh, that was my pal T.J. McKnight. This might be a little bit above his pay grade, but he could probably give me a name at Karlson Plumbing you could call."

"Would you mind giving him a call?" I asked and Erik reached for his phone.

Thirty-nine

Erik called his pal T.J. and ended up leaving a message. "Hi T.J., it's Erik. Hey, some things came up in that White House apartments case we're working on. I'm hoping you can put me in touch with someone. Give me a call when you've got a minute. Thanks."

"Any idea when he might get back to you?"

"He'll call back as soon as he has a minute. For all I know, right now, he could be up on a ladder soldering copper fittings with a torch."

"Thanks for making the call. See if you've got any more items signed by Kelly after his death."

Erik moved to the top of his stack and started turning pages over. It only took a couple of minutes. He shook his head once he was finished and said, "That appears to be the only item. I suppose it could have been an honest mistake. Maybe Kelly signed the blank form, and someone else filled in the specifics a couple of weeks later."

"I doubt it. The little I know of the guy, he strikes me as someone who wouldn't be signing a blank form.

What if his signature was—" Erik's phone rang, and I stopped.

"Hi T.J., thanks for the quick call back, and sorry to bother you at work. I just have a quick question. We're going through some forms from Woodbury giving approval on materials used in the construction of The White House Apartments. Do you know someone we could talk to who deals with getting approval in Woodbury? Yeah, that's kind of what I thought. Jared Karlson, he's the head honcho? Okay, no, don't worry. I promise I won't mention your name. Thanks for calling back so fast. Yeah, you too," Erik said and disconnected.

"Jared Karlson is the guy to talk to?" I asked.

Erik nodded. "Yeah, T.J. said he just left the job site and was heading back to the office. You thinking of going over there?"

"Yeah, I'd like to show him the document and get his take on it."

"Please don't mention T.J.'s name. Apparently, the guy is a real ass kicker."

"Not to worry. Let me have that file, and I'll head over there now."

Erik pulled the file from the stack and handed it to me. I placed it in a manila envelope to give it a little more professional appearance and headed out the door. The Karlson Plumbing building was over in the Midway industrial area, just off Fairview Avenue. I'd been past the place a couple of times, but other than my conversation with Erik's pal T.J., I didn't think I'd ever interacted with anyone there. T.J. had mentioned that they did commercial work as opposed to dealing with homeowners. Probably a good idea based on the number of apartment buildings that have been going up around town over the last couple of years.

The building was a one-story concrete block structure with three cars parked in front and an industrial van labeled Karlson Plumbing parked in the back. I drove into the front parking lot and went inside. There were two desks facing one another. One desk was empty, and a woman who looked fifty was seated at the other one. She had a number of files scattered in front of her, and at the moment, she was on the phone. She smiled, gave me a nod, and pointed to the chairs in front of her desk. I sat down and waited for a minute or two before she hung up.

"Hi, sorry to keep you waiting. How can I help?"

"Hi, I was hoping to be able to talk to Jared Karlson. I don't have an appointment."

"And what would this be concerning?"

"I'm a private detective. We're looking into a potential murder, and I have a question I'm hoping Mr. Karlson might be able to help me with."

Her eyes had widened at my mention of 'private detective' and remained that way. "Let me just see if he has a moment," she said and hurried away from her desk and down a hallway.

I could hear her voice from down the hall but couldn't make out what she was saying other than a few words I picked up on, 'you,' 'detective,' and 'murder.' That apparently got Jared Karlson's attention because a calmer version of the woman suddenly appeared and said, "Mr. Karlson will see you now. Please follow me." I followed her down the hall to a large office. She stepped aside at the door, and I walked in just as Jared Karlson stepped out from behind his desk.

He wasn't muscular like a weightlifter, but he was definitely solid looking, probably due to hard labor from the time he was about fifteen. He looked to be in his early fifties, and I wondered if the woman might be his wife.

"Hi, Jared Karlson. You're here investigating a murder?" he asked as he extended his hand.

"Nice to meet you, sir. My name is Dev Haskell. I'm a private investigator," I said as we shook hands. His hand was like squeezing a brick. "Yes, I'm investigating a murder, three murders, actually. Let me state, for the record, that neither you, your company, nor any of your employees are involved. I have a couple of questions about the victims, and hopefully, you can point me in the right direction regarding some paperwork I'm not all that familiar with."

"Paperwork? In a murder investigation?"

"Would you mind if I showed you?"

"No, not at all. Please take a seat," he said, stepping back behind his desk.

As I sat down, I opened the manila envelope and took out the application with Robert Kelly's signature.

"Did you happen to know a gentleman by the name of Jack Carter?"

Karlson nodded and said, "We'd done a few projects for him. I knew him to say hello and have a pleasant conversation, but I didn't really know him personally. He and his wife were killed two or three years ago in a car accident."

"You worked on his White House Apartment project, correct?"

He seemed to grow cautious and said, "We did some work there. We had contracted to do the entire project but withdrew after ninety days under mutually agreed terms. At the time, Carter was a silent partner, and although his involvement was the reason we submitted a bid and accepted the project, it became clear in short order that he was just that, a silent partner, and all decisions were being made by another individual."

"Would that other individual have been Odell Dankworth?"

"Yes," Karlson said and didn't elaborate further.

I pushed the form with Robert Kelly's signature across the desk to him. He took one look at it, glanced up at the right-hand corner where the date was, and shook his head. "I'm afraid I can't be of any assistance on this. We had withdrawn from the project prior to the date listed here."

"I understand that, in fact, that might even be good. My question is this. The form was approved by a Woodbury building inspector by the name of Robert Kelly. He was found murdered in his home on the twenty-second of March in 2020.”

“Yeah, I remember that.”

“The date Kelly approved this is April fourth. Am I missing something here that this would have Robert Kelly’s signature on the fourth of April, almost two weeks after he had been murdered, and then it got the approval stamp a week later?”

Karlson slid the form closer and read it for a moment. He paged through it, looking at a couple of other pages. He slowly shook his head and said, “This isn’t right. Obviously, there’s no way Kelly would have been able to approve these requests. Now, it could be that someone made an error and listed the wrong month. Which would mean the approval was actually in March.”

“But that would require two errors, the date on Kelly’s signature and then, a week later, the approval stamp dated the eleventh of April. Again, I’m not accusing anyone, and certainly not you. But it’s just not making sense to me.”

“And it’s not making sense to me, either. You’re on to something here. I’m not sure what exactly, but something is very wrong. Let me give you a number,” Karlson turned to his open rotary Rolodex file and flipped through. He wrote down a number on a pad of paper along with the name Donald Carroll and handed it to me.

“Don Carroll is with the City of Woodbury. Mention that file number in the upper lefthand corner, and he’ll be able to bring it up on his computer. Something is very wrong here. I'm hoping for their sake it's as simple as an incorrect date and the wrong month was added."

"Thank you," I said and folded the piece of paper. "Would you mind if I asked you one more question?"

"All right," he said, not sounding all that sure.

"Jack Carter. Are you aware of anyone who would have wanted to kill him?"

He shook his head. "Jack Carter had a sterling reputation. He was as honest as they come. I could never understand why, exactly, he got mixed up with Odell Dankworth. I don't know if he stepped in, in an attempt to make the best of a bad situation. Or if he was attracted by the idea of being a silent partner. Although, in short order, everyone knew he was involved with Dankworth, and no one could understand why. Anything else?"

"No, sir. Thank you for the phone number. I'll contact Don Carroll just as soon as I'm back in my office. Would you like me to keep your involvement private?"

"Actually, feel free to mention me. Proof positive that I want things working fairly."

"Okay, Thank you again for your time." I slipped the form back into the manila envelope and held out my hand. We shook hands, and I walked out to the entrance.

"Thank you for your help," I said to the lady seated at the desk.

"Enjoy your day," she replied.

As I climbed into my car, I saw her hurry down the hall toward Karlson's office.

Forty

Louie was down at the courthouse when I got back to the office. I brought Erik up to date on the Robert Kelly signature situation in about sixty seconds and then poured the last of the coffee into my mug. I turned off the burner, took a sip, and promptly poured the contents of my mug down the sink. I took out Jared Karlson's note with Don Carroll's phone number and made the call.

"Don Carroll," was how he answered.

"Hello, Mr. Carroll. My name is Dev Haskell. I'm a private detective working on a case, and I got your number from Jared Karlson at Karlson Plumbing."

"Oh yeah, I've worked with Jared a number of times and worked with his father for a number of years on various projects. You said you're a private detective?"

"Yes, sir, I'm working on a case, and one of the many things we're reviewing is the White House Apartments and the—"

"At no surprise. We seem to be looking at some aspect of that structure on almost a monthly basis. But as I recall, I don't believe Karlson Plumbing had much to do with the project. I think they came to a mutual agreement with the Dankworth organization and withdrew after ninety days. Other than some very basic work, they were no longer involved."

"That's my understanding as well. In fact, the only reason I spoke with Jared Karlson was to get his opinion as an experienced individual on a request that was approved by the building inspector from Woodbury."

"Would you happen to be familiar with the specific request?"

"Yes, sir, in fact, I have a copy of it in front of me, and I could give you the number."

"Yes, please. I'll bring it up on my computer." I read the number off to Carroll and waited. "This will take just a moment, and I'll have it in front of me. Yeah, here we are, The White House Apartments. Dankworth Building Brokers. Got it. How can I help you?"

"Here's what I don't understand. This had been approved by Robert Kelly."

"Yes, and he is no longer employed by the City of Woodbury."

"I'm aware of that. He was murdered in his home on the twenty-second of March, back in 2020."

"Beyond tragic. An excellent inspector. A wonderful person. I believe his murder is still listed as unsolved."

"Yes, it is. But looking at the file you have on your screen, you'll note that the application is dated the fourth of April 2020, and it was stamped approved the following week on April eleventh. My problem is, how could Robert Kelly approve this application if he had been murdered on the twenty-second of March, fully two weeks before the application was submitted?" I waited a long moment for a response. "Hello. Hello? Mr. Carroll, are you there?"

"You've got me wondering the same thing, and I don't have an answer for you. Strange, very strange. Could you give me your number, please? I'm going to have to look into this, and it may take some time."

"Yes, my name is Dev Haskell," I said, then gave him my email address and phone number.

"Thank you for bringing this to my attention. Hopefully, we're looking at a clerical error and nothing else. It just amazes me that no one caught it."

"I look forward to hearing from you, sir. Thank you for your time."

"Thank you, Mr. Haskell. I'll get back to you," Carroll said and disconnected.

As I hung up, Erik's cell phone rang. He smiled and answered, "Hi, how is your day going?" He rose from his chair and stepped out of the office. His call got me thinking, and I took out my cell phone and hit speed dial for Crystal.

"Oh, Dev, I was just about to call you."

"How is your day going?" I asked, taking a note from Erik.

"Well, I was wondering if you would be interested in getting together tonight. I made some chili, and I was going to make some garlic bread. Would you be interested in having dinner?"

"I would love to, Crystal. Is there a time that will work better for you?"

"How does 7:00 sound?"

"It sounds perfect. That will give me time to get Morton settled in."

"Oh, yes, your friend, Morton. I completely forgot. Tell you what, I'll bring dinner over to you if that will work."

"You don't have to do that. I can—"

"Not a problem, Dev. I'll see you around 7:00. Oh, and rest up."

"Not to worry," I replied, but Crystal had already disconnected.

Forty-one

It was mid-afternoon when I got a call from Aaron LaZelle. My cell phone was on my desk, and Aaron's name came up on the first ring. I let it ring three times before I answered. "Hi, Aaron. What's up?"

"Have you been listening to the news," he asked.

"No, actually, I've been working. Going over a number of files related to Jack Carter. I think I may have mentioned that his daughter wanted me to look through the events of her parents being killed."

"So you're up in your office?"

For some reason, the way he said it caused me to turn in my desk chair and look out the window. A police cruiser was parked at the curb just behind my car. "Yeah, other than a quick trip to see a plumber, I've been in here all day. Are you thinking you might have time for dinner tonight?" I asked, knowing he wouldn't.

"Oh, I only wish. I've got some news for you that will probably have some bearing on whatever you're working on for the Carter girl. You mind if I stop over?"

"No, glad to see you. I'm here for the rest of the afternoon," I said as I pushed my chair off to the side.

"I'll be there in a bit," Aaron said and disconnected.

I watched out the window as he climbed out of the passenger side of the cruiser. He waited for a couple of cars to pass and headed across the street. He glanced up at the window, but from where I had moved my chair, he'd be unable to see me. I rolled back behind my desk and said, "Hey, Erik. Just a heads up. Aaron LaZelle, my cop pal, is going to be here in about ten seconds." I could hear Aaron on the stairs. It sounded like he was taking them two at a time. A moment later, he stepped into the office. Morton gave him a look but remained on his pillow.

"Oh man, that was fast. Were you over in The Spot?"

"I only wish. Hey, Erik. How are things going for you?"

"Doing well, sir. How about you?"

"Just as crazy as always, and please, call me Aaron. Oh, and my condolences on having to work with Dev. It must be a chore."

"Actually, he takes pretty good care of me," Erik said.

"You just in the neighborhood?" I asked as Aaron dragged a client chair away from Erik and placed it alongside my desk.

"Not exactly. I wanted to ask for your help on something."

"Yeah, sure. You said you had some news regarding the Carter case?"

"Yeah, Louis LePew passed away this morning." Erik shot a look toward me. "I can't say I'm sorry to hear that. Good riddance. The more I look into the history, the more I'm convinced LePew is responsible for not only Jack and Kate Carter's deaths in the hit-and-run incident, but I'm also coming to the conclusion he murdered a building inspector from Woodbury named Robert Kelly. How did he die?"

"Initial indications are he was murdered. Suffocated by someone placing a pillow over his face."

"A pillow? Did you have anyone stationed outside his hospital room?"

Aaron shook his head, "No, never. He was in a coma the entire time. Our concern was his attempting to leave. We had about two days' worth of questions to ask, and now we may never get answers to those questions."

"Is there something we could help you with? Having gone over a number of files, we might be able to fill in some blank spots."

"Well, there is one thing you could help with right now. I spoke to Jamie Donovan on the phone. He confirmed what you had said about working on the vehicle, basically tearing everything out and reinforcing the thing for LePew."

"Yeah, that's right, and I hasten to add that LePew told him he wanted to drive the thing in a demolition derby."

"Yeah, Donovan mentioned that. What I'd like to do is view the vehicle with the idea that we take possession.

Donavan is onboard to testify if necessary, although with LePew dead, that may not be necessary. I'd like to take a look at it and possibly have a team show up for evidence processing and photographing," Aaron said as he grabbed a paper from the inner pocket of his sports coat and handed it to me.

"That's certainly not a problem. I don't own the thing."

"Yeah, but you apparently have a key to the storage facility."

I opened my desk drawer and took out the set of keys for the door at Seventh Street Storage and the vehicle. "Here, they're yours," I said and handed the keys to Aaron.

"Where'd you get these, anyway?"

I shook my head and said, "I wish I could tell you. They were sent to me anonymously. No idea where they came from or how they got here. They just showed up with a note that had the address typed on it. Nothing else." I glanced over at Erik, staring at the floor.

"You have time in your busy schedule to join me at the storage facility?" Aaron asked, although it wasn't a question as much as an order.

"Seventh Street Storage? Yeah, sure, you want me to drive?"

"No, let's take the cruiser. We'll get there that much faster."

"Happy to help," I said as we both stood. Aaron headed for the door, and I glanced at Erik, who quickly shook his head.

Forty-two

We waited for a bus to pass and then crossed the street. Aaron opened the rear passenger door for me and then climbed in front. A uniformed officer was behind the wheel, and as he drove down the street, Aaron asked, "How are things working out with Gustafson's nephew?"

"Actually, pretty well. He's a nice guy. Works very hard, and he's a bit of a computer nerd, so he spends a lot of time just keeping me straightened out."

"Nice," Aaron said. "You think his uncle has him with you just to keep an eye on what you're up to?"

"No, although that would sound a lot better. The real reason he put him with me is that Erik expressed an interest in getting into some aspect of Federal law enforcement. Tubby figured that, after a couple of days with me, he'd never want to get close to anything like that again. Too bad for Tubby, but that didn't exactly work out the way he'd planned. The guy works really hard at whatever he's involved in."

Aaron laughed for a second or two. "That's pretty funny. Of course, he's got a full-time job just trying to keep you in line."

"When you spoke with Jamie Donovan, did he mention the paint from the car in the hit and run?" I asked.

"He did, and in fact, he mentioned the color. It's a unique name. I've got it written down at my desk."

I brought out my phone and hit messages. "Casino White Pearl," I read from the screen. "That was the color of the Acura that Jack Carter and his wife were in when they were killed."

"You're thinking LePew was behind the wheel?"

"Unless we come up with something else, that's my thought. Have you run tests on the pistol that was in LePew's briefcase?"

"Tests are scheduled for today. They may have already run them. Someone from Woodbury was going to join the ballistics team for the testing."

"Well, keeping my fingers crossed. I'm thinking LePew for the murder of Robert Kelly as well as Jack and Kate Carter."

"Any thoughts on who may have paid him a visit overnight?" Aaron asked.

"I've got nothing to prove it, but at the moment, my money is on Odell Dankworth. The emails, there were four, between him and LePew back in 2020 regarding Robert Kelly. They seem to point a pretty strong finger. Add to that a bogus copy of the supposed business relationship between him and Jack Carter, transferring eve-rything to Dankworth upon Carter's death," I shook my head. "You should lock the guy up, Aaron."

"It would be nice to have something a little more solid than your opinion, Dev."

"Well, with any luck, the test results on this vehicle will get you just that much closer."

We turned into the Seventh Street Storage parking lot. Since there weren't any handles on the inside of the rear doors, I had to wait for Aaron to let me out of the back seat. The officer driving remained behind the wheel. Aaron and I walked through the lobby and out the door into the storage area.

Today, there was a couple in an SUV loading the rear of the vehicle with boxes. We got a friendly nod and walked down to unit 147. As I knelt down to unlock the door, Aaron said, "Do you know if Dankworth has a key to this unit?"

I opened the lock and shook my head. "I can't be-lieve that he does. If he did, the mere fact that this vehicle is still around suggests he has no idea." I stood and raised the metal garage door.

Aaron stared for a long moment and then took out his phone. "Yeah, Norris, I'm looking at the vehicle now. We need to bring it in and have it examined. Tie it to the LePew murder, and that should eliminate any time delays. No, if you'd take care of that, please. Yeah. I won't leave until they arrive." He glanced at the garage door next to the unit and said, "The unit is one-forty-seven. Just now, it's one of only two with an open door. Thanks. I'll wait here until they arrive."

"That was Manning you were talking to?"

"Yeah, he's sending a photo team over. By the time they're finished, hopefully, the tow truck will be here and haul it in. They'll examine that white paint. I want them to photograph this thing before they tow it out of here. Did you touch anything on this?"

"Yeah, I did, along with Jamie Donovan, Donnie Grogan, and Erik Gustafson."

"And Donovan did all the work on this?"

"That's what he said."

Aaron nodded. "He's going to drop off a file with the billing specifics and a video of the work being done. God, look at this thing. It's amazing," he said and walked alongside the vehicle as he peered inside. We examined the vehicle and then chatted for another twenty minutes before two officers stepped out of the lobby and headed toward us.

One of them, a woman, was carrying a large black briefcase. "Lieutenant LaZelle, nice to see you again. This is the vehicle?" she asked as she set the briefcase down and unzipped it.

"Nice to see you, Melanie. This is a friend of mine, Dev Haskell. He—"

"Oh, yeah, I've heard of you. Nice to finally meet you." We shook hands. "Lieutenant, we'll take a number of photos from different angles. We'll photograph the interior but through the windows. I don't intend to open any doors or lift the hood until after the tech team has been over it."

"Yeah, that's fine," Aaron said, and we stepped away from the vehicle.

She raised the lid on the briefcase, seemed to study for a moment, and took out a digital camera. She screwed on a lens, stepped in front of the vehicle, and began taking pictures. She adjusted the lens, bent down, and photographed the streaks of white paint on the front of the vehicle from different angles. From there, she moved along the side, doing just what she said, taking photos of the interior through the windows.

The other officer was kneeling next to the briefcase and attaching lenses to two other cameras. He stood and began photographing the opposite side.

"They're going to be at this for a while, and I've got to head back to the office," Aaron said.

"I'll follow you out," I said, not that I had another choice.

"I'm heading back to the station, Melanie. Thank you for arriving so quickly," Aaron called.

She was standing at the rear of the vehicle. She smiled, gave a quick wave, and continued photographing. We walked back into the lobby and out the door to the cruiser.

"Should I go back in and tell the woman in the lobby that the vehicle is going to be towed out of here?"

"They've already been informed, and when the officers following the tow truck arrive, they'll have a copy of the court order that they'll leave with them."

I climbed into the rear seat, and Aaron closed the door. Our ride back to my office was interrupted by a phone call to Aaron. "Yeah, what do you have?" was how he answered. He nodded a couple of times and said, "Yes. Yes. Incredible. Okay, make sure there are two officers. Yes, they're photographing it now, and then it will be towed in. Good. You have the warrant? Tell them to try his office first. All right, keep me posted, and thanks for the update."

He turned around in the passenger seat and smiled. "Could be just a coincidence, but I doubt it. Odell Dankworth was on security video entering Regions Hospital this morning at 4:27 am and departing at 4:42 am. I wonder who he might have been visiting?"

"Louis LePew."

"Good guess. We've got a warrant out. Officers should be at his office in the next half hour. It's turning out to be a rather nice day, don't you think?"

"That's very good news. I was down there a few days ago. Never got inside the office. I knocked a number of times, and no one answered, but I'm convinced Dankworth, or someone, was in there."

Aaron shook his head. "I have a feeling, the more we look into this guy, the sketchier he's going to become."

"I only wish LePew was alive so he could be charged."

"Well, I suspect, once this Dankworth is arrested and charged, that will more than make up for it."

"Let me know when you get him," I said as the cruiser came to the curb at the bus stop in front of my building.

Aaron climbed out of the passenger seat and opened my door. I got out and extended my hand. We shook, and Aaron said, "Once we have him locked up, let's think about dinner, just the two of us. And, yes, I'll buy."

"Wouldn't miss it for the world," I said, and we both laughed.

I stood and watched as they headed down the street.

Forty-three

I was barely in the door when Erik asked, "Everything go okay?"

"Yeah, just fine. They've got a team photographing the vehicle. They're going to tow it down to the station and go over it with a fine-tooth comb. Oh, and the big news, they just put out an arrest warrant on Dankworth. Turns out he's on security video at the hospital around 4:30 this morning and then leaving about ten minutes later. They'll be going through the LePew files they took from us and, no doubt, searching Dankworth's home and office. With any luck, he's going to be locked up for the rest of his miserable life."

"Would it be alright if I told Melissa about this tonight?"

I thought about that for a moment and said, "I don't see why not. Just make sure you tell her there's a warrant out on Dankworth, and we have to wait and see what happens. You can tell her about the vehicle but stress that it's suspected of being involved in the hit-and-run. We don't know for sure yet."

Erik nodded. "She'll be happy to hear this, and she'll probably have all sorts of questions."

"Well, plead the fifth. At this point, things are moving in the right direction, and we're all keeping our fingers crossed. Time will tell, but I'm probably talking weeks, if not months, instead of just days. Still, things are beginning to move forward."

Louie wasn't back in the office when we left. We both had what we hoped would be a hot dinner date. I drove Erik back to Tubby's so he could get cleaned up and touch base with Tubby. I stopped at Solo Vino, got two bottles of wine, and then parked in my driveway. I put the wine in the refrigerator, clipped the leash on Morton, and took him out on a nice long walk. I grabbed a hot shower and slipped into a nice shirt and trousers for a change. I had the kitchen counter set and was watching out the window for Crystal.

She climbed out of her car wearing a white, half-button crop top, jeans with the knees ripped, and white sandals. I hurried out the front door to help her carry dinner into the house.

"Oh, thanks so much for doing this," I said and took both grocery bags from her and followed her back up on the porch. "How did your day go?"

"No complaints, work went well, and I don't have to be in until late tomorrow morning," she said as she raised her eyebrows.

I followed her into my kitchen. After studying for a long minute, I decided that, despite the rips, the jeans were actually pretty nice. Her chili smelled wonderful. I'd set the counter for two. The wine glasses were out. She placed a basket of freshly made garlic bread next to the wine glasses. She placed the pan of chili on a burner and turned it to a moderate temperature. I filled the wine glasses, and we chatted for a half hour. The room gradually filled with a delicious scent, and my stomach growled.

Crystal laughed and said, "Oh, well, I'll take that as a compliment."

We were both careful not to consume too much wine. I topped up our glasses halfway through dinner and then cleared the table while Crystal loaded the dishwasher. We had apple pie for dessert and chatted about everything and nothing. We brought our wine glasses up to the bedroom. I emptied the bottle into our glasses, and we were snuggling beneath the covers just before 10:00.

I woke with a start in the middle of the night. My digital clock said 3:10, and my first thought was that Fat Freddy was pounding downstairs on the door, but then I realized Fat Freddy would still be pounding. I listened carefully, but all I heard was Crystal breathing next to me. I decided I must have been dreaming and gradually drifted back to sleep.

"You so much as move, and you're a dead man," a voice whispered. I felt something cold pressed against the side of my head. "Get your worthless ass out of bed, and don't wake that woman up."

"Who the hell—"

"Shut up, Haskell, and get out of the damn bed. Now!"

I nodded and held my hands out in front of me. The figure stepped back and waved what looked like a .45 toward the bedroom door. I slipped out of bed, naked. Crystal made a noise, rolled halfway over in the opposite direction, and continued breathing deeply.

I headed for the door, wondering who in the hell this was and where, in God's name, was Morton? My second question was answered the moment I stepped into the hall. Morton was right there, gnawing on a very large bone that still had pieces of meat attached to it.

I felt the .45 pressed against the back of my head. "Now, here's what you're going to do, Haskell. I tore LePew's house apart searching and never found what I was looking for. You took Louis LePew's briefcase. He had money in there that belongs to me, fifty-f-ing-grand. I want it back now. You so much as think about doing something stupid, and I swear to God, I will blow out what little brains you have, and then I'm gonna kill your girlfriend and your dog. You hear me? Now I just want my money, and I'll go."

"You're Odell Dankworth."

He pressed the .45 firmly against the back of my head, forcing my head down. "I don't think you heard me. I want my damn money, now!"

"I heard you. Okay, okay, just calm down, and I can get it for you. I've got it hidden, and I have to get a screwdriver from my bedroom."

"What do you need that for?"

"The money is hidden in a wall. I have to unscrew a panel."

"So help me, if you're playing a game, I'll kill all of you. I will, I promise you," he said and banged the barrel of the .45 against the back of my head.

"Okay, okay. I get it, but I have to unscrew the panel and—"

"If you're lying to me, I'm going to—" **BANG!**

I jumped as the .45 went off next to my head. As I spun around, the .45 dropped onto my bare foot and caused me to jump, knocking Dankworth into the wall. His eyes were up in the back of his head. He was limp and dropped to the floor with a thud. Naked Crystal stood behind him with the empty wine bottle in her hand.

"Oh, my God. Did I kill him? Is he dead?"

"Oh, thank you. No, no, he's not dead. Yet." I quickly rolled him face down, placed a knee on his spine, and put all my weight on top of him. "Can you get my jeans and bring them to me?" I said as I picked up the .45 and pressed it against the back of Dankworth's skull.

Morton walked over with the bone in his mouth and checked us out.

"Oh, you were a big help," I said just as Crystal hurried back into the hall with my jeans. I grabbed my cell phone out of the front pocket and handed it to her. "Dial 911. This guy's name is Odell Dankworth. The cops are looking for him."

"Okay. Yes. Yes. Okay. I think I can. How do you turn this on?"

I yanked Dankworth's arms behind his back, and tied them up with my jeans, then stood and took the phone from Crystal. I dialed 911 and turned on the hall light. We heard a siren a few minutes later, but it felt like it had taken hours. Crystal stepped out of the bedroom with her jeans on. She was in the process of pulling her white half-button crop top over her head. We heard footsteps on the front porch as Morton barked and followed Crystal down the stairs.

Dankworth moved his head and strained at my jeans wrapped around his wrists and arms. I bounced the .45 against the large red bump on the back of his head, and he screamed.

"Don't even think of trying to move, you worthless piece of shit," I growled.

"Haskell," a voice called from behind me.

I turned and recognized two officers, but I couldn't remember their names at the moment. It sounded like another siren was pulling up out front.

"You might want to slip into something a little less revealing," the officer said. He calmly took hold of the barrel on the .45 and gently removed it from my hand.

"Yeah, yeah. This piece of shit broke in and threatened to kill us. There's a murder warrant out for him. He suffocated a guy named Louis LePew in Regions Hospital yesterday. You can check with Lieutenant LaZelle in homicide."

The two officers looked at one another and nodded. The one with the .45 stepped off to the side and spoke into the radio attached to his vest. The other officer knelt down, untied my jeans on Dankworth's wrists, and slapped handcuffs on him.

Dankworth groaned as the cop patted him down, then rolled him over and searched his front pockets, belt, and trousers. I slipped my jeans on.

Two more cops came up the stairs. One of them smiled and said, "Well, Dev Haskell. Are we interrupting?"

"Sergeant Strehlow, very nice to see you again. Who did you piss off to get this gig?"

"The list is long, Dev. Very long."

Forty-four

Dankworth was checked out by a fire department Emergency Medical Team and then hauled away in handcuffs in the back of a squad car. Crystal and I gave basic information to the arresting officers. It turned out that Dankworth actually broke the glass in a pane in the backdoor window, reached in, and unlocked the door. Apparently, I'd been so eager to get Crystal upstairs and into the bedroom that I neglected to turn on the alarm system. Looking back, that was probably what saved Dankworth from being shot or, at the very least, the two of us exchanging gunfire.

It was almost 6:00 AM by the time the police finished up and left. Just now, Crystal was still in the shower, where she'd been for over a half hour. I had a second pot of coffee going after serving it up to everyone except Dankworth. I had already applied the first coat of patching plaster to the bullet hole in the hallway. I planned to let it dry for twenty-four hours before I applied a second coat. I had taped a piece of cardboard over the windowpane in the backdoor. I debated making breakfast for Crystal or offering to take her out, but I had a feeling I knew where our conversation was going to be headed.

Eventually, I heard the shower turn off and figured it would be better to give her some privacy rather than hurry upstairs and suggest a meet-up in bed to brighten up both our days. I heard her coming downstairs a half-hour later, and I hurried out to the staircase.

"Oh, Crystal, you look gorgeous. How about a coffee? And I would love to cook you breakfast or take you out if—"

"Thanks, Dev. No offense, but this just isn't working out. That awful man was going to kill you. No, strike that. He was going to kill me too, both of us."

"That's why I thought we could just discuss it over a nice breakfast. Start to get control of our emotions and—"

"Get control of our emotions? Dev, the police were here for two and a half hours. We were going to be murdered, and you're acting like this was just a normal night in your life. A man with a gun broke into your house. You apparently knew who he was, and he was going to **KILL US!**"

"No need to scream, Crystal. Everything is—"

"Ahh! Ahh! AHHHHHHH!"

"I know. I know. That's why I thought a nice breakfast—"

"Breakfast!" she screamed and hit me on the chest. "Are you crazy? Breakfast?" she said and hit me again. "All I want to do is get out of here and go home. It just keeps getting worse. I know you lied about saving those two little children in the treehouse. I was worried sick about you, and you just stood me up. We plan a romantic night together, and you have to run off and investigate someone. I get all dressed up and come over here, and you've locked yourself out and are nowhere to be found. You force me to drink two bottles of champagne. And now someone tried to kill us, and you want to go out for breakfast!"

"Okay, I get it. I can cook breakfast for us here, Crystal."

"No, Dev, you don't get it. You just don't get it!"

"Okay, what if we climb back into bed, and we can attend to each other's—"

"There, see! Climb back into bed? I can't deal with this anymore, Dev. I'm going home. Do not follow me. Do not call me. Please do not contact me! Ever!"

"Are you sure? I mean, with all those toys of yours, I could—"

"Ahh!" she screamed again and hurried out the door, slamming it behind her.

I figured it probably wasn't the best time to tell her she forgot her chili pan and the leftover garlic bread. I watched her drive off just as Morton came down the stairs. I gave him a head scratch and let him out the backdoor.

I got a text message from Erik. Apparently, things were okay on the Tubby front because he said he would be ready at 8:30. I ate the remaining bowl of chili and some garlic bread for breakfast, then grabbed a shower and put on a clean t-shirt. Morton and I were waiting at the curb when Erik stepped outside the gate at Tubby's.

"Hi Dev, have you been waiting long?"

"At least sixty seconds," I lied, which brought a smile to Erik's face. "How'd your evening go?"

He reached into the back, gave Morton a head scratch, and said, "Cheeseburgers at McDonald's again, but it was nice to see Melissa. She has some exam coming up that she had to study for, so I had a quiet night at my uncle's, watching tv and looking around on the internet. What about you?"

"I'll tell you when we get in the office. Hopefully, Louie will be there, so I'll only have to go through it once."

"That doesn't sound good. You okay?"

"Yeah, not a bother."

Fortunately, I parked behind Louie's Ford Fiesta, which meant he was already up in the office. He was on his computer when we walked in.

"Hey, Good morning. Fresh coffee on, fellas," was how Louie greeted us when we walked in.

"Dev's going to tell us about his evening. Said he didn't want to have to say it twice," Erik said as he filled his coffee mug and then reached across the desk and filled my mug. He dripped a trail of coffee across the desk once he finished.

"So, a big night?" Louie asked.

"Let's just say, interesting." I went on to describe Crystal's dinner and how we enjoyed one another's company. I skipped our romantic interaction and told them I woke up to a .45 pressed against my head.

"What? Who the hell did that?" Louie asked.

"Well, apparently, Odell Dankworth was able to dodge the police and their arrest warrant and decided to pay me a visit."

"Dankworth? What did he want?"

"He never really said. He was just upset that we had been checking into Louis LePew and the Robert Kelly murder. He actually put a hole in the backdoor window and reached in to unlock the door. He woke me up by placing a loaded .45 against my head. Made me climb out of bed and took me out into the hallway. He was all wound up and reading me the riot act when Crystal snuck up behind and hit him over the head with an empty wine bottle. If it wasn't for her, I don't think I'd be here right now." My phone suddenly rang before either one could respond. Aaron LaZelle.

"Hi, Aaron."

"Are you okay? I just learned about your late-night visitor."

"Yeah, I'm fine. One of the more interesting nights I've had in a while."

"I'm not referring to Crystal. I meant Odell Dankworth," Aaron said.

"Oh, my misunderstanding. Yeah, I'm okay. Crystal was pretty upset, as you might imagine."

"She's okay?"

"I think she might be once she calms down, but that might take a couple of days or even weeks."

"Any idea why he was there?"

"I think he was aware we were closing in on him. Between what we think might have happened on the Robert Kelly murder, him suffocating LePew, and the arrest warrant, I'd say he was pretty desperate."

"Good Lord. But you're okay?"

"Yeah, it will be interesting to see how I sleep tonight, but, yeah, I'm okay. Is he behind bars?"

"He will be. Standard policy, he's getting checked out by the medical team. I don't know if they'll do an x-ray on the head or not. God bless the woman you had over."

"Yeah, Crystal. Thank God she was there. She was pretty upset afterward."

"Understandably. Listen, if you need anything, don't hesitate to call."

"Thanks, Aaron, and don't forget, now that Dankworth is locked up, you're buying dinner."

"Yeah, I guess I did say that. Okay, chat later," he said and hung up.

"Erik, have you talked to Melissa about this?"

"When would I do that? You just told us about it a minute ago."

"Oh, yeah, I guess that's right. See if she can stop over later today. I'd like to go over this with her and let her know. The word is liable to spread in the city attorney's office, and I want to give her the facts."

"I'll call her in a bit," he said.

Since I never went back to sleep after Dankworth woke me, I drifted off in my desk chair. When I woke, there was a BBQ sandwich from Roosters on my desk. "Oh, look at this. Did Louie get this?"

"No, I did," Erik said. "I wanted to tell you thanks for all you've done, and well, I'm glad you're okay after your run-in with Odell Dankworth."

"Yeah, well, with any luck, he won't be seeing the light of day for at least twelve years."

"I called Melissa. Apparently, you're the talk of the office over in the courthouse."

"Hopefully, on a positive note."

"Oh, I think so. She said she'd stop over after 4:00."

"Okay, good. I've got something for her, and that will give me time to enjoy my lunch and then run an errand."

"Anything I can do to help?"

"Yeah, relax, take it easy, and realize how lucky you are to have your uncle."

Aaron called just as I was about to start in on my sandwich. "Hi, Dev. I only have a minute, but just got the word and wanted to let you know that the pistol in the LePew briefcase is the same weapon that was used in the murder of Robert Kelly in Woodbury back in 2020. Always nice to get a cold case off the books."

"No kidding? That's great news. I only wish LePew was alive so he could spend the rest of his life behind bars."

"I hear you. The tech guys are going over that battering ram vehicle as we speak. They got confirmation late yesterday on the white streaks, Casino White Pearl."

"So it was him that killed Jack Carter and his wife."

"We'll never be a hundred percent certain, but yeah. I'd say so. Hey, I gotta run. Thought you'd want to know. You got time for dinner tonight?"

"I do, and Aaron, I tell you what, I'll buy. Which McDonald's do you want to go to?"

He laughed. "I'll give you a call later and let you know. Behave until then," he said and disconnected.

I ate my sandwich and then drove home. I measured the pane of glass in the backdoor, phoned the dimensions into the hardware store, and then went upstairs. The patching plaster I'd set in the bullet hole was drying nicely. I looked around and decided there was just one more thing I had to take care of.

Epilogue

I saw Melissa pull in front of my car a little after 4:00. She climbed out and hurried across the street. I just barely heard her coming up the stairs. She knocked on the door as she opened it and stepped inside.

Erik was out of his chair before she could even say hello. They focused on one another, kissed, and then he held her hand and led her over to the client chairs.

"Thanks for coming over, Melissa. It's great to see you."

"Are you kidding? Everyone is talking about you, Dev. I never expected things to go this way, but that stinky LePew person is dead, and Mr. Dankworth is in jail awaiting trial, and the charges against him are continuing to pile up."

"Well, you should know that a lot of that would not have happened except that Erik dug into the files you provided, which led to him finding more information in more files, and that ultimately led to the arrest of Odell Dankworth. This isn't over by any stretch. It could well be six months to a year before Dankworth goes to trial.

But he'll be up on a number of charges, so be patient and don't worry. He definitely is going to be locked up."

"Yes, and not the least of those charges will be breaking and entering your home. Assault and attempted murder charges are being filed as we speak. I'm just so glad you're okay. I lost my folks to him. That's way more than enough to last me for the rest of my life."

She reached over, and Erik wrapped both his hands around her hand. They were lucky to have one another, and there was a part of me that felt envious.

"As it stands now, Melissa, we're pretty much done with our investigation. Things will probably surface when the police or the prosecutors from your office have questions. I'm willing to help them in any way possible. Thank you for asking me to help. Your dad never gave up on me, and God knows no one would have blamed him if he had."

She suddenly stood, stepped over to me, wrapped her arms around me, and gave me a kiss on my forehead. "Oh, Dev, my dad always knew you were a wonderful person."

"Well, everyone makes a mistake once in a while," I said. I reached down and grabbed a brown paper grocery bag. "I have a little something for you here, but there are some stipulations." She gave me a questioning look. "You can't mention this to anyone. Both of you have to keep this quiet. My suggestion would be you apply it toward your law school tuition, a little bit at a time." I handed the grocery bag to her.

"But what in the world is in—Oh my God! Dev? What? Where?" Erik leaned over, peered in the bag, and they both sat there for a very long moment with their mouths open. "Where did this come from?"

"It's almost fifty thousand dollars, and it came from your mom and dad. Dankworth and LePew were just minding it."

The End

Thanks for taking the time to read the Dev Haskell mystery <u>P. I. Apprentice</u>. If you enjoyed the book please consider leaving a review, it really, really helps.

Don't Miss the sample of <u>Rebel Without A Clue</u>, the next book in the Dev Haskell series on the following page.

Sneak Peek

Rebel Without a Clue

Second Edition

MIKE FARICY

Prologue

orton and I stopped for just one in The Spot at the end of our walk. Since Morton couldn't see above the bar, he did his usual straining against the leash and almost tore my right arm from the socket as he charged along the bar toward Louie's stool. He rounded the corner of the bar, came to a screeching halt, and stared at Louie's empty bar stool. He quickly glanced around and then gave a whine when he couldn't see Louie anywhere.

"Get you a beer?" Mike, the bartender, asked as he grabbed a clean mug from the back of the bar.

"Yeah, thanks, the usual IPA, Mike."

"Louie still working?" he asked, sounding surprised.

"No, he's got a bit of a head cold, so he's at home in recovery." Louie was home convinced he had contracted Covid. I was pretty sure he had just picked up a head cold. The result of spending last night passed out in his car across the street from the office. I didn't want to mention Covid for fear Mike would make me drink my beer outside.

"Here you go, Dev," he said as he slid the beer mug across the bar. "Put it on your tab?"

"No, surprisingly, I've actually got some cash. Better give me a bag of pork rinds, too, while I'm thinking of it."

At the sound of the words 'pork rinds,' Morton's tail began to wag and slap against the side of the bar. I opened the bag, poured half into my hand, and bent down to Morton. He inhaled the things in about a half second. Not one of them fell to the floor. I settled onto Louie's stool, glanced around the bar at the dozen or so people, and took a sip of beer.

I was halfway through my beer when the front door opened. In stepped a woman with long dark hair and a beautiful figure. She was clad in very tight jeans and a gray tank top with half the buttons undone, revealing a very enticing cleavage. She took a couple of steps, scanned the crowd, and then headed down the bar. The conversation level definitely lowered as heads turned to watch. Some woman in a booth punched the guy she was with on the shoulder to get his attention back.

I figured the dark-haired beauty was meeting up with one of the three guys in the softball uniforms who had come in a few minutes earlier, but she sauntered right past them, causing all three heads to turn and follow her as she came around the corner, struck a pose, and said, "Hi, you wouldn't happen to be Dev Haskell, would you?"

She didn't appear to be serving a court document or an arrest warrant, so I said, "Yeah, I am, and you are?"

Morton was on his feet and immediately shoved his nose between her legs. "Oh, how cute," she said. "My name is Tracey Wilde. I got your name from a friend. You investigate stuff, don't you?"

"Yeah, I'm a private investigator. Morton sit," I said, and surprisingly, he did. "Are you thinking you might need help with something?"

Her dark blue eyes flashed, and she said, "Not exactly. It's kind of a long story. I've just separated from my husband, and I'm thinking about maybe filing for divorce. Do you do that kind of thing, investigate husbands?"

"Well, if you're filing for a divorce—"

"I'm just thinking about it. I haven't done it yet. That's why I want someone to check him out. He started his own business, and he works all sorts of crazy hours. At least that's what he's telling me, but I think he might not be telling me the truth."

"So you think he's having an affair with someone?"

"Maybe. I just don't know. That's what I want to find out."

"Has he been abusive to you?"

"No, well, at least not yet."

"Are you worried he might be abusive?"

"I just want to be careful. I told him I didn't want to live with him anymore, told him he had to move out."

"And did he?" I asked. My first thought was that telling her husband he had to move out seemed like a pretty strong response to someone working long hours in a new business.

She seemed to think about that for a moment, then nodded and said, "Yeah, he moved a couple of months ago. I had to tell him a number of times, but he eventually got the message. I sold the place as soon as he was out."

"Okay, I think it might be best if we met at my office or a place of your choice if you'd feel more comfortable somewhere else."

She smiled and said, "I guess your office would be okay. Should I call your secretary and make an appointment?"

Since I didn't have a secretary and my calendar was completely open, I pulled my wallet out and handed her my business card. "Call any time, and I'll adjust whatever is scheduled so we can meet."

"How about if I just show up at 10:00 tomorrow morning?"

"Sure, I'll move some things around, and that should work. Maybe call before you come just to be sure I'm in the office. I'm working on a couple of big cases, and it's possible something might come up, but I should probably be there."

She glanced at my business card and said, "Mmmmmmm, I like this. Okay, sorry to interrupt your evening." She glanced over at the four empty stools between the other single guy in the place and me. A half-finished beer was on the bar in front of him. He'd been too busy study-ing her figure to have touched the beer recently.

"Not a problem, you're really not interrupting. I just stopped to talk to the bartender. I'm looking into some-thing for him," I lied.

"Oh, cool," she said and held out her hand. I ex-tended my hand to shake hers. She immediately wrapped both soft, warm hands around my hand. She smiled, raised her eyebrows, and rubbed her thumbs on the palm and the back of my hand as she said, "Thank you. I look forward to getting to know you a lot better. Have a nice evening. I'll be thinking of you, and I'll see you in the morning." She waited a moment before she stepped back, blew me a kiss, and headed toward the front door. Multiple heads turned as she walked past. As soon as she stepped out the door, one of the guys at the end of the bar called my name and gave me a thumbs-up.

"Was that the latest hot number you're seeing?" Mike asked as he stepped in front of me.

"No, just a new client. She's like all my clients. She's just excited to be involved with me."

"Well, if she ever comes in again, I'll have to set her straight. You ready for another beer?"

"I'd love one, but I'm gonna take a pass and head home."

"They'll all think you're going after that sexy chick."

"You can tell them she begged me to stop over, and I didn't want to disappoint her."

One

The following morning, I was up almost an hour before my alarm went off. Three different times over the course of the night, I woke up to check the time and then went right back to sleep. There was no way I was going to get back to sleep now, so I shaved, showered, and put on clean jeans and a pressed shirt in anticipation of my 10:00 appointment with the lovely Tracey Wilde. I checked the clock, only five hours to go. I looked her up on Facebook and Instagram. I couldn't find her on LinkedIn. Her Facebook page had a number of pictures of her. In fact, that was about all there was on her site. Pictures of her in formal dresses, pictures with a number of different men I presumed to be friends. Pictures of her working out in a bikini and drinking champagne in bed. There were a half-dozen shots of her walking on an ocean beach. A bunch of pictures of her sitting around a swimming pool and three images where she was leaning against an expensive-looking blue coupe. All the images appeared to be professionally taken, and I wondered if she might be a fashion model.

Her Facebook site didn't have any personal information listing a job or where she was from. There was nothing indicating she was married or in a relationship. I'd get the lowdown on all that during our 10:00 meeting. As soon as Morton finished his morning task and ate his breakfast, we hurried down to the office. Louie wasn't in, but that wasn't really a surprise. I wished him a speedy recovery but hoped he didn't make an appearance until my meeting with Tracey was finished. I had ninety minutes before the meeting, when I started to clean the office.

I put on a fresh pot of coffee, emptied the wastebaskets, recycled the beer cans along with an empty bourbon bottle, and rinsed out both coffee mugs. I borrowed the vacuum from the hairdressers across the way and vacuumed the place probably for the first time in close to three years. I used paper towels to dust the tops of the file cabinets. I tossed a pair of insulated overalls, two fishing poles, a tackle box, and a softball jersey into the back closet. I placed a stack of old files on my desk and set Louie's yellow legal pad next to the stack of files so that it looked like I was involved in a number of cases. I began staring out the window at 9:45. Fifty minutes later, I'd pretty much given up and had just decided Tracey wasn't going to make an appearance when my cell phone rang.

"Haskell Investigations, how can I help y'all?" I answered, faking a Southern accent and crossing my fingers.

"I'd like to speak with Dev Haskell, please," a voice that sounded like Tracey said.

"One moment, please," I replied, then pressed one of the keys on my laptop to make a bell sound before I said, "Dev Haskell."

"Oh, hi, Dev. Glad I got you. This is Tracey. Sorry I'm calling so late. In fact, I'm just pulling up in front of your office. I forgot I had a massage scheduled this morning."

"Not a problem. Come on up. I'll have a coffee ready for you."

I glanced out the window just as a dark-blue two-door coupe pulled to the curb behind my 2012 Dodge Charger. I'd bought my car at the police auction two years ago for seven grand. I pulled the binoculars from my desk drawer and scanned the coupe just as the driver's door opened, and beautiful, sexy Tracey stepped out. She was wearing heels, a short black leather skirt, and a white blouse that revealed a good deal of her wonderful cleavage. She carried what looked like a white bakery box. I quickly rolled my desk chair back as she waited for a guy in a pickup to pass.

He slowed, honked, gave her a wave, and headed up the street. She crossed the street and stepped into the building. A moment later, I heard a slight creak on the staircase as she made her way up to the second floor.

There was a soft knock on the door as it opened, and Tracey stepped in. If she was surprised by the look of the place with Louie's picnic table desk, my scratched antique wooden desk with mismatched client chairs, or Morton's ragged pillow that he'd just jumped off of, she didn't let on.

"Hi, Dev. Hope I didn't screw up your morning," she said as Morton inserted his nose beneath her short black leather skirt. She smiled at him, scratched his head, and handed me the bakery box. "I thought I'd better bring a little treat since I know you're really busy, and I'm really late."

"It's not a problem. I had more than enough to do," I said as I nodded toward the stack of files and Louie's legal pad. I set the bakery box on my desk, opened it up, and stared at four delicious muffins.

"I hope you like blueberry muffins."

"I love them. How did you know? Grab a seat and let me pour you a coffee. Do you take it black?"

"Mmm-mmm, if you have a little cream and sugar, I'd love it."

"Not a problem," I said and opened the top file drawer. I'd borrowed a bowl of plastic cream containers and sugar packets from a restaurant last year, and since Louie and I took our coffee black, the bowl was still full. I set the bowl in front of Tracey, filled Louie's mug for her, and set it on the desk. I filled my mug and settled into my desk chair.

Tracey seemed to be searching for something in her black leather purse. I was just about to ask what she was looking for when she smiled and said, "Oh, finally, here you go," she said to Morton and held out a large dog biscuit. Morton snatched it from her hand and hurried back to his pillow.

"Oh, man, he'll probably want to go home with you. Thank you, that was very nice."

"I think he's just a sweetie."

"Give it some time," I said. "So, you said last night you wanted me to take a look at your husband. Let's start with a little background information. Do you mind if I take some notes?" I flipped the page on Louie's legal pad and wrote Tracey's name at the top.

"No, I guess that's okay. Well, let's see. I grew up on the East side. Went to high school at Johnson. Took a couple of semesters at the U and didn't like it at all. I got into modeling, and that's worked out very well."

"You still involved in modeling?"

"Yes, but when I first started, I was taking any job offer I could get. After a couple of years, I landed a position with an agency. That led to some film work and industry work. After a year of that, I started my own agency, representing myself, and I've been doing that ever since."

"So, you're self-employed?"

"Yes, through the agency I run."

I made a two-word note on the legal pad, 'Agency/Self.' "What was your maiden name?"

"Oh, I never changed it. I kept my own last name. I told my soon-to-be ex-husband that I didn't want to change my name, and he said I could call myself Little

Red Riding Hood for all he cared, just as long as I married him."

"That sounds nice."

"Yeah, he's a nice guy, or at least he was, but we've both changed. I guess that happens. Anyway, I kept my name. My full name is Tracey Desiree Wilde. My last name ends with an 'e.'"

"And could you spell your middle name for me?"

She did and then added, "I thought long and hard about dropping the second 'e' at the end, but then decided I'd be dealing with misspellings for the rest of my life, so I just let it go."

"And how long have you been married?"

"It's been almost three years."

"What's your husband's name?"

She smiled and said, "Percy Riggs. His middle name is Eugene." She spelled his name out for me.

"You said he moved out. Where did he move to?"

"He's still in town. He lives on the third floor of a house on Lincoln Ave. Maybe a mile or so from the Cathedral. I don't know the address. Do you know that area?"

I nodded and said, "Yeah, I'm from the city, and I live four or five blocks up the street from the Cathedral, so I'm familiar with the area."

"You live in an old house?"

I nodded. "Yeah, it's coming up on a hundred and fifty years old. Speaking of which, I've got your phone number, but give me your address and your email address." I wrote them down and asked, "This is the house you and Percy lived in?"

"No."

"You own this home?"

"Yes, I moved a month or two ago. I've been so busy it feels like forever."

"How does Percy feel about you two?"

She shook her head. "He thinks that, given enough time, I'll want to get back together. I understand him thinking that, but it's getting to the point that the last thing I want to do is have him move back in, and we'll have to go through this all over again. Do you know what I mean?"

Having been dumped by uncountable women, I understood exactly what she was saying. "It's never any fun. So, tell me, what does he do? You said he started his own company."

She nodded, drank some coffee, and said, "He's always been a tech person. He's got a master's in computers, or the internet, or something like that. I'm not sure what it is. He's always worked in the computer world and has done pretty well. He started his own company not quite a year ago."

"What's the name of it?"

"His company? He named it after himself, Technical Percy."

"Technical Percy, that's the name of his company?"

"Yeah, and I get what you're probably thinking, but that's what he named it."

"And you told me that he's working a lot of hours."

"An unbelievable amount of hours. Seven days a week, fourteen or sixteen hours a day. He'd come home and go to bed. No interest in me. I mean, a couple of nights, I dressed in a negligee and waited for him to come home. He just looked at me and said he was too tired and that he'd catch me in the morning. The next morning when I woke up, he had already gone to his office."

We chatted back and forth for another hour. We each had a blueberry muffin, and I told Tracey I would check out her husband. No one was more surprised than me when she counted out ten one-hundred-dollar bills on my desk and said, "Let me know when you need more."

She gave me a lingering kiss on the cheek, said goodbye to Morton, and strutted out of the office. I watched her out the window as she climbed into her blue two-door coupe. I grabbed my binoculars, repeated the license plate number to myself until I'd written it down, and watched as she disappeared up the street.

TWO

I turned on my computer and Googled Technical Percy. The site popped up with a photo of Percy Riggs seated at a circular desk in shirt sleeves. He appeared to be in shape, not necessarily muscle-bound, but certainly not a lard ass. He was a nice-looking guy, smiling at the camera, and my first thought was, *If I was looking for a tech guy, I'd maybe contact him.* He was surrounded by three large computer monitors with all sorts of what looked like complex information on the screens. Along with a phone number, there was an address over in the Midway Industrial District. I wrote down the address and headed out to the car with Morton.

The Midway area was home to a number of small factories back in the 1920s and 30s. University Avenue ran more or less through the middle of the area. Obviously, things had changed over the course of the last century, and many of the four and five-story factory buildings that weren't torn down had been converted to condos or office buildings. Some structures had been torn down over the past thirty years and replaced by apartment buildings.

Technical Percy was located on North Hampden Ave. Not what you'd call a charming neighborhood, although there was nothing wrong with the area. It was just all older industrial structures. The address was a windowless, four-story brick building that had been painted a tan color. There was an entrance door in the center of the building and a mostly empty parking lot in front of the building. I pulled into the parking lot and parked next to a green Jeep Liberty with a rusted passenger door. A quick glance around didn't reveal any cars that gave the impression of fancy, which got me thinking of the two-door blue coupe that Tracey was driving.

Inside, a small lobby featured an elevator and a glass-enclosed sign listing the various businesses. Technical Percy was up on the fourth floor in unit 412. I pushed the button for the elevator and waited, then waited some more. I pushed the button three more times over the course of the next few minutes and finally decided that the staircase might be the better option. The factory, or whatever had been here before, had been divided up into small offices and theoretically updated. Clearly nothing had changed on the staircase since the original construction.

I made it up to the fourth floor and walked down the hallway. The offices all had wooden doors, so it was impossible to see inside. I walked past the Technical Percy office and down to the end of the hall counting twenty-four office doors. Only five were labeled with company names, one of which was Technical Percy. I walked back to the office, knocked as I opened the door, and stepped inside.

If the building hallway and the staircase appeared to be pretty low rent, Technical Percy looked like it came from a different universe. There were desks, electric cords, and computer screens everywhere in the large room. I made a mental note that there were no windows in the room. Three people, one of whom was Percy, were seated at desks, typing away on keyboards.

He looked just like his online photo. Fit and in shape, although you'd never describe him as muscular. He focused in on me staring wide-eyed at all the technology, and said, "Hi, can I help you?"

"I think I'm in the wrong place. I was looking for a friend of mine, Kevin O'Brien," I lied. "He doesn't happen to work here, does he?"

"No, I'm sorry, there's no one here by that name. What company does he work for? I can look it up and tell you where they are."

"Oh, thanks, but I don't know the name of the company. He just gave me the unit number, and I was sure he said 412."

"Sorry, wish I could help."

"Yeah, me too. What do you guys do, anyways?"

"Some aspects of tech."

"You lost me right there," I said. "Sorry to interrupt. Have a nice day."

"You do the same, sir. Hope you find your friend."

"I'll just give him a phone call. Thanks again," I said and stepped back into the hall.

My first impression was that Percy Riggs appeared to be a nice guy. I took the stairs down to the ground floor and headed out to the parking lot. Morton was half-asleep in the backseat. He raised an eyelid as I opened the driver's door, saw it was me, and went back to sleep. So much for security.

I pulled my phone out and called my pal, Dave McGovern, in the Department of Motor Vehicles. He'd been arrested for driving under the influence two years ago, and I'd put him in touch with Louie, who was able to get the charges dropped on a technicality. Dave was able to keep his job and said he owed me a favor for the rest of his life.

"McGovern," was how he answered my call.

"Hi Dave, Dev Haskell calling. Just checking in. How are things?"

"You know, Dev. Same day, different shit. Let me guess. You need some information on a license plate."

"Not exactly. I'm looking for the license number on a vehicle owned by a gentleman named Percy Riggs." I spelled the name for McGovern and added, "He's a St. Paul resident. I believe he lives on Lincoln Ave."

I could hear McGovern's fingers on his keyboard. A moment later, he said, "Yeah, this must be him, unit two at 716 Lincoln Avenue. Does that sound right?"

"Yeah, Dave, that sounds right. You have a license number on his car?"

"He's driving a white Chevy Equinox, a 2018. You got a color crayon and a clean spot on the wall?"

"Yeah, go ahead." I wrote the license plate number on my hand, told Dave thanks, and looked around the lot. There was a white car four spots off to the left. I backed out of my place and pulled alongside. Sure enough, it was a Chevy Equinox, and the license plate matched the number Dave McGovern had given me. I gave a quick look around, didn't see anyone, and climbed out. I walked around the vehicle, looking in the windows. There was nothing to see other than a long-handled brush to knock snow off the car.

I climbed back in my car and drove over to Lincoln Avenue. 716 was a three-story brick structure. I guessed the place was at least a hundred years old. There was a door off to the side that looked like an enclosed entrance that led up to the third floor. I went around the block and turned into the alley. The backyard housed a three-stall garage, an oak tree, and was fenced in by a six-foot wooden fence. All in all, it was a nice-looking place.

I drove back down to the office and pulled in behind Louie's faded Ford Fiesta. Morton and I hurried up the stairs to see Louie. He was seated at his picnic table desk, eating a blueberry muffin. His legal pad was in front of him.

"Hey, how are you feeling? It's great to see you."

"None the worse for wear. I tested negative for Covid the last two days and again this morning, so I finally decided to come into work."

"I can hear you're still plugged up."

"Yeah, I'm thinking I might give The Spot a pass tonight and head over to the gym and grab a sauna."

"You belong to a gym?"

He nodded and said, "Yeah, not that I ever use it."

"It's just good to see you back."

"Well, there's only so much time I can take watching the damn TV before I start to lose what's left of my mind. You look like you've been busy with all the files. New client?"

"Yes and no. Yeah, I've got a new client. A woman has me looking into her soon-to-be former husband. Just a quick glance today, and he seems like a pretty average guy. He started a tech business and is apparently working his ass off. She was in here this morning, and I stacked up those files and stole your legal pad just to make me look busy."

"But she hired you, right?"

"Yeah, and paid me in advance, in cash. So I'm not complaining. You got a court appearance later today?"

"No, fortunately. Things have been a little slow the last week or so, which turned out to be just fine. I'm in court tomorrow, and I have to get some things lined up. Hopefully, I'll be free of this cold by then. God, I'll tell you, I've been behaving at home the last couple of nights, and it's not fun."

"Well, maybe cut back on the times you spend sleeping in the car."

"Yeah, it's just that, at the time, that was the better choice than trying to drive home."

We spent the rest of the afternoon working. Louie had six or seven sneezing jags that went on for a dozen or more sneezes. Each time, I envisioned a cloud of cold germs heading my way. When he wasn't coughing and sneezing, I was searching the internet for information on Percy Riggs. There wasn't much other than he apparently had quite the reputation as a tech guy. He was involved in helping students in a local high school. He served on the board of directors for his church and volunteered to deliver Meals on Wheels.

Just before 5:00, Louie shut down his computer and stood up from his desk.

"You going to grab a sauna?" I asked.

"Well, I was thinking maybe it would be okay to head over to The Spot for just one. Care to join me?"

"We'll meet you over there," I said.

Three

I took Morton on our usual three-block walk. He got up close and personal with two fire hydrants and a tree. Along the way, we were passed by a black SUV. The first time, I really didn't pay any attention. The second time it passed, I figured it was maybe someone who didn't know the neighborhood. The third time I saw it, the car didn't pass us. Instead, it was parked a block away from The Spot and appeared to be watching Morton and me as we entered.

Once we stepped into The Spot, instead of heading down the bar to Louie, I stood by the small window with the red neon 'OPEN' sign and watched. A minute later, the SUV drove past. The same bald guy I'd seen previously was behind the wheel as the car headed up the street.

"Everything all right, Dev?"

"What? Oh yeah, Mike. Everything's fine. Hey, I'll have a beer and better give Louie a refill."

"Coming right up," he said as Morton pulled me down the length of the bar and around the corner to

Louie. When Morton turned the corner, Louie reached down with his handful of pork rinds.

"I gotta tell you, Louie. You were really missed by your biggest fan. I tried to take your place, but he wasn't all that thrilled."

"Who can blame him?" Louie said just as Mike delivered my beer and set a fresh drink in front of Louie.

"It's great to finally be back," Louie said and raised his glass. He drained what was left in the glass, placed it off to the side, and slid the fresh drink in front of him. Apparently, his idea of 'Just having one' was off the table. "Hey, congratulations on the new client. I know things have been a little slow for you the last couple of months."

"Hopefully, this is a sign they'll be picking up. You've been busy, haven't you?"

Louie nodded. "Yeah, up until a few days ago, but sooner or later, things will pick up, and then I'll be complaining about that."

"Feast or famine," I said. We chatted for another twenty minutes and finished our drinks. Louie served Morton the rest of the pork rinds and turned down my offer for another drink. We said good night to Mike and walked out to our cars.

Louie had always been the type of driver you preferred to have at least a block ahead of you. Tonight was no different. I watched him as he drove up the street and eventually turned at the stoplight. I glanced around for the black SUV, but thankfully, I didn't see it. I lost count of the number of times I checked my rearview mirror on the way home. I pulled into the driveway and parked in the garage for a change. No sign of the SUV as we headed for the back door. I ate cold pizza for dinner while standing at the kitchen counter and then settled in front of the TV. Apparently, whatever I was watching didn't quite keep my interest because I woke up just as the 10:00 news was ending.

Morton was already upstairs and stretched out on the bed. I set the alarm and was back asleep in a couple of minutes. I woke ten minutes before the alarm went off. I was dressed and downstairs finishing breakfast when Morton made his entrance. He got his routine head scratch before I let him outside and filled his food and water dishes.

We were down at the office well before Louie arrived. I made a fresh pot of coffee and sat drinking a mug while looking out the window in search of a black SUV with a bald driver. He never appeared, and I chalked it up to me getting hyper about a new client. Not to mention a *sexy* new client. Just as I watched Louie pull up behind my car, my phone rang.

"Dev Haskell," was how I answered, followed by a sip of coffee.

"Hey, Baby, just checking in. Did you find anything out yesterday?" a woman asked.

"Tracey?"

"Yeah, good morning. Oh, you're not in a meeting or something, are you?"

"No, no, just finished up with a client, and I'm watching him get into his car. I always like to make sure they're safe when they leave."

"Oh, my God. You are so good. What did you find out yesterday?"

"I learned that Percy has a very large office with a lot of high-tech equipment."

"You were actually in his office?" she asked, sounding more than a little surprised.

"Yeah, it's quite the place. He had two other people in there. I'm guessing employees. He does have employees, doesn't he?"

"I think so, but I don't know for sure. They could be contract people, you know, just hired for a specific project for a day, a week, or a month. He never really talked much about what he did all day, every day." She suddenly sounded like she was talking to someone else. "Okay, I'll be there in just a minute. You've got the beach ball?" I heard a man's voice but couldn't make out what he was saying. "Oh, sorry about that. I just wanted to check in and see if you uncovered anything."

Uncovered anything? "I'll keep you posted, Tracey. We both better get back to work. Talk to you later."

"Yeah, let me know if you find out anything," she said and disconnected just as the office door opened, and red-faced Louie stepped in carrying a bakery box. He gave me a wave as he walked around his picnic table and collapsed into his desk chair. He took a couple of minutes to catch his breath, then cleared his throat and said, "Good morning, brought us a little treat. I figured you could use some sweetening." He stepped over and set the box on my desk. "Fresh caramel rolls. They were just arranging them on the tray when I walked in. Check them out," he said and opened the box. There were four cinnamon rolls covered with caramel sauce. "Go ahead, help yourself, Dev."

"Oh, Louie, this is perfect. Thank you," I said, reaching in and taking one of the rolls. It was warm to the touch and slightly sticky. I set it on my desk and licked my fingertips.

"Here, let me top up your coffee," Louie offered and grabbed my mug before I could reply. He topped it up and set the mug in front of me. Then he noticed his mug still off to the side of my desk where Tracey had left it yesterday morning. Fortunately, it was empty of creamy coffee. He filled it up, took a sip, then grabbed a caramel roll and settled in at his picnic table desk. "Mmm-mmm, delicious," he said over a mouthful of caramel roll.

"So, to what do I owe the pleasure?" I asked and nodded at the caramel roll on my desk.

"What? I can't spring for a little treat in the morning just to get our day started off on the right foot?"

I took a bite of the gooey roll. The caramel sauce was still warm enough to leave a sticky drip that landed on my chin. "Thanks for getting these, Louie. What's up?"

"Okay, okay, bear with me. I got a call from a distant acquaintance. He can be a bit of a pain. Let me rephrase that, he can be a major pain, okay? Anyway, he asked me to put in a good word for him and see if you might have some time to check into something. He wouldn't tell me what it was."

"You said the guy was a pain?"

"Yeah, always has been, even when we were in school, but he's been very successful in the business world, and now he's even more full of himself. Pictures himself as a ladies' man. I think women think of him as their bank. I don't know if he's got an employee problem, or he's been hacked, or is he hacking someone. If you don't want to get into it, believe me, I understand."

"Oh, no, I'll be happy to check it out, Louie. I can always tell him no. Give me the contact information, and I'll give him a call."

"Oh, thanks, Dev. Really appreciate it. Just remember, there's no pressure from me if you don't want to take whatever he's got going. Here's his number, and thanks." Louie handed me an envelope with a name and number scrawled on it. He glanced at his watch and said, "I better head down to the courthouse." He crammed the rest of the caramel roll into his mouth, licked his fingertips, and gave me a wave as he headed out the door.

I watched out the window as he climbed into his faded Ford Fiesta and drove away. I took a sip of coffee, looked at the number, and placed a call to Louie's acquaintance, a guy named Ernest Stanton.

Four

The woman answered saying, "Rebel Investments."

"Hi, I'm calling for Ernest Stanton," I said.

"Who may I say is calling?"

"My name is Dev Haskell. I'm replying to a request from Mr. Stanton."

"Please hold while I transfer your call," she said and then did just that, transferring my call before I could even say thank you.

"Mmm, Ernest Stanton, and this is your luck day," a voice said. Then it sounded like he swallowed something.

"Mr. Stanton, my name is Dev Haskell. I'm a private investigator, and I office with an acquaintance of yours, Louie Laufen."

"Humph, Louis. Yes, he mentioned you. I have a bit of a problem here. Would you be available to meet with me sometime this week?"

"I think I can do that. If you want to schedule a day and time, I should be able to adjust my schedule."

"Wonderful, give me a moment, and let me check my calendar. Would you be available tomorrow, Wednesday, at 11:00?"

"I think so. Let me check my schedule. Hold on just a moment, please," I said, then glanced out the window at a young woman pushing a stroller. I watched as she walked around the corner and disappeared behind a hedge. "Yes, sir, thanks for waiting. I can make that."

"Good, we're downtown at 400 Robert Street."

"I know the building," I lied. "I'll see you tomorrow morning at 11:00, sir."

"Looking forward to it, Mr. Haskell. Thank you for the call, and please give my regards to Louis."

"I'll be sure to do that, sir," I said just as he disconnected. I sat back in my chair and thought for a moment about how strange life was, coming from virtually no business to suddenly two new clients in as many days. One of whom paid me upfront in cash. Which reminded me that I wanted to knock on the door where Percy Riggs was renting. I took Morton for a brief walk, and then we drove past Percy's office. Since I saw his car in the parking lot, that gave me the all-clear to knock on the main door of the house where he rented.

Because of the narrow streets in that older section of town, parking was allowed on only one side of the street. Lucky for me, it was the same side that Percy lived on. I pulled in front of the house and parked. Morton had a look on his face suggesting maybe we were going for a walk.

"Sorry, pal. This shouldn't take too long," I said as I locked the doors and headed up the winding brick path to the front door. The door was oak with a large six-foot panel of beveled glass and a brass doorknob. A black, post-mounted mailbox with the image of a pony express rider just below the brass flap labeled 'LETTERS' was bolted down on the front stoop. I pushed the doorbell and heard it chiming inside.

A half-minute later, a woman appeared in the hall-way. She was just an inch or two over five feet tall, with neatly arranged brown hair. She wore expensive-looking slacks, a designer blouse, and a string of pearls. She opened the door to the small entry and then said, "Yes?" from behind the beveled glass door.

"Hello, sorry to bother you. Is Percy Riggs home?"

She nodded and said, "Percy lives up on the third floor."

I shook my head and placed a hand behind my right ear, signaling I was having trouble hearing her.

She repeated herself, only louder.

I gave the same signal with my hand behind my ear, only this time I said, "I'm sorry, I can't hear you."

She gave a somewhat disgusted look, hooked a brass chain to the beveled glass door, and then unlocked the door and opened it no more than an inch. "I said, Percy lives up on the third floor."

"Oh, okay, sorry to bother you. Is this his entrance? I'm just in town for the day, and he told me that he had moved here recently."

"His entrance is around the side, but I'm sure he's at his office. He seems to work eternally."

"Yeah, that sounds like Percy. I have his office address on my GPS. I'm sorry to bother you. Ummm, if he's not home, is it possible to leave a note at his door?"

"Well, the door heading up to his apartment will be locked, but there's a mail slot you could drop the note through."

"All right, again, I'm sorry to bother you. Thank you for your time."

"Shall I tell him you stopped by?"

"No, I've got an hour. I can head over to his office. If I remember, it's on Hampden Avenue North in the Midway district." She nodded. "Anyway, I've got the address on my GPS. Thank you, and have a nice day," I said. I gave her a wave as I stepped off the front stoop and walked back to my car. She continued to watch me until I drove away.

I drove a block over to Grand Avenue, took a right, and two blocks later took a left onto Dale Street. A block later, I drove down Summit Avenue, one of the nation's most famous Victorian mansion streets. Four blocks later, I took a right and headed down Ramsey Hill to the entrance to 35E. I had just pulled onto the entrance and was checking my side-view mirror. The lane next to me was clear of traffic, but as I pulled onto the freeway, I caught the momentary image of a black SUV pulled to the curb just before the entrance ramp. No one ever stops there. Was it the same SUV that I thought was following me yesterday? There was no way to tell, so I accelerated and then checked my rearview mirror a half-dozen times as I sped to the Randolph Avenue exit. I never did see the SUV and decided it probably wasn't the bald guy from yesterday.

I drove down Randolph to my building, made a U-turn at the intersection with The Spot bar, and parked just across the street from my office. I sat in the car for ten minutes to see if the black SUV would appear. It never did, so Morton and I headed up to the office.

To be continued . . .

Thank you for taking the tine to check out <u>P.I. Apprentice</u>, Needless to say, things are about to get even crazier. It might be a good idea to grab a copy and see what happens. Enjoy the read and thanks!

Books by Mike Faricy
Crime Fiction Firsts

A boxset of the first four books in four crime fiction series:

Russian Roulette; Dev Haskell series

Welcome; Jack Dillon Dublin Tales series

Corridor Man; Corridor Man series

Reduced Ransom! Hot Shot series

The following titles comprise the Dev Haskell series:

Russian Roulette: Case 1

Mr. Swirlee: Case 2

Bite Me: Case 3

Bombshell: Case 4

Tutti Frutti: Case 5

Last Shot: Case 6

Ting-A-Ling: Case 7

Crickett: Case 8

Bulldog: Case 9

Double Trouble: Case 10

Yellow Ribbon: Case 11

Dog Gone: Case 12

Scam Man: Case 13

Foiled: Case 14

What Happens in Vegas… Case 15

Art Hound: Case 16

The Office: Case 17

Star Struck: Case 18
International Incident: Case 19
Guest From Hell: Case 20
Art Attack: Case 21
Mystery Man: Case 22
Bow-Wow Rescue: Case 23
Cold Case: Case 24
Cash Up Front: Case 25
Dream House: Case 26
Alley Katz: Case 27
The Big Gamble: Case 28
Bad to the Bone: Case 29
Silencio!: Case 30
Surprise, Surprise: Case 31
Hit & Run: Case 32
Suspect Santa: Case 33
P.I. Apprentice: Case 34
Rebel Without a Clue: Case 35
Puppy Love: Case 36

The following titles are Dev Haskell novellas:
Dollhouse
The Dance
Pixie
Fore!
Twinkle Toes
(*a Dev Haskell short story*)

The following are Dev Haskell Boxsets:
Dev Haskell Boxset 1-3
Dev Haskell Boxset 4-6
Dev Haskell Boxset 7-9
Dev Haskell Boxset 10-12
Dev Haskell Boxset 13-15
Dev Haskell Boxset 16-18
Dev Haskell Boxset 19-21
Dev Haskell Boxset 22-24
Dev Haskell Boxset 25-27
Dev Haskell Boxset 28-30
Dev Haskell Boxset 1-7
Dev Haskell Boxset 8-14
Dev Haskell Boxset 15-19
Dev Haskell Boxset 20-24
Dev Haskell Boxset 25-29

The following titles comprise the Jack Dillon Dublin Tales series:
Welcome
Jack Dillon Dublin Tale 1
Sweet Dreams
Jack Dillon Dublin Tale 2
Mirror Mirror
Jack Dillon Dublin Tale 3
Silver Bullet
Jack Dillon Dublin Tale 4
Fair City Blues

Jack Dillon Dublin Tale 5
Spade Work
Jack Dillon Dublin Tale 6
Madeline Missing
Jack Dillon Dublin Tale 7
Mistaken Identity
Jack Dillon Dublin Tale 8
Picture Perfect
Jack Dillon Dublin Tale 9
Dublin Moon
Jack Dillon Dublin Tale 10
Mystery Woman
Jack Dillon Dublin Tale 11
Second Chance
Jack Dillon Dublin Tale 12
Payback Brother
Jack Dillon Dublin Tale 13
The Heist
Jack Dillon Dublin Tale 14
Jewels To Kill For
Jack Dillon Dublin Tale 15
Retirement Scheme
Jack Dillon Dublin Tale 16
The Collector
Jack Dillon Dublin Tale 17

Jack Dillon Dublin Tales Boxsets:
Jack Dillon Dublin Tales 1-3
Jack Dillon Dublin Tales 4-6

Jack Dillon Dublin Tales 1-5
Jack Dillon Dublin Tales 1-7
Jack Dillon Dublin Tales 6-10

The following titles comprise the Hotshot series;
Reduced Ransom! Second Edition
Finders Keepers! Second Edition
Bankers Hours Second Edition
Chow Down Second Edition
Moonlight Dance Academy Second Edition
Irish Dukes (Fight Card Series)
written under the pseudonym Jack Tunney

The following titles comprise the Corridor Man series:
Corridor Man
Corridor Man 2: Opportunity knocks
Corridor Man 3: The Dungeon
Corridor Man 4: Dead End
Corridor Man 5: Finger
Corridor Man 6: Exit Strategy
Corridor Man 7: Trunk Music
Corridor Man 8: Birthday Boy
Corridor Man 9: Boss Man
Corridor Man 10: Bye Bye Bobby

Corridor Man novellas:
Corridor Man: Valentine
Corridor Man: Auditor

Corridor Man: Howling
Corridor Man: Spa Day

The following are Corridor Man Boxsets:
Corridor Man Boxset 1-3
Corridor Man Boxset 1-5
Corridor Man Boxset 6-9

All books are available on Amazon.com
Thank you!

Contact the author:
- Email: mikefaricyauthor@gmail.com
- Twitter: @Mikefaricybooks
- Facebook: Mike Faricy Author
- Website: http://www.mikefaricybooks.com

Published by

MJF Publishing